Day of the Tiger

CHUCK MCCRARY IS A WISECRACKING FORMER GREEN BERET turned private investigator with a special genius for helping people in trouble–especially if they can pay him for his efforts.

OPPOSITES ATTRACT, RIGHT? Tank Tyler is a mega-wealthy investment manager and Pro Football Hall of Famer. Al Rice, a victim of drugs and self-pity, has been a miserable failure since being kicked off the football team years ago. The two men share a sordid secret that ruined Al's life and turned Tank's dreams into nightmares for sixteen years, in spite of his success—a secret that still entangles the lives of these polar opposites.

Now Monster Moffett, a sadistic loan shark who once mangled Al's hand with a ball-peen hammer when he couldn't repay his loan, again targets Al. Moffett even threatens Al's mother, Doraleen Rice. When Doraleen begs Tank for help, he hires private investigator Chuck McCrary to protect both Doraleen and Al.

Chuck exposes a human sex trafficking ring and forced prostitution in the sleazy world of high-priced "Gentlemen's Clubs"—a world where Chuck will need more than brawn, balls, and bullets to sort out this mess.

Moffett kidnaps Doraleen Rice to hold as collateral for her son's debt. Chuck uncovers Moffett's hideout, but he can't wait for the FBI. With gun in hand, he invades the heavily-armed gang's stronghold alone, but he hasn't counted on facing a knife-wielding African warrior. Now he faces deadly odds of ever seeing the light of day.

Also by Dallas Gorham

I'm No Hero

Six Murders Too Many

Double Fake, Double Murder

Quarterback Trap

Dangerous Friends

Day of the Tiger

McCrary's Justice

Yesterday's Trouble

Day of the Tiger

A Carlos McCrary, Private Investigator, Mystery Thriller

By Dallas Gorham

ISBN-10: 1530435544
ISBN-13: 978-1530435548

18021601

Cover art by Michael By Design www.MichaelByDesign.com.

Editing by Marsha Butler www.ButlerInk.com.

Day of the Tiger

A Carlos McCrary, Private Investigator, Mystery Thriller

It is better to live for one day as a tiger than to live for a thousand years as a sheep.

—Tibetan Proverb

Chapter 1

ALFRED RICE CRINGED as the man in black raised the ball-peen hammer above his left hand. "No, for God's sake, Monster! I paid you the interest. I'll pay you the rest, I swear." He struggled to free his arms. Panic rose in his throat like bile.

"Crummy forty thousand dollars. That pays the interest to last month, you moocher. I told you I want the whole two hundred grand. I don't trust you no more." The man in black, Montgomery "Monster" Moffett, raised the hammer again. The industrial fluorescent lights high above the table cast multiple shadows across Rice's arm. "You're thirty days past due. This is the late fee."

"Monster, I need both hands to work," Rice pleaded.

"Hold him steady." Moffett's men jammed Rice's forearm tight against the table. Moffett's eyes blazed and his breath came quicker as he smashed the back of Rice's hand with the hammer, shattering the fourth metacarpal bone. The blow crushed the veins and capillaries surrounding the bone. Skin ripped at the ragged edges of the ugly crater in Rice's brown skin. Subcutaneous bleeding oozed into the crater, filled it, and spilled across the back of his hand like red lava spreading across a brown mountainside. Moffett licked his lips at the whiff of blood.

Rice shrieked like a banshee. Pain dominated his senses and became the focus of his universe. His vision blurred.

"You don't work, loser; you hang out in strip clubs instead of making money to pay me back." Moffett swung the hammer again.

Rice's second metacarpal bone splintered, and his scream echoed off the concrete block walls. He stared wide-eyed at the second crater gouged by the hammer. Blood pooled, escaped, and mingled with the flow from the first wound. The red stream dripped off the back of Rice's hand. A red slick spread across the table top. Sobbing, he pleaded with Monster. "I swear on my mother's life I'll pay you the rest, Monster. I'll pay you, I swear."

"You should've thought of that before you welshed on a debt." Moffett swung the hammer again and pounded a third crater between the first two. "You owe me two hundred large. You're past due. You got two weeks."

Rice's vision turned to red. He slumped to one side.

Moffett swirled the bloody pool with the hammer, smearing streaks across the Formica. He laid the gruesome hammer head on Rice's wrist. He seized the frightened man's ear and twisted it savagely. "You hear me, loser? You listening to me? Huh?"

Rice mumbled through the bubbles that formed on his lips. He tried to nod, but it hurt his ear.

Moffett tapped the victim's wrist with the side of the hammer, leaving a red smear. "In two weeks' time, I turn Teddy loose on you with his knife. He'll carve you a reminder to pay your debts. Two weeks after that, I break both your arms. Two weeks after that... Well, you did swear on your mother's life, didn't you?"

"That's not what I meant. You can't—"

Moffitt twisted Rice's ear again. "You don't tell me what I can't do, loser. You understand me?" He waved at the other two men, who stepped away from Rice.

Moffett released Rice's ear and shoved his head away, knocking him off the metal chair.

Rice peered up from the concrete floor. "You stay away from my mother. Just stay away. Do whatever you want with me. Maybe I deserve whatever I get, but not my mother." His eyes narrowed. "You touch a hair on her head and I'll kill you if it's the last thing I ever do."

Moffett kicked him in the stomach. "Yeah, and I'm the Tooth Fairy." He laughed when Rice vomited.

Rice collapsed in a heap, sobbing as he cradled his ruined hand in the crook of his other arm.

"Throw this bum out."

Chapter 2

"I OWE AL RICE A DEBT I CAN'T REPAY." Tank Tyler paused to ascertain that I was listening.

I looked east out the window of Tank's sixty-first floor office in Port City's newest skyscraper, admiring the view of Seeti Bay. The sea breeze had scrubbed the late afternoon air to a clean, crisp blue beyond the window wall. The knife edge of the horizon beyond Port City Beach appeared to be at arm's-length. "Can you see all the way to Bimini?"

"Not quite. Hey, I didn't ask you here to admire the view. I have a friend who needs help." He paused. "Earth to McCrary. Earth to McCrary. Come in, McCrary. Hey, you're the McCrary of McCrary Investigations. I said I have a friend who needs your professional services. Did you even hear me?"

I pivoted from the window. "Don't get your panties in a wad; I heard you. You owe Al Rice a debt you can't repay, yada, yada. I got it. Tank, you have more money than Tom Cruise. I would've said you have more than you can count, but you're a Certified freakin' Public Accountant with a computer for a brain. If you owe this Rice guy a debt, write him a check for crissakes."

He sighed. "Some debts can't be paid with money. God knows I've tried."

"How so?" I sipped Tank's expensive beer.

He waved the question off. "That's personal. It's enough for you to know that Al is in big trouble. I hope you can help him, and I'll pay you to tackle it." He lapsed into silence, tilted his glass for the last of the twelve-year-old, single-malt Scotch, then rattled the ice cubes.

I rotated the Pilsner glass in my hands and gazed out the window. One thing I'll say for Tank: He stocks the best private bar in Port City. "You pay the freight and I'll walk your dog."

He smirked. "Black people don't own dogs."

"Tank, how many times I gotta tell ya? I'm the funny Mexican; you're the studious African American CPA. Besides, you told me you owned a Border Collie when you were a kid." I sipped my beer. "Sure, I'll help your friend. What's his problem?"

"Al has so many problems I don't know where to begin." Tank shrugged. "First, there's Monty Moffett, otherwise known as 'Monster.'"

Despite me being a tough guy, that sent a frisson down my spine. I knew Moffett by reputation, although I had never encountered him personally. "Al is involved with Monster Moffett?"

"Yeah. Is that bad?"

"Doesn't get much worse. What do you know about Monster Moffett?"

"Only what I read in the newspaper. Is he as bad as his nickname?"

"Worse. Moffett is the biggest bookie and loan shark in Port City, both businesswise and physically. This guy is nearly as big as you. Must be six-foot-five and outweighs you by fifty pounds. Of course, he's mostly fat and you're all muscle. But even so, he scares the hell out of most people."

"Does he scare you?"

I shrugged. "Maybe he would if I had good sense, but I have more balls than brains."

"I would've said that you have balls *instead* of brains."

"You sure know how to hurt a guy. Especially a guy who is, uh, what's that big word I learned? Intellectually challenged. You forget: I have copious brawn to go with my extraordinary balls."

"So, you'll help Al even with Monster Moffett in the picture?"

"You forget: Under this business suit and tie I wear a red cape and a blue leotard with a big red S on it."

"I thought you only wore that to go nightclubbing."

I grinned. "The bigger they are... Moffett is ruthless and sadistic, but his nasty temper makes up for it. I'd do the world a favor to knock him down a notch or two. I suppose Al owes him money?"

"Yeah, and he hasn't got a pot to piss in. A couple weeks ago Moffett sent two wise guys to haul Al to someplace in the warehouse district. Moffett took a ball-peen hammer to Al's left hand. Poor guy was in surgery for three hours. Over a hundred stitches and God knows how many steel pins. He'll never shuffle a deck of cards again, that's for sure." Tank set down his glass and cracked his knuckles. "Last week Al came to my office with a cast up to his forearm. He told me every agonizing detail."

"If you want me to help him," I asked, "why'd you wait until last night to call me?"

"Frankly, I didn't know what to do. I've bailed him out more times than I can count. It never works. You know that old definition of insanity..."

"Doing the same thing over and over, thinking this time you'll get different results. Yeah, another old joke I tell better than you."

Tank smiled. "Sometimes when you don't know what to do, the best thing to do is nothing."

"That sounds more like a bumper sticker than an excuse."

"In my defense, Moffett did give him two weeks. I knew Al had another week before Moffett came after him."

"So you procrastinated."

Tank stared at his empty glass. "I'm not proud of it."

"What changed?" I asked. "Why did you wait, then call last night in a hurry to meet?"

Tank walked over to the bar. "You ready for another?"

I raised my empty glass. "Last one, I have to drive."

Tank opened the bar refrigerator, slid out another Amstel, and handed it to me. "If I give Al money to pay this loan, Moffett will increase his credit line." He poured a little Scotch and slid ice cubes down the side of the glass. "He's done that before. Every time Al gambles or cooks up another hare-brained scheme, he gets deeper in debt to Moffett. When it comes to borrowing money from a loan shark like Moffett, Al's like an alcoholic who can't stop drinking."

I tilted the Pilsner glass and poured the Amstel gently down the slope. Didn't want to bruise the beer. "How much does Al owe Moffett?"

"Two hundred thousand dollars."

Two hundred thousand dollars was petty cash for Tank, but the way he said it called for a whistle, so I whistled. "What does Al do for a living?"

Tank swirled his drink, rattled the ice. "Anything and nothing. He's full of grandiose schemes. He does an occasional drug deal, he gambles, and he's been arrested twice for shoplifting. He tried to flip houses during the last real estate crash. Lost a bundle, of course."

"Al doesn't sound like the type of guy you'd pick for a friend. In fact, he sounds like the polar opposite of conservative, uptight CPA Thomas Tyler." I poured the remainder of my beer. "How'd you become friends with a man like that?"

"We played football together for the UAC Falcons for two years. Al attended Carver High School here in the City where his mother teaches English and his father was head football coach. Al was a sophomore, a year ahead of me. I showed up fresh off the farm from Florence, Alabama, and Al took me under his wing. He drove me to his house for a home-cooked meal." Tank stared out the window, lost in the past. "I was a fish out of water. Hell, I'd never visited a city larger than Huntsville, Alabama, except for recruiting trips in high school. Al taught me how things work at a big university in a big city."

"What went wrong with Al?" I asked. "How did he end up such a loser?"

"It was sixteen years ago. Not relevant anymore."

"But he didn't finish college, did he?"

"Nope. He quit after he was kicked off the team in the spring semester of his junior year."

"Why'd he get kicked off?"

"Not important now."

"Could be relevant. Sometimes things like that gnaw on you for years; they color everything you see in the world."

"Drop it, Chuck. It's not important. Trust me on that."

Whenever someone tells me to trust them, it often means they don't know what the hell they're talking about. I tried another tack. "So, you two played together for two seasons."

"Yeah."

"What happened to him after he got kicked off the team?"

"He dropped out."

"Why?"

"Not important now."

I shrugged; I would come back to the subject later. "Using my unsurpassed analytical mind, I surmise that, for whatever reason, Al's life went downhill and yours skyrocketed. Consensus All-American your junior year, Bronko Nagurski Award for best defensive lineman in the known universe your senior year, and the UAC Falcons won the National Championship that year."

I pointed to the Falcons team picture on the wall. "And where was Al while all this glory was heaped on you?"

"I lost track of him for a few years."

"But not for long, I'll bet. You were a first round NFL draft choice with a multi-million-dollar contract. It was all over the sports pages. Al had to know about it. Stop me if I get this wrong."

"So far, you're right on the money."

"Hurray for me." I lifted my glass and toasted myself. "You'd be amazed how many long-long friends and relatives you find once you win the lottery."

Tank grunted. "You got that one hundred percent right."

"So Al materializes out of the blue to congratulate his old, but newly-rich friend. You feel guilty about your success—you're rich; he's poor. You're a big football star; he got kicked off the team. How'm I doing so far?"

"Batting a thousand."

"Then Al plays the guilt card. He asks you to bail him out of a little mischief. You help him out and one thing leads to another. Eventually it becomes a habit for you both. You're a rich man, so why not? I get that. That about right?"

"Yeah, pretty much." Tank stared into his glass.

I threw up my hands. "So why am I here? Why'd you call me last night?"

"Something intervened."

"What is this, big guy, twenty questions? What intervened?"

"More like *who* intervened. Al's mother, Doraleen, called me yesterday afternoon. Moffett showed up at her house and threatened her if Al doesn't pay. Moffett told her that Al swore on her life that he'd pay. He told her Al's two weeks was up tomorrow. She was at her wits end, so she called me. She was so scared she could barely talk. I went out to her home and installed better locks. Then I called you."

I drank Amstel while I decided what to say. "And here we are."

"Yeah, here we are." Tank sighed. "I've fretted over this mess ever since Al's mother called. I'm convinced that throwing money at Al—or at his creditors—is a short-term solution for a long-term problem. I tried that before, and it doesn't make any long-term difference to Al. I want to do something different this time." His eyes were moist. "That's why I called you."

"What am I supposed to do, psychoanalyze him? Read his aura? Adjust his chakras? I'm a poor dumb private investigator with a room-temperature IQ."

"For starters, I want you to help Al's mother."

I inhaled the Amstel's hoppy aroma; at least something in this room was perfect. I made a get-on-with-it gesture to Tank.

"Doraleen was a second mother to me while I attended UAC. I call her Momma Dora. She invited me for Thanksgiving my first year at school. I couldn't afford to fly back to Alabama, and it was too far to drive there and back in four days. After that I spent every holiday but Christmas and Spring Break with Al's family. We became real close."

"Even after Al dropped out?" I asked.

"Even then. Momma Dora said that my ties with Al and her went deeper than football."

"And you stayed in touch all these years."

"Like I said, she's a second mother." Tank's brown face creased in a grin. Sometimes he looks like he has forty-eight teeth. Guy is a real-life toothpaste ad. "Besides, Momma Dora makes the world's best chili." The grin faded. "A stray bullet killed Al's father while we were at UAC. For the last few years, ever since Al became unreliable, I've visited once a month. I help around the house and do things she needs a younger person for. I hang Christmas decorations on her roof or change a light bulb in a ceiling fixture. Al... he doesn't visit Momma Dora often enough. Even when he comes, he's not good for much anymore." He sipped his Scotch. "Momma Dora regards me as the son who turned out all right."

"What makes Al unreliable? Drugs?"

"When he can afford them. Alcohol when he can't."

"Al have any brothers or sisters?"

"Momma Dora and her husband William tried to have children for years. They had lost hope. Then Al came along. She said Al was a gift from God, never repeated."

I tugged a notepad from my jacket. "What's Al's full name? Albert? Alfred? Alexander?"

"Alfred Lord Tennyson Rice."

"For real?"

Tank grinned. "What can I say? Momma Dora's an English teacher.

I scribbled it on my notepad. "Do you have a picture of Al I could borrow?"

"Momma Dora will have one."

"What about on your phone? You have a picture in the contact list?"

"Yeah, I forgot that one."

"Send it to my phone." He did, and I examined the photo. "That's one I can use. Now to the assignment at hand. What should I do about Monster Moffett? Wave a magic wand? Sprinkle pixie dust? Join hands and sing Kumbaya? My voice sounds best in a large choir where it's drowned out."

Tank stood at the window and spread his hands. Standing there in his three-pieced, blue pin-striped suit, he was the world's largest financier—physically anyway. His bulk blocked the view. "I don't have a clue how to help this family, but I gotta do something even if it's wrong. If Al continues on this path, I guaran-damn-tee you, he'll end up dead. I could live with Al being dead—karma and such. But for Momma Dora... an old woman shouldn't bear a loss like that. I can't let it happen. Not if there's any way under heaven to prevent it."

"From Moffett's reputation, he won't back off unless someone kills him. Then his ghost will haunt you. If that's what you want, big guy, that ain't gonna happen. I don't do hits, even when the guy deserves it." That was almost true.

"God, no. That's not what I mean. Besides, if Moffett fell into a bottomless pit, Al would find another jerk to gamble with. No, this situation requires a more original approach."

"Performing a personality transplant is outside my area of expertise."

"Nobody likes a smart ass. Come with me to meet Momma Dora. She's a wise old bird; hell, she earned a Masters in English Lit. Maybe she'll know what to do."

Chapter 3

Doraleen Rice took a deep breath when the doorbell rang. Surely it wasn't that horrible man again. She peeked through the peephole and sighed with relief. Tank and a white man, who must be his friend Chuck McCrary, stood at the door. She trembled as she opened the solid oak door. She jumped when it clunked against the brass security bar. "You haven't seen Race Car out there, have you, Tank? I let her out an hour ago. She should be back by now. I'm worried about her, what with that… that gangster making threats yesterday."

Tank scanned the front yard. "No, Momma Dora, I don't see her." He faced Chuck. "Did you spot a white Persian cat out front?"

"Nope."

Doraleen closed the door to swing the brass security bar open. She reopened it wide enough for the two men to enter. "Come in, come in, boys. Hurry inside."

She slammed the door behind them, threw the two dead bolts, and swung the door guard across the matching knob screwed to the door edge. "I'm not used to this door safety thing, Tank." Standing on tiptoe, she reached her arms as far around Tank's neck as she could and leaned her cheek against his muscular chest. Tank wrapped arms the size of tree trunks around her slender shoulders. She burst into tears.

I STOOD NEAR THE DOOR, shifted my weight from one foot to the other, while this tiny woman and my giant friend comforted each other. I felt as out of place as a hooker in church. Glancing around, I noticed the new door guard was expertly installed. One dead bolt was newer than the other. Those must be the extra locks Tank installed.

Tank patted the old woman's shoulder and kissed the top of her head. "There, there, Momma Dora. I'm here. Everything will be all right."

"I'm frightened, Tank. While I waited for you and your friend to arrive, I kept worrying, 'What if that Moffett man comes back before they get here?' What would I do—what *could* I do?"

She stepped back and smoothed her palms down the front of her brick-red dress. She held out her hand. "I'm Doraleen Rice."

She presented a firm handshake and cold hands. To my eye, she had aged like fine wine with skin smooth as a burnished oak barrel. The tiny lines that etched the corners of her eyes reminded me of wood grain, not wrinkles. She could have been anywhere from fifty to eighty. Her red dress and salt-and-pepper Afro hairstyle could have been Little Orphan Annie, but all grown up. I handed her a business card, one without the crossed swords on it. "I'm Chuck McCrary. I'm here to help." Instantly I felt stupid. I remembered that old joke: I'm from the government; I'm here to help.

"Let's sit. We have a lot to discuss." She led us into a living room that resembled a set from a 1980s television sitcom. The one modern piece in the room was a huge HD television with a cable box on the table beside it. A bottle of sherry and three stemmed glasses with gold rims sat on the coffee table next to the TV remote.

Mrs. Rice lifted the bottle. "Will you have a sherry, Chuck?"

"No thanks, ma'am, I have to drive." I didn't mention that I don't like sherry. No sense hurting the lady's feelings.

Tank wasn't as tactful as I. "You know I don't drink sherry, Momma Dora." He glanced my way. "Momma Dora sets out a glass for me anyway. She says she wants to be hospitable in case I change my mind." He patted her hand.

"Chuck, I'm old enough to be your mother—maybe your grandmother, but don't make me feel old by calling me 'ma'am.'

Please call me Doraleen. Since you don't want sherry, Tank will brew you both fresh coffee while we get acquainted."

I raised an eyebrow at Tank. He grinned. "Don't act surprised, Mr. Gourmet Cook. Despite what you think, I'm not helpless around a kitchen. I know how to brew coffee. You and Momma Dora talk." He removed his suit jacket and draped it across a chair back.

"Thanks, coffee is fine, ma'am. I mean, Doraleen. Just so you know, I call every woman *ma'am* no matter her age, high school English teachers in particular. It's the way I was raised."

Doraleen smiled back, but the smile didn't reach her eyes. She had other things on her mind. She waited until Tank left the room. "Tank is such a good man. He's a second son to me. I don't say it in front of him because it embarrasses him, but I love that boy like I'd borne him myself. How did you and Tank meet?"

"We're both friends with Bigs Bigelow," I responded. "Do you know Bigs?"

"Oh, yes. He and Tank played together on the Pelicans defensive line—the 'Bigs Brigade' the newspapers called them. Bigs is a fine, fine man. Did you know that he retired from football and became a police detective?"

"Yes, ma'am. I met Bigs when I was a police detective."

"So Bigs introduced you to Tank?" She poured herself a sherry.

"Yes, ma'am. I came into a chunk of money a while ago, thanks to a sizable bonus a client paid me. I didn't make millions like Bigs, but I asked him to recommend somebody to keep me from blowing my nest egg on wine, women, and song."

"Bigs got rich playing for the Pelicans," Doraleen said, "but, more important, he *stayed* rich once he retired from football. That's not easy to do."

"I always say 'I can resist anything but temptation.'" If she saw the humor, she didn't let it show. My comedic genius often goes unappreciated. "Tank made sure I resisted temptation," I finished lamely.

Doraleen sipped her sherry. "Many of Tank's friends from professional football wasted their good fortune and wound up destitute. So did my William, God rest his soul. I remind my students that the quality of our decisions determines the course of our lives. My William played two years for the Miami Dolphins and wound up with nothing to show for it but bruises and memories. At least they were good memories. Of course, William made his bad money decisions before I knew him. I would never countenance such nonsense." She leaned toward me. "Tank told me once how William's bad experience inspired him to do better while he was in college. Did you know Tank passed the CPA exam on the first try?"

"No, ma'am, I didn't know, but I'm not surprised."

"Tank is modest, isn't he?"

"Yes, ma'am." If Tank were in the room, I would have said he had much to be modest about. Doraleen would not have found that remark amusing either.

Doraleen's eyes sparkled. "Tank takes his profession seriously; it's almost a mission to him. He says one must respect the money." She leaned back. "So you are Tank's client." It was not a question.

"And friend. We often work out at Jerry's Gum together, and we watch football together."

"Tank tells me you're a private investigator."

"Yes, ma'am. McCrary Investigations."

"Do most private investigators earn enough to require an investment manager like Tank?"

I shook my head. "Not the ones I know. Most make a so-so livelihood like anybody else. I'm the exception. Sometimes, my clients give me a bonus when a case works out better than expected. I send that bonus money to Tank. He invests it for me. My account must be small potatoes compared to his other clients, but I add to it every month." I glanced over my shoulder to ascertain what had delayed Tank. My collar felt tight.

"Mighty oaks from little acorns grow, Chuck. Never forget that." Her eyes sparkled. "What makes you exceptional?"

"My strength is as the strength of ten, because my heart is pure." I knew she would recognize that quotation.

"You're an Alfred Lord Tennyson fan?"

"All-arm'd I ride, whate'er betide, until I find the Holy Grail."

"*Sir Galahad*, Tennyson's most famous poem. Did you know Al's full name is Alfred Lord Tennyson Rice?"

"Yes, ma'am. Tank told me."

"You view yourself as a knight errant."

"And I have dimples."

Doraleen smiled. Or maybe smirked. "Tank warned me that you fancy yourself a humorist."

"Guilty as charged."

"I'm sure you're quite droll, Chuck, but I don't have a sense of humor."

"You could have fooled me."

"What?" She raised a hand to her chest. "Oh, that was another *bon mot*, wasn't it? It was irony."

"I thought so. Mistakenly, it appears."

"If ever a damsel in distress needed a knight errant like Sir Galahad to gallop in on a white horse, it is I."

I grinned. "Spoken like a true English teacher."

"You shall be my Sir Galahad." Doraleen glanced at the door. "I don't mean to be rude, Chuck, but I'm worried about Race Car. Ever since that horrid man came here yesterday to threaten me, I've been on pins and needles. I think about things I've seen on TV and in the movies... you remember the horse's head scene in *The Godfather*?"

Everyone who'd ever seen that movie remembered the scene.

"That scene scared the heck out of me," I said. My stomach knotted when I remembered another time I'd found a client's dog slaughtered by a mobster with a sadistic streak like Moffett. I forced the dead dog's image from my mind.

"Race Car isn't a prize racehorse, but she is every bit as precious to Al and me. To Tank too, for that matter. We found her following the graveside service at William's funeral. This forlorn, dirty little kitten walks up to us in the middle of that forest of tombstones. God knows where she came from. She rubs against Al's leg and he picks her up. She licks his hand and purrs, and Al was smitten. He said, 'It's Dad. He sent this kitten to tell us he's okay.' We searched the cemetery to see if there was a momma cat anywhere, but it was like the kitten had dropped from the sky—or from Heaven. Al named her Race Car.'"

"Race Car?" I repeated. "An unusual name for a cat."

Doraleen smiled. "William played wide receiver. He was so fast that his nickname was Race Car Rice. We named her in tribute to my William. But Race Car's old. There's no telling how much longer she'll live."

"Would you like me to find her, Doraleen?" I asked.

She set down her sherry and snugged the shawl around her shoulders. "I'll go with you. Race Car can get nervous around strangers. I notice you carry a gun. Even if that... that man is out there, I'll be safe with you." She followed me to the door.

I flipped back the security bar and opened the two dead bolts. "Normally, I'd hold the door for you, Doraleen. In this case, let me go first—for security." I hauled the door open and jerked to a stop in mid-stride, barring Doraleen's path with my arm.

An off-white Persian cat sprawled in macabre repose on the concrete, fluffy fur streaked with crimson splotches. Bloody streaks marked a trail where the pitiful pet had fought her way up the steps and across the porch and collapsed near the door. Ragged stumps were all that remained of her tail and ears. Race Car raised her head. Her mouth opened in a soundless meow.

Doraleen pushed past my arm with surprising strength. "She's alive!"

Chapter 4

I DREW MY GLOCK AND SCANNED THE STREET AND SIDEWALK; no one was visible in the streetlights. I stuck my head inside the door. "Tank! Get out here—front porch. It's an emergency."

I leapt down the porch steps and ran to the sidewalk where I could see around the Bougainvilleas that sprawled across Doraleen's front yard. A set of taillights sped away a block up the street. The SUV squealed a right at the corner and was lost to view. I debated chasing it in my own minivan, but I-95 was two blocks away. The SUV would vanish before I had it in sight.

I holstered the Glock and jogged to the front porch where Tank was cradling Race Car in his arms. Blood stained his shirt sleeves and vest.

Doraleen stood beside him, stroking the cat's back.

"Doraleen," I asked, "do you have a regular vet for Race Car?"

She blinked away tears. "What…? My vet?" She shook her head as if to clear it. "Yes, yes, of course." She eyed her watch. "She might be closed."

"Let's go anyway," I said. "If the clinic is closed, they'll have an emergency contact number on the door. We'll drive my van. Tank, you sit in back with Race Car. Doraleen, get your purse and lock the house."

Doraleen didn't move. She continued to stroke Race Car's matted fur.

I patted the sweet old lady on the shoulder. "Doraleen," I said softly, "we need to get Race Car to the vet. Get your purse and lock the house. Please."

She kept stroking the cat.

Tank stepped back, moving with Race Car out of reach. "Momma Dora, we need to go. Now."

"Okay. I'll be right back." She pushed the door open and went inside.

I thumbed my remote and the rear door of the minivan slid open. I followed Tank to the vehicle, slid the bucket seat back, and waited while my giant friend wedged himself in and slid the door closed. I opened the passenger door as Doraleen hurried down the porch steps. I helped her into the van, closed the door, and trotted around to the driver's seat.

Doraleen clicked her seatbelt. "Head to I-95 and drive south. It's the second exit."

I STOPPED IN THE CLINIC'S EMPTY PARKING LOT and read the veterinarian's emergency contact number by my headlights. I punched in the number and handed the phone to Doraleen.

"Dr. Willsey? It's Doraleen Rice… Yes, ma'am. Race Car, a white Persian… Something terrible happened to Race Car. We're parked at your clinic. Can you come down and help her? Someone cut off her ears and tail. Thanks. We'll be waiting."

She handed the phone back to me. "Ten minutes." She twisted where she could reach Race Car in Tank's lap. She stroked the cat's back. "There's a bench on the front porch. I'll carry Race Car and wait with her up there."

"You'll get blood on your dress, Momma Dora. I'll hold her. I'm already bloody."

Doraleen opened the passenger door and spoke over her shoulder to Tank. "She'll feel safer in my lap. I don't mind the blood."

I followed both of them to the bench and waited until they sat. "Once the vet gets here, I'd like to go back to your street and locate the place where… that is, the crime scene. Search for evidence."

Doraleen patted Tank's knee. "I'm safe with Tank. You go on. If it rains, it might wash away clues."

I PARKED AT THE CURB IN FRONT OF DORALEEN'S HOUSE. I yanked on rubber gloves and shined a Maglite. Blood drops marked a faint trail on the concrete. The trail led down the sidewalk to Doraleen's next door neighbor. Four more drops and a blood smear clustered on the pavement. I sniffed the air and followed a scent until I knelt on the sidewalk near a plumbago hedge. I sniffed again. Shining the Maglite under the hedge, I spied an empty tuna can. That's how the bastard attracted Race Car. Any cat within smelling distance would come to him, even one who was nervous around strangers.

I played the beam back and forth under the hedge. A white scrap of fur lay in the mulch. I jerked an evidence bag from my pocket and picked up the white object. A cat's ear. My stomach felt like a fist-sized rock. *Oh, God, that poor cat.* I bagged the ear and found the tail and the other ear nearby. Bagged them too. I wasn't sure what I would do with them. When I found the bastard who did this, maybe I'd make him eat them.

I bagged the tuna can. Maybe I could pull a fingerprint off it.

As I set the evidence bags in the van, a light rain began to fall.

Chapter 5

AL RICE SWIGGED MORE IRISH WHISKEY, swished it around in his mouth, and stared at the stripper dancing on the stage behind the bar at the Orange Peel Gentlemen's Club. *What was her name? Brandy. Yeah, it's Brandy. Or maybe Amber. What the hell difference does it make?* This might be his last drink in his entire life. He'd never see Jasmine again—even if her name *was* Jennifer now. Tomorrow would be two weeks since Moffett had smashed Al's left hand to smithereens. Moffett had threatened to send Teddy to do even worse if he didn't pay. Teddy, now he was one bad dude. Always playing with that creepy knife. A warrior's weapon, Teddy called it.

And Rice hadn't paid. Two hundred thousand dollars, by God. Moffett might as well demand that Rice pay off the national debt. That was as likely to happen. What the hell… it was too late. It was always too late for Al. Too late for something. Too late for anything.

The surgeon who repaired his crushed hand had given him a prescription for forty Oxycodone pills for the pain. "Take one every six hours, as needed," he'd said. That was supposed to last ten days. Fat chance. He'd swallowed eight pills the first day.

Then Cinnamon, another stripper at the Orange Peel, slipped him a note that she wanted to score some Oxycodone. After her shift, Rice met her in the parking lot and sold her the rest of the pills for money and a blow job. The BJ wasn't even good. He was too high to enjoy it. At least the money was good. For the last few days, he'd drunk his way through the cash while he ogled Jasmine and the other strippers. *Who says you need*

Oxycodone for pain? Irish whiskey is nearly as good. Rice's biggest pain was that Jasmine or Jennifer or whatever-the-hell her name was—wouldn't give him the time of day. And why the hell did she change her name? He had barely gotten used to calling her Jasmine.

He downed another drink and set the glass on the bar too hard. He waved at the bartender with his right hand. He raised his voice above the music. "Billy! I'll have another."

Billy leaned across the bar. "Pay for the drinks you already drank, Al. You can't run a tab forever."

"How much I owe you?"

"$48.50."

Rice belched. "$48.50. Sure thing, sure thing. I have it here… somewhere." He patted his jacket pockets, then his pants. He stood up from the barstool. Stuffing his right hand into his left front pants pocket, he twisted around, then tilted and staggered to regain his balance.

A man two stools down peeled his attention from the stripper, regarded Rice from the corner of his eye, and carried his drink to an empty table.

Rice lurched into another man at the bar. "Whoa. Sorry, sorry." He grasped the bar. "Let's see… Aha. Here we go." He managed to slip a credit card from his pocket, and tossed it on the bar.

The other man frowned, dropped a few bills on the bar, and walked out.

"Al, you're running off my customers." Billy stuck the credit card in a terminal. He punched the keys, studied the screen for a moment, and scoffed. He slid the card back across the bar. "Declined, Al."

Rice drained the last of the Irish whiskey. *Better enjoy it; it might be the last drink I'll have. Ever.* He reached in another pocket, found another credit card, and pushed it across the bar. "Try this one."

The bartender stuck the card in the terminal. "Declined. You got any cash, Al? You owe me $48.50."

"$48.50," Rice repeated.

The previous night Rice had drunk himself into oblivion at that same bar. He had awoken this morning in his car with no memory of how he got there. Now he wouldn't get enough alcohol to dull the pain of the real world again. How could he enjoy his last night on earth?

He lifted his hand. "See this cast?" He had trouble saying "cast." It sounded more like "cash."

Billy shouted above the music. "No, but I'd like to see cash."

"No, no, no. Not *cash*. I said, 'See this *cast*.'" He waved the cast.

"Yeah, I seen it lots of times. What about it?"

Rice slid back onto the barstool. "It was a pres... a present."

"Yeah, so what?"

"A present... from Monster Moffett." Rice held the cast in front of his face and studied it with bloodshot eyes. "You know good ol' Monster, don't you, Billy?"

"I seen him around."

"He's gonna kill me tomorrow, y'know. That's why I'm here to enjoy the girls tonight."

"Yeah, right, and I'm gonna be elected president." The bartender shook a finger at Rice. "Listen, Al. Your troubles with Monster Moffett don't mean shit to me. I got troubles of my own. You gonna pay your tab or what?"

"Sure, sure, sure..." Rice slid his hand into his shirt pocket and fished out a clump of crushed bills. He dropped them on the bar and tried to smooth them out with his right hand. "Oops." He pinned a bill under his cast and pressed it out. "Too goddamn dark in here to tell what kind this is, Billy. You got a light?"

"If you weren't drunk, you could tell." Billy pulled a penlight from his shirt pocket. It was a twenty.

"How much I owe you?" asked Rice.

"$48.50."

Forty... eight fitty," Rice repeated. "I thought that was it." He pushed the twenty across the bar. He pinned another bill under his cast. "Let's see what this one is."

Billy shined the penlight again.

It was another twenty, which Rice laid carefully on the first bill. He yanked another bill out.

A five, and Rice lined it up on the two twenties. "Here you go. Let's call it even." He attempted to pick up the remaining bills. "I need something to tip the dancers, Billy."

The bartender seized Rice's wrist. "You owe me $48.50, not $45. How much more you got there?" He pried the bills from Rice's fist and counted them. "Four more bucks." He snatched the bills off the bar. "I'll keep the extra fifty cents for a tip. Sheesh."

"Okay… Okay… So my tab's paid. How about my other drink?"

"Go home, Al." The bartender walked away.

"You gonna call me a cab?"

The bartender stopped at the far end of the bar. "What the hell are you gonna use to pay for a cab?"

Rice found that uproariously funny. "Just kidding, Billy. I don't need a cab; I have my car. Don't matter none. Got no home to go to. Oops, Momma wouldn't like that. Lemme rephrase: It doesn't matter, because I have no home to which I could go." He guffawed. "No home to which I could go."

The bartender walked around the bar and grabbed Rice's arm. "Gimme your keys."

Rice stared at him.

The bartender searched Rice's pockets until his found the keys. "I'll keep these until tomorrow. Come back sober and I'll give them to you." He walked Rice toward the door. "Like the song says: *You don't have to go home, but you can't stay here.* Beat it, Al."

Rice stumbled out the door and stopped in the middle of the sidewalk, swaying. He staggered to the wall and leaned on it. Oh, Christ, what would happen to him now? Tomorrow Moffett would send Teddy Ngombo after him. He couldn't go home. He couldn't confront Momma like this. He'd been there a couple of days ago. He couldn't bear to see that expression on her face again. He should've showered at Momma's. He couldn't remember why he hadn't. God knows, he needed a bath. He hadn't bathed in days, ever since his landlord stuffed his clothes in a plastic garbage bag in front of his apartment. He'd tried the door, but the goddamn landlord changed the lock. That was a week ago, but it seemed like forever. He didn't remember what he did with the clothes.

He slid down the concrete block wall and plunked down on the sidewalk. He belched and then vomited. He leaned to one side and passed out.

Chapter 6

I RETURNED TO THE VETERINARY CLINIC. I tapped on the glass door. The doctor unlocked the door from inside and let me in.

"You must be Chuck McCrary. I'm Dr. Willsey, Sharon Willsey." She was a plump, middle-aged woman with salt-and-pepper hair. She wore green scrubs and bright orange sneakers. She shook my hand.

"Nice to meet you, Doctor. I know Doraleen appreciates you coming down after hours."

"She's a sweet old lady with a sweet old cat. I'm glad I could help. Follow me." She led me down the hall.

"How is the patient?" I asked.

"Race Car is recovering from the anesthetic. Doraleen and Tank are with her. I cleaned and cauterized the wounds and gave her an antibiotic to guard against infection. Race Car is old for a cat and this was a shock to her system. I'll keep her a couple days for observation. That's all I can do. If there are no complications in the next two or three days, we'll let nature take its course and hope she recovers. Here we are." She opened a door to the treatment room.

Doraleen sat in an upholstered chair with Race Car asleep on a white cloth on her lap. The old woman stroked the cat's side, avoiding the bandages on her ears and tail.

Tank stood next to her with his hand on her shoulder. "What did you find out, Chuck?"

"I'll tell you later. Right now, I need to talk to Doraleen." I swiveled to Dr. Willsey. "Can we go home now?"

"Yes." She lifted the unconscious cat from Doraleen's lap. "Ms. Rice, once the anesthetic wears off, Race Car will go back to sleep on her own and sleep the whole night. I'll examine her again first thing in the morning and call you with an update."

I UNLOCKED DORALEEN'S FRONT DOOR and handed her keys back. "Tank, would you please see if that coffee is any good." I opened the door and switched on the light. "Why don't you change those bloody clothes, Doraleen? Tank and I'll wait for you in the living room."

We were drinking coffee when Doraleen joined us. She'd slipped into a colorful Chinese silk robe and fuzzy pink slippers. "I'll pour another sherry."

I waited until she sat beside Tank and sipped her wine. "Doraleen, do you feel like answering questions?"

"Of course. What do you want to know?"

"Do you know where Al is?"

"I hadn't seen Al in weeks until day before yesterday. He appeared at my door drunk. Said he'd been kicked out of his apartment and was living in his car. I made him spend the night, though he didn't want to. I tried to get him to take a bath, but he was too drunk and too stubborn." She pivoted to Tank. "You know how he gets when he's been drinking—or worse."

Tank nodded.

Doraleen sighed. "When Al woke the next morning, he couldn't wait to leave my home—his home too, if he would stay here and clean up his life. I insisted he eat breakfast." She tugged a handkerchief from a pocket and twisted it in her hands. "He told me that Moffett threatened to harm me. I told Al that I had a little money. I offered to pay Moffett if Al came back home, sobered up, and got a real job. Al laughed. He said I could never get enough money to pay Moffett." She leaned a little closer to Tank. "How much does he owe?"

"Two hundred thousand dollars."

"Jesus, help us."

"Doraleen, did Al say where he was going?" I asked.

"No. I asked him what he intended to do, where he wanted to go. He walked out anyway." She peered down at her sherry.

"Al is a sheep without a shepherd. He's like the bumper cars at the old amusement parks when I was a little girl. External forces bump him around willy-nilly. He never takes control of his own life."

"Tell me about Monster Moffett contacting you yesterday," I said.

She sipped her sherry first and blotted her eyes with a handkerchief. "Al told me he made a terrible mistake. He swore on my life that he would pay his debt to this… this… *creature.* Al meant it as a figure of speech to indicate his resolve to honor his debt. But this Monster man seized upon the statement and threatened to do me harm. When Al told me, I didn't take it seriously."

She smiled at Tank. "You know the lies Al tells to try to get out of trouble. He'll spin any tall tale he thinks will work. Always, whatever the trouble is, it's somebody else's fault. Al is never responsible for any of his messes."

"Right," Tank agreed.

"I thought Al had fabricated another fantasy. But yesterday afternoon after Al left…"

"What happened?"

"After I got home from school, the doorbell rang. I opened the door, and this awful man was standing on the porch, holding Race Car in his arms. He asked if she belonged to me." She wiped another tear. "I said she did, and he handed her to me and said…" Her voice broke. "He said, 'Who will take care of the cat if anything happens to you?' He said Al owed him money and Al swore on my life that he would pay."

"Can you describe the man?" I asked.

"A little shorter than you, medium build, dark-skinned black man, like a real African from Africa. Looked like tribal ritual scars on his forehead and around his eyes. Long hair in dreadlocks, like he might never have cut it in his life. Thin mustache, otherwise clean-shaven. Oh—he had another scar, not a ritual one, on his right cheek, like this." She drew her hand down her cheek at an angle. "It was frightening."

Tank said, "That's not Moffett, is it?"

"No," I replied. "Among other differences, Moffett is white." I pivoted to Doraleen. "Might the scar have come from a knife fight?"

"I suppose so. It was puckered like it hadn't been stitched professionally, if at all. The man's appearance was quite fearsome."

"You say he spoke to you. Did he have an accent?"

"He spoke careful English, like it wasn't his first language. He had an accent, but I couldn't tell you where from. It wasn't one I recognized like French or German. That's why I thought Africa. Although there was a hint of British English."

"Did this guy give you a name?"

She shook her head.

"What made you think he was Monster Moffett? What did he say?"

"He said Al owed the money to 'us.' I asked him who 'us' was, and he said 'Monster Moffett.'" She waved the handkerchief. "I just assumed. He certainly *looked* like a monster."

"Tell me what he said."

"He said Al had sworn on my life that he would pay and I was collateral on Al's loan. 'We take Al's oath seriously.' Those were his exact words. 'We take Al's oath seriously.' He said Al better take it seriously, because they know where I live." She sobbed for a time.

Tank and I waited helplessly while she recovered.

She wiped her eyes. "He said I'd better make sure Al pays the money or I would regret it for the rest of my very short life." She twisted the handkerchief in her fingers. "Those were his exact words. 'You'll regret it for the rest of your very short life.'" She raised her handkerchief to her face and cried again.

Tank wrapped his arm around her and patted her shoulder.

I felt terrible for her. I wrote the man's description on my notepad. I could identify the thug from a description that good. But so what? Doraleen couldn't prove anyone had threatened her. I remembered my days on the job. The cops would listen to her complaint and tell her there was nothing they could do. Even if I found the guy, roughed him up, and told him to stay away from Doraleen, Moffett wouldn't let that go. Al didn't deny that he owed Moffett the money. My hands were tied.

I texted the description to Kelly Contreras, a police detective I'd worked with over the years.

I drank cold coffee and waited for Doraleen to calm down.

This muddled situation reminded me of Iraq and Afghanistan, and I said the same to Tank.

"I don't see the similarity."

"We went into Iraq and Afghanistan with good intentions and vague goals. Put boots on the ground and killed a bunch of people—mainly bad guys, but civilians too. Made few friends and lots of enemies. Lost a bunch of our own people, including many of my brother soldiers. We blew hundreds of billions of dollars building infrastructure—good intentions again. Then we declared victory and hightailed it out of both places. Both countries collapsed into chaos."

"I don't get the analogy."

"It was Vietnam all over again. Blood and treasure wasted because the underlying causes of Iraq's and Afghanistan's troubles remained in place."

"What underlying causes?" Tank asked.

"Don't get me started. My grandpa Magnus McCrary served in Vietnam and he told me people still don't agree on what went wrong there. As for Iraq and Afghanistan, who knows? I was a dogface grunt. But neither country has ever experienced democracy or self-government. Both indigenous populations regard themselves as a religious sect or a tribal member, rather than as a citizen. Both had cultures of corruption, nepotism, and cronyism. Nothing changed in the few years we were there."

"So how does Al's situation remind you of those?"

"You hired me to help Doraleen. You're okay with throwing your treasure and my blood into the mission. Great. We have the best intentions, but what does true help look like? Al's two weeks are up tomorrow and we don't know where he is. Suppose I find him, how will I know when the case is over? How will the world be different? What will have changed in Doraleen's life? Will Al be sober and debt free? For how long?"

Doraleen stopped crying. "Al's been sober before, Tank. Lots of times. It's never lasted. And you've paid off his debts lots of times. Nothing changes because my son doesn't change." She twisted the handkerchief in her hands. "He's the same old Alfred Rice."

"Tank, we don't have a clearly defined mission here. I can guard Doraleen for a while, but not for the rest of her life. You ruled out paying off Moffett. The only crime I might prove would be cruelty to animals. I have nothing to give to the police." I spread my hands. "All I can do is find Al and bring him to a safe place. But what do we do for the second act?"

"What do you recommend, Momma Dora?" asked Tank. "What can we realistically do for Al?"

"Al's time is up tomorrow, and this Monster Moffett man will be searching for him. Find Al before he does. The rest, we'll work out once Chuck gets Al safe."

"All right, Act One is clear enough," I said, "find Al before Moffett does."

Chapter 7

"WHAT WAS AL'S LAST ADDRESS?"

Doraleen rattled it off, and I wrote it down. "I'll go tomorrow. Ask if he gave a forwarding address. Does Al still have a phone?"

"I don't know. I call his number but it goes straight to voicemail."

"That's good. That means his account is active or you'd get a message that the number wasn't in service. Maybe his phone is dead and he hasn't recharged it because he's living in his car."

"Everybody owns a car charger," Tank said. "That can't be why it went to voicemail."

"Work with me here, Tank. Look on the bright side." I smiled at Doraleen. "He might have lost the charger or it could be broken. The important thing is the account is active and Al can turn his phone on in the future. Let's keep that option open for Al. Call his cell phone company tomorrow morning and tell them Al went on vacation and forgot to pay his bill. Tell them he asked you to pay it. Use your credit card to bring his phone bill current."

Doraleen sat straighter. "I can do that. Anything else I can do to help?"

"Yes. Leave another voicemail. Tell Al that you hired a private investigator to protect him from Moffett. Give him my name and cell number; it's on my card. Ask him to call me ASAP. Maybe we'll get lucky."

"What about me?" Tank asked, "What can I do?"

"Did you bring a handgun with you?"

"Not with me, no."

"Doraleen, do you own a gun?"

"Oh, heavens, no. Guns frighten me. William owned one, but after he passed, I turned it in at a police department buy-back event. I was glad it was gone from the house. Sorry."

"That's okay; I have an extra one for Tank to use."

I unclipped the Glock from my belt. "Keep this. Stay here tonight and drive Doraleen to school tomorrow before you go to work. Moffett won't try anything at the high school. I'll have Snoop pick her up tomorrow afternoon after school and babysit her until I find Al." I pivoted to Doraleen. "I'll send you a text with Snoop's picture so you'll recognize him. He'll call for you in the school attendance office."

"Snoop?"

"Nickname. His real name is Raymond Snopolski. He's a former police detective like me. He was my partner when we were both in the Port City Police, and he's better with a gun than I am. You'll like him, and he'll keep you safe."

"Okay, I'll wait for this Snoop in the attendance office. What else can I do?"

"What kind of car does Al drive?"

"A silver Toyota sedan."

"What year?"

"I don't remember, but it's ancient." She smiled. "And it was filthy when he was here. I have the license number."

I was surprised at that. "Great, what is it?" I wrote it on my notepad. "I'll have the police issue a BOLO on it."

"I don't want to seem ignorant," Doraleen asked, "but what's a BOLO?"

"Be on the lookout. The cops will help me find his car. They'll call if anyone spots it."

"They'll do that for you?"

"I'll tell Detective Kelly Contreras that Al's life is in danger, and he can help the PCPD bring down Monster Moffett if we find him… Yeah, they'll do it." *I hope.*

Chapter 8

I SQUEEZED MY DODGE CARAVAN INTO A PARKING SPACE up the street from the Albemarle Arms apartments on NW 77th Street. I moved the Browning .380 clipped to my belt around to my back. I wore a navy-blue sports coat to hide the gun. I locked the van and set the car alarm. No one paid any attention. Not surprising since the minivan was six years old, dingy white, and identical to a million others. It might as well have a neon sign on it that blinked to potential thieves: *Nothing inside here worth stealing.*

I walked up the cracked sidewalk and stopped at the three-story apartments. Faded terra cotta paint peeled off the walls of the concrete block and stucco building. Four neglected Sabal palms with the stumps of old fronds clinging to the trunks stood silent sentinel on each side of the sidewalk that led to the front porch. I struggled to remember what they called those stumps. Then it came to me: *boots*. The next hurricane to hit Port City would snag those overgrown crowns like Velcro and toss the trees through a window or onto a car. A pink Bougainvillea ran wild to the left of the sidewalk and covered the windows up to the second floor. At least their thorns were a good deterrent to burglars.

The faded *Albemarle Arms* sign had a *For Rent* placard hooked on the bottom, swinging in the morning breeze.

I knocked on the office door, waited, and knocked again. I climbed the steps to the third floor balcony and found apartment 3-H. I knocked on the door, waited, knocked again. Maybe the landlord had not rented Al's apartment yet. I jiggled the doorknob but it was locked. Some of Al's things might be inside, things that might provide a clue to his whereabouts. I debated whether to pick the lock or find the super and spoof him. I didn't want to be caught breaking and entering. At least not yet. You catch more flies with honey than with vinegar. Yeah, spoofing was the way to go.

I returned to the office door and knocked again. I called the emergency contact number on the office sign.

"Albemarle Arms. This is Reggie speaking."

"I'm at the office door. Where are you?"

"In back. I'll be right there. Give me two minutes."

Reggie was a middle-aged black man with gray hair cut short. Reminded me of Obama in his second term, except for the beard. Reggie's stubble was white, which would've given him a scholarly aspect if he weren't wearing a dirty khaki industrial uniform and work boots and carrying a tool belt in his hand. "Can I help you?"

"Are you Reggie?"

"Yeah, Regivius Larkin. I'm the superintendent. Everybody calls me Reggie."

"I'm looking for Al Rice."

Reggie scoffed. "When you find the bum, tell him he owes me fourteen hundred dollars in back rent. He don't live here no more. I evicted him a few days ago." He swiveled to open the office door.

"Did he leave a forwarding address?"

"You're kidding, right?"

I shrugged. "I had to ask."

"Why you wearing a piece? You a cop?"

"You're not supposed to notice my gun when I clip the holster to my back."

"You was facing the other way when I walked up, son. I spied the bulge in the back. You ain't the first cop I ever seen, y'know."

"I'm not a cop. I'm a runner for a bookie. Al Rice's bookie. Sometimes I carry enough cash to need protection. My boss owes Rice two thousand dollars. You know where I can find him?"

"No, and if I did, why should I tell you?"

"I might help you collect that back rent, that's why."

Reggie gave the matter some thought. He shrugged. "Come on in." He led me inside. He dropped the tool belt on a battered desk and plopped into an equally-worn chair. "Rice owes me fourteen hundred dollars, plus eviction expenses."

"My boss owes him more than that," I said. "When I find him and pay him, he'll have the money to pay you and move back into his apartment."

The superintendent frowned. "How do I know you ain't shitting me?"

"First tell me if you have any information about Rice. If you can't help me, it doesn't make any difference whether I'm shitting you or not."

"I might know a thing or two about Al Rice. I might know how to find out more if you pay the back rent."

"If you're only the super, why do you care if Al pays or not? Are you the landlord too?"

"Nah, but he give me a cut of the rents I collect. If I get the fourteen hundred back, I keep a hundred forty."

"Tell you what, Reggie, I'll make you a better deal." I tugged two hundred-dollar bills from my pocket. "You help me out and I'll give you these."

The super reached for the bills and I drew them back. "First you help me out."

"You don't act like no bookie. You sure you ain't a cop?"

"I'm not a bookie; I work for a bookie. And, yeah, I used to be a cop. I make more money working for the bookie."

"You on the shady side of the law now, and you carry a gun. How I know you'll give me the money after I help you?"

"Did Al Rice leave any stuff here?"

"Yeah. I threw his clothes in a trash bag for him and he left without them."

"Did you clean out his apartment after he left?"

"Nah, I cleaned out the refrigerator so's it won't stink. I'll wait on the other stuff until I rent it to someone else."

"I'll give you a hundred now to tell me what you know and the other hundred once you show me Rice's stuff and let me into his apartment."

"You going to a lot of trouble to pay a debt. Why you not wait for Rice to find you?"

"Not good for my boss's reputation. He pays off his winning customers. It's good for business. Do you want the hundred or not?"

Reggie stared at the two bills in my hand. "Deal." He pocketed one. "Rice, he like to hang out at a strip club in the neighborhood. He sweet on one of the strippers. He talk about her all the time."

"What's her name?"

"Don't remember."

"Reggie, if Al was sweet on a girl and talked about her a lot, he must've mentioned her name."

"I said I don't remember."

"Then tell me the name of the club."

"Don't remember that neither."

I began to shove the other hundred back in my pocket.

"Wait, wait." Reggie waved his hands. "I don't remember the name and that's the God's honest truth. But how many can there be, man? I know he usually walked there. Al, he said he had two DUI's and wouldn't risk a third one. Since he walked, it has to be close. That's good information, right?"

I held up a hundred. "Al have any friends?"

"When he had money, Al had lots of friends—black, white, and brown. Not that I knew any names. When he was broke—which was most of the time—he din't have no friends. He'd get late on his rent, then he'd catch up. Then he'd get late again. Same old, same old. I gave up when he got two months behind. I changed the lock and threw his ass out."

"How long did he live here?"

Reggie scratched his head. "Almost two years."

That was plenty of time for stuff to accumulate in Al's apartment—credit card slips, old letters, bills. Lots of potential there. "Where are his clothes?"

"In the apartment. I changed the lock and left his stuff in a bag outside the door. I stuck a note on it for him to take them and leave. State law don't let me keep his clothes. Wouldn't be worth nothing anyway. Next day, the note was gone, but the clothes was still there. I set them inside the apartment door. If he don't show before I rent the apartment, I'll toss them in the dumpster."

"Let's look in the apartment."

Reggie opened the door and stood in the opening, blocking it. He stuck his hand out. "Time for that other hundred."

I held up the bill. "If you were searching for Al, where would you start?"

"At that strip club. All he talked about was that stripper what worked there and how he knew she loved him but pretended not to." The super snatched the bill. "Stripper's name was Jasmine, not that the information does you much good. Half the strippers in town are named Jasmine and the other half are named Tiffany." He cackled as he stuffed the bill in his pocket. "Lock the door behind you when you're finished."

"Thanks, Reggie." I handed him a business card, one without the Welcome Wagon logo. "If you think of anything else, give me a call. There's another hundred in it."

Reggie read my card. "Din't figure you was no bookie. Why you really wanna find Rice?"

"Very bad guys are after Al Rice. He's in danger, and I want to find him and keep him safe."

"How I know you ain't one of them bad guys your own self?"

"His mother hired me to find him."

"Why should I believe you?"

"Look at this face. Is this the face of a bad guy?"

He laughed. "You got me there, white boy. Knock yourself out."

I set the bag of clothes to one side while I searched the two-room apartment. The front room had a kitchenette on the left wall and a dinette set with a yellow Formica table and four chairs upholstered in yellow plastic. The other side of the room held a battered couch that might have been purple when it was new, sometime in the first Bush administration. A worn easy chair that might have matched the couch years ago sat beside it at an angle facing the small television. A side chair that didn't match anything sat at the other end of the couch. Two empty beer bottles were adding to the rings on the coffee table between the couch and the television. An uneven set of Venetian blinds hung in the jalousie window that overlooked the walkway.

The refrigerator-freezer was empty like the super said. The cabinets in the kitchenette held mismatched tableware. I checked inside the coffee cups and found coffee grounds and stains. I searched the underside of the plates; nothing taped there. One cabinet door had a two-year old calendar hung inside on a finishing nail. The drawers held nothing of interest. The cabinet under the counter held a couple of battered pots and pans. I found a baggie of marijuana stuck in a teapot. A pot stash stashed in a pot. Ha. I left it there for the next tenant. Happy birthday. Or happy something.

The bathroom medicine cabinet held a toothbrush, toothpaste, shaving gear, and a half-empty ibuprofen bottle. I examined the pills. They were ibuprofen. Nothing in the toilet tank or taped underneath it.

The bedroom closet and shelves appeared empty. I ran my hand along the top shelf and found a red envelope addressed to Al. It was a Christmas card from Doraleen. It had a long, handwritten note inside that expressed her love, invited Al to move back home, and promised to get him into rehab. I stuck the card back in the envelope, which was postmarked two Christmases ago. I debated what to do with it. If I gave it to Doraleen, it might make her sad. On the other hand, it proved Al cared enough for his mother to keep the card. I stuck it in my pocket.

I stripped the bedclothes off and shook them out. Nothing. The pillowcases were empty. I flipped the filthy mattress and there it was: a small address book. Names and phone numbers with few addresses. Mostly first names and some with only initials. I stuck it in my pocket for further study if my other leads failed.

In the nightstand I found three credit card bills postmarked several months earlier. None had been opened. I read the charges: liquor stores, drug stores, convenience stores, and bars. Not a single charge at a grocery store. None reflected any payments on the account balance. The most recent bill contained a notice that the card would be cancelled if the minimum were not paid within ten days. That bill was two months old.

I told my smartphone, "Find strip clubs near me." A map flashed on the screen. Three strip joints were within walking distance of Al Rice's apartment.

Chapter 9

AL RICE WOKE WITH A SPLITTING HEADACHE. At least that meant he was alive. *Teddy hasn't found me yet.* He squinted against the sunlight and closed his eyes. His mouth felt Sahara-Desert dry. Where was he? He moved his hand. Rough pavement. Was he lying on a street? He listened for traffic noise. Nothing. He rolled over and banged his head. He opened his eyes. The door panel of a car. He was in the parking lot behind the Orange Peel. How the hell did he wind up here? He thought back to the previous night. What was that god-awful smell? He glanced down at his jacket. Christ, he had vomited on his jacket. That explained the smell, stronger than the smell of his unwashed body. He felt for his keys. Not in his pants. Oh, yeah. That prick Billy stole his keys. *What did he say? Come back tomorrow when you're sober and I'll give your keys back? Yeah, that was it.* Al glanced at his wrist for the time, then he remembered he'd sold his watch. He yanked his phone from his jacket. The screen was dark. Christ, it wasn't charged. He'd forgotten to charge it for the last few days.

He reached a hand up and brushed the car door handle with his fingertips. Out of reach. He slumped onto his back and wondered if the Orange Peel was open yet. He couldn't buy a drink, but he could get his keys back. Maybe there was a bottle of something in his car; he couldn't remember. He squinted. Damned sun hurt his eyes. It was pretty high; perhaps the Orange Peel was already open. He rolled onto his shoulder and reached again for the door handle. *Crap. Still out of reach. God, my head hurts.* He struggled to his knees, grasped the door handle, and levered himself to his feet.

Suddenly he needed to pee. He glanced around, spotted the dumpster enclosure, and staggered inside the wooden fence. He finished and stumbled back to his car.

Glancing at his filthy jacket, he shrugged it off and draped it across the hood. He patted his rear pocket. At least no one stole his wallet while he was passed out. He had his suspended driver's license in case he needed it to reclaim his keys. He planted a hand on the wall to steady himself. If only his head didn't hurt so bad… If only his mouth wasn't so dry… If only he wasn't so hungry… If only, if only, if only. His life was a series of bleak *if onlys. Why does this always happen to me?*

He stumbled his way to the entrance to the Orange Peel. Locked. He scanned his surroundings. Across Charles Boulevard a bank sign flashed the time and temperature. *Eighty degrees already. Fifteen minutes until opening.* He made his way to a bus bench fifty yards away and slumped down, head in hands. He felt as miserable as he'd ever been in his life. He had no plans beyond getting his keys back. At least that was a goal, any goal, for a man with no goals.

A man he didn't know unlocked the glass door to the Orange Peel. The bank sign marked five more minutes, then he wobbled to the door and tugged on it. The man had locked it behind him. Rice shaded his eyes with his hands and pressed his nose to the glass.

The man inside said, "We open in ten minutes."

"I need my car keys. I left them here last night."

"Ten minutes."

"I need my damn keys."

"Ten minutes."

Rice banged on the door with his fists. "Give me my damn keys, or I'll break the stupid door down." He sobbed.

The man hurried over and opened the door. "Okay, okay, I'll get your keys. What's your name?"

"Al Rice."

"Show me your ID."

Rice displayed his driver's license.

"Stay there. I'll get your keys." He disappeared through the entrance curtain. A minute later, he returned. "Here you are."

Al's gut rumbled. He'd better make nice to the guy. "Thanks. Say... I'm sorry I lost my temper. It's been a hard few days."

The man smiled. "Hey, everyone has a hard day once in a while. Maybe today will be better. Have a nice day."

"Can I... Can I use the bathroom before I go?"

"Sure. It's over there."

Rice used the bathroom and slurped a long drink of water from his cupped hand under the faucet. He was still thirsty, but he knew from long experience that his thirst would disappear with time. He slurped another drink from his palm before he left the bathroom.

"Thanks, buddy."

"Come back to see us, Mr. Rice."

"Yeah, sure thing."

Steadier now, he walked back to his car. He stared at his key ring. It held three keys: the key to the Toyota, a key to his old apartment, and a key to his mother's house. Tears rolled down his cheeks as he stared at the keys, a reminder of his crummy past, his miserable present, and his hopeless future. He fumbled the key to his old apartment off the key ring. He bounced it in his hand and hurled it across the lot. It tinkled and bounced its way into the hedge.

He blinked the tears away until he could find the keyhole and unlocked the car door. *Shit.* He'd left his jacket on the hood. Lifting his jacket, he stared at the vomitus dried on the front. *Christ, I don't want that in the car.* He staggered to the dumpster, lifted the lid, and tossed the jacket inside. One more thing he'd lost.

Returning to his car, he searched the glove compartment; sometimes he kept a half-pint there or maybe a joint. Not today. He felt under the front seat. Nothing there either. He sat in the driver seat, draped his hands over the steering wheel, and laid his forehead on the backs of his hands. Tears rolled down his cheeks. He stared at the two keys on his key ring. There was one place he could go...

Chapter 10

ALL THREE STRIP JOINTS WERE ON CHARLES BOULEVARD, a north-south thoroughfare one block west of the Albemarle Arms. The Crazy Lady was two blocks south of 77th Street. The Orange Peel three blocks north of the Crazy Lady, and two blocks further north, the Fuzzy Bare.

I parked my van near Charles Boulevard and walked toward The Crazy Lady. I searched for Al and his car along the way. The first block was a smorgasbord of small businesses: a dry cleaner, a pizza shop, and a used CD and DVD store. There was also a storefront church. I entered each one, displayed Al's picture on my phone, and asked if anyone had seen Al or knew him. No luck.

The first business on the next block was a heating and air conditioning installation and repair company. I skipped it and the other stores on the block and headed for the Crazy Lady. The top row of the marquee said *2-4-1 Drinks Til 8 p.m.* The next line promised *Free Lunch Til 5 p.m.*

As I approached the entrance, the doors whooshed open from both sides. Rock music with a heavy beat boomed in my ears.

The interior designer had been keen on purple and pink. Purple carpet, purple and pink upholstered chairs, and more purple drapes on the windowless front wall. Publicity photos of the dancers in provocative poses were displayed on the pink walls.

There were two people on my side of a freestanding purple wall twenty feet from the front door. The first was a doorman in a purple and white striped muscle shirt over purple slacks. His shiny bald, black scalp resembled a rippling ocean in the pink and purple flashing lights. He was over six feet tall and muscled with bulk built by countless low-weight repetitions. I call them "show muscles." They weren't working muscles like a boxer develops when he spars and exercises for months. Purple Guy would intimidate people who didn't know better. That was good enough for a strip club bouncer and sufficient for ninety-nine percent of the people he encountered. I was the other one percent.

Purple Guy flashed a professional smile with gleaming white teeth as he stood beside a podium in the center of entrance wall. "Welcome to the Crazy Lady," he said in a voice that carried above the music, "where your fantasies can come true."

"That's good to know." I showed him my phone and leaned close to Purple Guy's ear. "I'm looking for this guy. His name is Al Rice. You seen him lately?"

"You a cop?"

"No, private investigator."

"If you're not a cop, you can't come in here carrying a gun."

"You're not supposed to spot my gun when it's clipped in the back."

"I have X-ray vision, like Superman."

"I have a concealed weapon permit."

"Sorry, sir. We don't allow guns inside."

I returned to my van and locked the Glock in my custom built-in gun safe. I fastened a Browning .380 in an ankle holster and returned to the club.

"Welcome back. There's a twenty-dollar cover charge, sir."

"I'm not here for the girls. I want to know if you know Al Rice or if you saw him lately."

Purple Guy kept his professional smile. "For that you get a free lunch. Pay Erica at the cash register over there." He pointed toward the second person visible in the entrance area, a well-toned woman with chemical blonde hair and amazing boobs on an elevated platform behind the register. Clearly, he wouldn't talk to me until I was a paying customer, if then.

Erica was visible from the knees up wearing a pink bow in her hair. A long string of purple pearls dangled on either side of her right breast. She appeared to be nude; then I noticed the pink bikini bottom she wore. She was dancing in place to the rock music that emanated from behind the wall. She held her arms out and undulated like pink coral in an ocean current. *Go, Erica, go.*

"Erica accepts all major credit cards," Purple Guy added with another professional smile. "And there's plenty more like her behind that wall."

I bowed to the inevitable. That's why God invented the expense account. "Thanks."

Erica accepted my twenty-dollar bill and I realized why the club had her stand on a platform. She bent over to open the cash register. Her ample breasts became a metronome for the music when she slipped the bill into the drawer. A nipple ring flashed from her left breast. "Would you like change for tips?"

"Maybe later."

She closed the cash drawer with a smile. "Give me your hand and I'll stamp it for you." She picked up a rubber stamp in one hand and grasped my hand with the other, squeezing gently. I think this was supposed to thrill and delight me. "This stamp will give you access to the pleasures of the Crazy Lady behind that wall. All of them," she added breathlessly and winked. My nose was level with her breasts. Her nipple ring was decorated with rhinestones. Like I might not notice.

"Ooh, your hand is nice and strong! I love a man with long fingers." She winked and shimmied like she could barely refrain from throwing me on the floor and having her way with me right then and there. She stamped the back of my hand with a purple heart.

That's all I needed, another Purple Heart. Twisting back to Purple Guy, I flashed Al's picture. "*Now* do you know this guy?"

"He seems familiar. Why d'you want to know?"

"Believe it or not, his mother hired me to find him." I laughed, just a regular guy.

Purple Guy laughed with me. "His momma wants to find him? You gotta be shitting me."

"God's honest truth."

"You got identification?"

I flashed Purple Guy my credentials and handed him a business card. "Have you seen him?"

"Maybe." Purple Guy rubbed his thumb and forefinger together. "His momma throwing him a birthday party or something?"

"Something like that." I showed him a fifty-dollar bill.

The entrance doors slid open and two men walked in.

"Welcome, gentlemen, to the Crazy Lady," Purple Guy said, "where your fantasies can come true. Nice to see you again." He gestured them toward Erica, she of the bouncing boobs and promising pleasures. Erica jiggled happily for the new suckers.

Purple Guy appraised the fifty and found it beneath contempt. "If Momma wants to find her boy bad enough to hire a private eye, it's gotta be worth more than a lousy fifty bucks."

I added another fifty to the pot. "Where is he?"

Purple Guy stuck the bills in his pocket. "I didn't say I knew where he was. I said he seems familiar. I seen him, but it's been a few weeks. What'd you say his name was?"

"Al Rice."

"Yeah, that's the guy. He's on our no-fly list."

"No-fly list. What's that—no terrorists allowed?"

He, like many people, didn't recognize my humor. "I'll show you; it's pretty cool." He stepped over to the podium. A computer screen was mounted in the top. Purple Guy swiped a finger across the screen and scrolled through pictures of faces, all men. "There." He pointed to Al's picture, a drunken grin on his face. Al's name displayed across the bottom. "He's on the no-fly list."

"What does that mean?"

Purple Guy pointed to a purple door in a pink wall to my left. "Go check in the office. They'll explain. Knock once and walk in."

I CLOSED THE SOUNDPROOF DOOR BEHIND ME, and the music shut off like someone had yanked the plug. The quiet was a welcome relief. Compared to the pink and purple main showroom, the office appeared mundane. Beige carpet, white walls, a reception desk, visitor chairs, and a fully-clothed, middle-aged secretary who reminded me of my banker. "May I help you, sir?"

"I'm Chuck McCrary, private investigator." I handed the woman a business card, one without a magnifying glass logo. "The doorman said you could tell me about your no-fly list."

Banker Lady read my card and entered the information on a keyboard. "Yes, Mr. McCrary. I don't find your name on the list, and, if I may say, you don't act like an undesirable customer. May I ask the nature of your interest in our no-fly list?"

I showed her Al's picture. "I'm looking for this man. His name is Al Rice and he used to live in this neighborhood. His mother hired me to find him and bring him home. Your doorman showed me his picture on your no-fly list."

"What's his name again, please?"

"The name on his driver's license is Alfred Lord Tennyson Rice." I didn't tell her Al's license was suspended for DUI. That was on a need-to-know basis. "He goes by Al."

"I see why," she said with a smile. She tapped her keyboard. "Yes, Mr. Rice was discharged from the club three weeks ago and told not to return. We placed his picture on the podium computer so the doormen ensure that we don't admit Mr. Rice again."

"So your no-fly list is people you banned from the club for bad behavior?"

"Precisely."

"It's important to Al's mother that I find him. May I ask why he was, uh, discharged?"

Banker Lady said, "Yes, you can ask."

"Why was he discharged?"

She flashed a saccharine smile, held out her hand, and said nothing. She and Purple Guy had a lot in common.

I laid a twenty in her hand.

Banker Lady made the twenty disappear and consulted her computer screen. "On several occasions Mr. Rice became drunk and behaved inappropriately toward a dancer. Finally, the owner instructed that he be discharged."

"Was that dancer's name Jasmine?"

Banker Lady smiled again, held out her hand again, and said nothing again. At least she was cheaper than Purple Guy.

This time it took two twenties.

"Yes, it was Jasmine. How did you know?"

"An acquaintance of Mr. Rice told me he was in love with a dancer named Jasmine."

She peered at Chuck. "The feeling was not reciprocated. Miss Jasmine told me she didn't know Mr. Rice, but he was obsessed with her. That's why the owner discharged him."

"May I speak to Miss Jasmine? I am very respectful and would talk to her here in the office, if that is acceptable." I held up two more twenties.

Banker Lady eyed the twenties wistfully and sighed. "Sorry, I already said more than I should."

I smiled at her. "It's the dimples. Works every time."

"It's a moot point; that particular Miss Jasmine no longer dances here."

"There's more than one Jasmine?"

The woman held out her hand. I gave her another twenty. She motioned for another one and I protested. "My client isn't made of money. That info is worth twenty."

Banker Lady shrugged and accepted the bill. "All dancers choose stage names. That's standard in the industry. Jasmine is a common name in the business, along with Candy, Kitty, Tammy, and so forth. Sometimes we get a new dancer and another girl already uses the same name. We ask the new girl to pick a new name. The week after Miss Jasmine left, we hired another dancer named Jasmine."

"Where is the first Miss Jasmine dancing now?" I held up two more twenties.

She shook her head. "I wish I knew; I could use the money. But it's not my department."

"Do you have her publicity photo I might see? Or purchase?"

Banker Lady pursed her lips.

"I'll pay you to print me her picture."

"How much?"

I held up a twenty.

Banker Lady raised an eyebrow and shook her head.

I added another twenty with the same reaction.

The third twenty did the trick. Banker Lady snagged them and tapped her keyboard. "You didn't get this from me. Printer's over there."

"Thanks." An eight-by-ten cheesecake photo of a woman dressed as a French maid stereotype emerged from the printer. I zoomed in on her face, and photographed it with my phone. I folded the photo and slipped it in a pocket.

"How soon after Rice landed on the no-fly list did this Jasmine leave?"

"Like I said, I already told you more than I should."

I offered a twenty-dollar bill.

Banker Lady scoffed. "You're kidding."

I added another twenty. "Forty bucks is my limit."

Banker Lady made the money disappear again and tapped her keyboard. "That Miss Jasmine received her locker key refund one week after Mr. Rice was added to the list."

"Did that particular Miss Jasmine give you a forwarding address?"

Banker Lady smiled. "I would love to sell you that information. However, if we had that information, we wouldn't release it for liability reasons—stalkers and such. Actually, people like Al Rice."

"I understand. How about a phone number? Surely, as her employer, you have the dancers' phone numbers in case you have a scheduling problem."

"That would be worth a bundle, but we don't have it. It's another moot point, because our dancers are not employees. We don't pay them; they pay us to work here."

That was a surprise. "Are the tips that good?"

"A good dancer with a good personality clears five hundred dollars a day, more on the weekend, all cash. Each dancer pays us one hundred dollars a day to work here; two hundred on Saturday night. We don't even ask their real names. I issue them a locker key and assign them a makeup table in the dressing room. They come and go."

"With the money so good, why would anyone quit?"

"Drugs, alcohol, pregnancy, boyfriends. You name it." Banker Lady shrugged. "These girls—they're not like you and me. They don't think like normal people."

"I understand. Did this particular Miss Jasmine quit or was she, uh, asked to turn in her locker key?" I read her expression. "I'm out of twenties. Will you take two tens?"

She would. "That's not my department. Our owner re-issued Miss Jasmine's locker to another dancer."

"Who's the owner?"

Banker Lady's face blanked. "I wouldn't know, sir."

"The owner told you to add Al Rice to your no-fly list and he had you re-issue Jasmine's key to another dancer, and you don't know his name?" I drew out a fifty this time. Then I added another fifty to it. "Who's the owner?"

Banker Lady appeared decidedly uncomfortable, even fearful. "You could give me a fistful of hundreds and I wouldn't know. There's not enough money in Fort Knox."

That was interesting.

BANKER LADY WORRIED THAT SHE HAD MAKE A MISTAKE in talking so much. She was always doing that, but Private Eye Guy, as she thought of Chuck, was cute and friendly. Private Eye Guy was bound to find Jasmine soon, and word would get back that he'd visited the Crazy Lady. The doorman would say that he'd sent Private Eye Guy to the office. She chewed on her lower lip while she considered what to do. She couldn't turn back the clock. She made a phone call. "Some guy came by asking about Jasmine... No, the other one, the redhead."

Chapter 11

RICE STARED AT THE GAS GAUGE IN DISBELIEF. *No, no, no. Not this too.* He slammed the steering wheel with his palm and groaned. He snatched a quick peek over his shoulder and jerked the car toward the right lane. The engine sputtered once more and died. Cars honked and swerved as he cut across the traffic and bumped over the rumble strip onto the shoulder, still coasting at forty miles per hour. The power steering died with the engine. He fought the wheel and wrenched the car onto the grass beside the highway. It bounced to a stop.

He slammed the steering wheel again and again, cursed his rotten luck. *Why is everything always stacked against me?* He shoved the door open and the warning bell clanged an alarm. Tears rolled down his cheeks again and he switched off the ignition. The radio died and he heard the traffic roar. People zoomed by who didn't care whether he lived or died. He stared at his keys, struggled to remember what he needed them for. *Momma, that's the key to Momma's house.*

He tried to get out. The seatbelt was fastened, mocking his inability to move. He found that funny. He chortled and slapped the car seat with glee.

He fumbled the seatbelt open and staggered upright. He locked the doors from habit and stumbled across the rough ground, headed for the next exit. *Got to get to Momma's before Teddy catches me.*

He made his way to the access road and stopped to catch his breath. He couldn't stay on a main street; Teddy might find him there. Teddy knew where his mother lived and he knew where

Rice had parked the night before. This access road lay on a straight line from the Orange Peel to Momma's house. It was the first place Teddy would look. Rice turned up the first cross street and scurried into the residential neighborhood. It was farther this way, but he had a better chance of arriving alive.

He came to an east-west boulevard. A hundred yards of open space, a hundred yards of danger, to reach the other side. He strolled into a convenience store. He found the water fountain and took a long drink. He stared at the sausages rotating on the warmer. He peeked at the coffee dispenser. The cashier up front didn't have a good view of the back of the store. No, he'd better not risk it. *I'm a coward. I've always been a coward. I'll always be a coward.* He visited the restroom before he resumed his odyssey. He huddled in the shadow of the porte-cochere over the gas pumps and scanned up and down the boulevard. The street cleared momentarily. He jogged across the frightening expanse of open pavement and dashed up another residential street, his breath ragged in his chest.

The sun dropped lower and the lengthening shadows made him feel marginally safer crossing the next wide boulevard. *Teddy is driving me like a wolf who's cut a buffalo from the herd.* He revolved that thought in his head. *Momma. Momma will know what to do.* If he could just get to Momma's house…

Chapter 12

I WAITED FOR ERICA TO COLLECT COVER CHARGES and make change for two more men. She handed them each a fistful of bills and stamped their hands. "This stamp will give you gentlemen access to the pleasures of the Crazy Lady behind that wall. All of them." She faced my way. "Hello, handsome. How can I serve you?"

I had deposited all my twenties with Banker Lady. I handed Erica a hundred. "You can give me a hundred bucks worth of fives."

"It is my *pleasure* to serve you." She winked and snapped up my hundred. She bent over the cash register and positioned her fingers on the keyboard. She lifted her face, her nose inches from mine. I smelled her chewing-gum breath: Juicy Fruit. "You know, handsome, two hundred would get the girls to go twice as far."

I admired her training; she must work on commission. "Why not?" I handed her another hundred. She grinned from ear to ear. I would need to reload my money clip at an ATM.

Erica counted out forty bills into my hand. "Would you like me to show you what to do with those?"

I smiled back. "Please do."

"Let's say that a dancer shows you extra special attention," she waved her breasts millimeters from my face, "or gives you an extra move you like," she did a bump and grind, "stick one or two bills in her bikini—if she's still wearing it." She presented her hip to me, inches from my fistful of dollars.

I stuck a five-dollar bill in her waist band. "Like this?"

Erica winked again. "Like that." Five dollars and an elastic waist band transformed me into the funniest, cleverest man she had ever met.

"And if she's not wearing her bikini?"

"She'll come around after her show and ask how you liked it. She'll be in a bikini then. Have fun."

"I'm sure I will. Oh, by the way, do you know where this girl is dancing now?" I showed Jasmine's picture to her. "She used to dance here. Name is Jasmine. She quit a couple weeks ago."

"Yeah, I remember her. No, don't know where she went. Girls come and girls go."

I made my way around the purple wall and entered the main showroom. I glanced both ways and stood against the wall while my vision adjusted to the gloom. Ever since the Green Berets, I've liked a wall at my back.

Two naked women, one black and one white, were dancing on the free-form stage four feet above floor level. Actually, they weren't quite naked; they each wore purple high-heeled shoes, a string of purple pearls, and a pink hair bow. The stage was shaped vaguely like a four-leaf clover with a dance pole mounted in the center of each lobe. Each dancer eyeballed the other for cues and they moved simultaneously to opposite poles and performed a choreographed routine. Both women were impressive physical specimens. They worked their way up and down the first two poles. Then they danced to the other poles to work the entire stage.

One long bar for drinkers snaked its way around the stage, in and out, hugging the contours of each lobe. The customers were all races and ages. Six topless women roamed the showroom with serving trays. Three Asians, a Caucasian, a black, and one woman who may have been Latina. Poster children for diversity. Each woman wore a pink bikini bottom, a pink hair bow, and a string of purple pearls. Must be a uniform for the personnel who weren't dancers. Or perhaps the servers took turns dancing.

The last time I visited a strip joint was in Germany with my fellow Green Berets. The German joint fronted for a brothel, which was legal there. I didn't know how things worked in

South Florida, but I didn't feel any more comfortable here than I had in Germany.

I remembered the advice of an instructor in Special Forces. "Always be polite and respectful, but make a plan to kill everyone in the room if necessary." Danger usually comes from people, not the environment. Most customers were men, although there were several couples. Most of the men were harmless, except one man who was with a date. At least she was dressed like a date instead of a hooker. I examined the environment: walls, floors, furnishings, lighting, sound system—even the ceiling. Another Purple Guy emerged from the door beside the stage and stood at the rear of the showroom. He could be the first guy's fraternal twin brother, except he was white. His muscles were more business-like than the first Purple Guy. He would be trouble in a fight.

Having formed my kill plan, I nodded to White Purple Guy and went to the lunch buffet. I picked a sturdy plastic plate and searched for something that was safe to eat. The salad bar was as clean as one would expect, although the lighting was poor. The requisite sneeze shield was spotless. I felt the stainless steel counter; the refrigeration was working. Food poisoning would be bad for the club's business. I selected a scoop of potato salad that came pre-made from a food purveyor. I found a tub of coleslaw and, applying the same logic, plunked a scoop on my plate. That was all I felt safe eating. I passed on the hot buffet. Too bad, the chili smelled delicious. I slid into a chair at a corner table in the rear of the showroom, against the wall.

A topless Asian girl materialized at the table. "My name Tammy, and I be your server today." She had a thick accent from somewhere in Asia I couldn't pin down.

I did a double take. She was the spitting image of Miyoki Takahashi, my girlfriend. I peered closer and there were one or two minor differences in the shape of their ears, and this girl Tammy was younger than Miyo. But in the dimly lit showroom floor, anyone who didn't know Miyo well would have been fooled. I wondered if Tammy was legal. I don't mean legal *age*, although she seemed young, but of legal immigration status. I didn't think there was a work visa category for Asian strippers to do highly-skilled work that couldn't be done by U.S. citizens.

She lay two napkins and a set of cutlery on the table. "What you like drink?"

"You have iced tea?"

"Sweet or unsweet?"

"Unsweet."

"We have it, and I bring to you." She winked, shimmied her petite breasts with a seductive smile, and strutted away. Lots of winking and shimmying here. Part of good customer service, no doubt.

The other customers ogled the dancers, glancing away when a server came over to them. I focused on everyone else. One recorded song segued into another and the two dancers made a big flourish to kick off their shoes. They danced naked to enthusiastic applause. Go figure. I studied the interactions between the customers and the wait staff until Tammy arrived with my tea. The black, white, and Latina servers seemed at ease with the customers; the Asian girls, less so. Was it because of their limited English, or was there something else going on?

"Here you are." She laid the tab on the table. Twenty dollars for iced tea. It must be really good tea.

I handed her the tab and a credit card.

Tammy read the card before setting it on her tray. "Carlos. That a great name. Can I get you something else?"

"My friends call me Chuck."

"I like be your friend. I call you Chuck." She giggled. It almost sounded sincere. "If you like, we be more than friends later, Chuck." She winked and shimmied.

"Maybe later. For now, I came here to watch Jasmine dance. Will she be on later?"

"Jasmine waiting tables, Chuck. She and I dance in fifteen minutes."

"Where? I don't see her."

"Over there." She pointed. "She serve that couple."

"That's not Jasmine."

"Yes, that Jasmine. We always dance together. Manager like to mix the Asian and the black girl."

"Listen, Tammy, I haven't been to the Crazy Lady in a while, but I remember Jasmine. She was a white girl with red hair. Could there be two dancers named Jasmine?"

Tammy laughed. "You must mean the old Jasmine. She quit. That black Jasmine been here about a week."

I handed Tammy a five-dollar bill. "Thanks for the information."

By the time Tammy returned with my credit card bill, the two women who had been dancing when I arrived finished their performance. They retrieved their bikini bottoms from the stage, twirled them on their index fingers, grabbed their shoes in the other hand, and jiggled their way off the stage. I added another five-dollar tip to the credit card.

"Thank you, Chuck. I see *you* later." Another wink and shimmy. She must like me a lot.

I finished my tea and made another trip to the salad bar. More potato salad and coleslaw to salve the hunger pangs until I ate a real lunch.

Tammy pranced back to the table. "I go on in few minutes, Chuck. You like more iced tea before I dance?"

"Good idea."

Tammy grabbed my first empty plate and carried it away.

Another two dancers mounted the stage. One costume was a caricature of a sexy female cop complete with a rubber nightstick which she fondled suggestively; the other dancer dressed as a scientist in a white lab coat and fake horn-rimmed eyeglasses. She carried a model of an Atlas rocket which she handled like she was in love with it.

I scanned the room with an occasional glance at the dancers while I ate. I nibbled my so-called food.

During their second dance, the cop and the scientist peeled out of their costumes, collected tips from the customers near the stage, and ended wearing a bikini and high heels. The third song they danced, collected more tips, did another choreographed pole routine, then removed their bikini bottoms, ending wearing only their shoes. The fourth song, they kicked off their shoes—again to enthusiastic applause when they mounted the poles and danced wearing a hair bow and purple pearls. Maybe the men in the audience had a foot fetish.

I pushed my second plate aside. There is a limit to the amount of potato salad and coleslaw a man can eat and remain sane.

During the second song of the Cop and Scientist's set, the two dancers who had performed when I first entered made the rounds to collect tips from the customers. They stopped at my table. "I'm Belinda and this is Bathsheba. How did you like our performance?"

"I loved it. My old favorite dancer was a beautiful redhead named Jasmine who was dancing here last month. You girls are just as good." I stuck a fiver in each girl's bikini waist band. "Did either of you know that other Jasmine?" I held up two more fives.

Bathsheba said, "I only been here a week." She asked Belinda, "You been here a while. Did you know her?"

Bathsheba appraised the bills in my hand. "Stick them down my bikini if you want."

"That's okay." I handed her the bills and she handed one to Belinda. "Me and my partner split everything. Tell me what you *really* want, big guy. And don't jive me; I got a good bullshit detector."

I gave her the full dimple treatment in case the five-dollar bills were insufficient. "I'm looking for this man." I showed both girls Al's picture. "His name is Al Rice. He had a thing for Jasmine—not the black Jasmine working here now, but the redheaded one who used to work here. Maybe if I find the redheaded Jasmine, I'll find Al Rice. It's worth a hundred bucks to find either one."

Bathsheba studied Al's picture again. "Yeah, I knowed him. He used to come 'round here mooning over the redheaded Jasmine."

"Do you know where I can find either one?"

"I know where you can find the redheaded Jasmine."

"Where?"

"Show me the money."

Chapter 13

I CALLED TANK. "Have you heard anything from Al?"

"No. Where are you?"

"I'm in my van running down a lead on Al. Are you at work?"

"Yeah, but I'm spinning my wheels; I'm worried too much about this Al and Momma Dora situation. You want to bring me up to date?"

"Can you take the afternoon off?"

"I cleared my appointment book for the rest of the week. This is top priority."

"How long since you worked out?"

"Last Friday. Meet me at the gym?"

"Half an hour," I responded.

"I'll bring my pistol. We can go shooting later."

"Yeah, my calendar is clear until seven-thirty tonight."

KENNEDY CARLSON GLANCED UP FROM HIS PAPERWORK. "You here to lock up your pistol so you don't shoot yourself in the foot?"

I unclipped the holster and handed it to my friend. "Like *that* could happen twice."

I shook his hand. "Tank's meeting me here for a workout. He'll be here soon. He's bringing a gun too."

"You two gonna hunt varmints?"

"You read too many outdoor magazines, Ken. Nah, we have a duel with bad guys in the middle of Bayshore Boulevard at ten paces. Right after we have a workout and a sauna."

I WAITED UNTIL TANK AND I WERE ALONE in the sauna to tell him what had happened since I'd left Doraleen's house the previous night. "I'll follow that lead at eight o'clock tonight. Maybe I'll get lucky."

"You might get lucky another way too. Visiting strip clubs is hard duty, pun intended."

"Yeah, but somebody's got to do it."

"Perhaps I should go with you. Make sure you don't get in any trouble." He grinned.

"You between girlfriends?"

"As a matter of fact, yes. But I have my eye on a WNBA forward for the Port City Flames. She's six-two and built like a brick backboard. Graduated with honors from UAC."

"Where'd you meet her?"

"I haven't exactly met her. She sat at another table at a UAC alumni fund-raiser for the athletic department last month. I caught her eye, but we didn't get to talk."

"I guaran-damn-tee you she knows who you are. Call her. You can't hurry up good times by waiting for them."

"The WNBA season begins in two weeks. They're in training camp."

"They don't train twenty-four hours a day," I said.

"I'll call her once the season opens."

"Tank, you never struck me as the shy type."

"I'm not shy. I'm… *patient*."

"Uh-huh, and I'm the president of Patagonia."

"Can I come with you tonight or not?"

"A three-hundred pound, six-foot-six black man wouldn't make anyone nervous or anything, would it?"

"I weigh two seventy-five."

"Like that's a *biiig* difference. Nah, since you're sleeping alone anyway, stay with Doraleen again."

Tank wiped his forehead and neck with a towel. "I called her on the way over here. She paid Al's cellphone bill and left the voicemail for Al like you said, but he hasn't called. Snoop picked her up at school and she's home safe. Snoop's with her."

"How the hell did Al get into this mess?" I asked.

The giant shrugged and a towel fell off his shoulders. "One thing leads to another. I remember at UAC, Al was money-hungry. He figured to play in the NFL from the time he was a junior in high school."

"Was he that good?"

"Oh, yeah. State high school All-American in his sophomore year. National high school All-American his junior and senior years. Notre Dame offered him a scholarship, and he had offers from Alabama, Florida, and a couple others I don't remember." He chuckled. "Momma Dora saved the recruiting letters in a drawer and showed them to me when we first met. She was proud of Al. So proud..." He sighed.

"So he selected UAC?" I prompted.

"Yeah, he had friends in Port City. The friends were the wrong people for an impressionable young man to hang out with, but that's another long story."

"I have time for a long story."

"Not important." Tank stood. "I'm overheated. I'm gonna shower. I'll be back in a few.

"I need a break too."

When we returned to the sauna, I asked again. "You were telling me about Al."

"Another reason Al stayed in Port City was a girl he was serious about. Al wouldn't leave her."

"They met in high school?"

"Yeah. Love at first sight he told me."

"So what happened to their relationship?"

Tank shrugged again. "Al didn't give me the details, but whatever it was, by his junior year, she had moved to New York. Al said she was chasing a rainbow. That was the first thing that shook him so bad that year."

"What happened to the girl?"

"Don't know."

"What was her name?"

"Janice Jackson."

"You remember?"

"Oh, yeah. Pretty as a picture and graceful as a deer. A white girl. Mr. William, Al's dad, he wasn't keen on Al dating a white girl, but Momma Dora accused him of acting un-Christian."

"So you lost track of her." I wiped the sweat off my brow.

"No reason not to. When she was Al's girl, I saw her a lot. Once she broke up with him, I didn't. Simple as that. Besides, she'd left town."

"I think it's dry in here, don't you?" I poured water on the rocks.

"Al wanted to get rich quick. He planned to jump to the NFL a year early, score a big signing bonus, and buy his parents a new house." Tank took a long pull on his water bottle. "Then Mr. William got killed."

"How did William die?"

"New Year's Eve of Al's junior year, some idiot was shooting bullets in the air to celebrate the New Year. What goes up must come down. Mr. William got hit by a stray bullet. Million-to-one shot." He crushed the empty bottle.

"I read about those in the newspapers every year, but I never knew anybody personally that was a victim. That must have been devastating to Al."

"And to Momma Dora," Tank said. "Al and I were in New Orleans to play in the Sugar Bowl. His parents were there and my folks. The team had a curfew like we do before a big game. Coach kept us in the hotel, but he let us stay up 'til midnight. Then we hit the sack. Momma Dora and Mr. William went out with my parents to celebrate New Year's in the French Quarter near Jackson Square. Then, maybe two in the morning, while Al and I were sound asleep…" He lapsed into silence.

"Since y'all were asleep at the hotel, how did you learn about the accident?"

"We didn't know Mr. William was in the hospital until after the game. Coach put the team's hotel room phones on 'Do not disturb' the night before, and he made us leave our phones in the hotel until after the game so we wouldn't be distracted. Momma Dora and my parents stayed at the hospital all night sitting in the emergency room, praying for Mr. William." Tank wiped his eye with the back of his hand. "He didn't die right away; he hung on for a long time. Following the game, Dad waited outside the locker room to drive us straight to the hospital where Mom had stayed with Momma Dora. Mr. William died before we got there." He stood and gathered his towels around his giant frame. "This is depressing, Chuck. I'm ready to shower and hit the shooting range. How about you?"

We showered, dressed, and retrieved our guns and phones from Ken's office. I had a text from Bigs Bigelow:

BOLO found Rice car. Call me.

I called. "Bigs, I got your text. Where is Rice's car""
"Abandoned beside I-95."
"Where?"
Bigs told me.
"Are you there now?"
"No, but we could be in ten minutes."
"I'll meet you there," I said. "And Bigs, thanks."

Chapter 14

RICE'S OLD TOYOTA SAT ASKEW ON THE GRASS near the shoulder of I-95 northbound. An unmarked car had parked ten yards behind it, red and blue lights flashing. I drove my minivan onto the grass in front of the Toyota. Tank parked his Porsche on the far side of me. Kelly Contreras and Bigs Bigelow, her partner, were standing to the right of the Toyota, away from the furious traffic speeding by five yards away.

Bigs and Tank hugged each other. The back-pounding between the two huge men must have registered on the seismograph at UCLA. "Tank, haven't seen you since the Super Bowl." Bigs grinned at me. "Hey, buddy. Tank been taking good care of your money?"

"Absolutely. He padlocked my wallet and gives me a twenty-dollar allowance every week for school lunches."

"If he doesn't treat you right, you tell me and I'll come smack him around." He laughed and waved at Kelly. "I don't think you've met my old friend Tank Tyler. Tank anchored the other end of the defensive line from me on the Pelicans before he became a world-famous CPA and money magician." He slammed Tank on the back with a blow that would topple an ordinary-sized human.

Kelly shook Tank's hand. "Bigs has told me so much about you, Tank. It's an honor to meet you."

"He hasn't mentioned you at all, Kelly, for which omission I will chastise him severely. Wow." He circled to Bigs. "You been holding out on me, bro. Why didn't you tell me you had such a beautiful partner?"

"Frankly, Tank, I didn't think about it; I've been married all my life." He winked at Kelly. "You want me to fix you up with her?"

"Guys, I hate to interfere with the matchmaking," I interrupted, "but we have a missing man in danger. Can we get back to business?"

She blushed. "Sure, Chuck. I ran the plates and compared it to the VIN. It's Al Rice's car. It's locked, and there's no sign of foul play. From what we can see through the windows, it appears that Rice was living in the car."

"He was," said Tank. "I know that for a fact."

"Al Rice's driver's license is suspended so he cannot legally drive," Kelly said. "Of course, we have no proof of who drove the car here."

I pointed at the traffic cameras overhead. "Anything on the traffic cams?"

She shook her head. "They're monitored in real time to spot traffic accidents and other tie-ups, but they're not recorded. I spoke to the traffic control guys; they didn't notice who got out of the car."

I walked around the Toyota, inspected the interior. I didn't notice anything Kelly hadn't seen. "Hell, maybe he ran out of gas." I peered through the wire fence beside the freeway. "Maybe those businesses over there have security cam footage of this area."

"I wish I could spend the time to canvass them, Chuck," said Kelly, "but there's no evidence a crime was committed here. Unless we can tie this to Moffett, we have other cases to work. I'll call a wrecker to haul this car to impound. After you find your friend, tell him he can reclaim his car there."

"I will."

"And, Chuck, about that description you texted me last night, did you get my reply?"

"No. When did you send it?"

"At nine this morning."

"Sorry, never got it. These cell phone thingies will never catch on. They're too undependable."

She laughed. "The guy you asked about is a bad dude named Teddy Ngombo who works as muscle for Moffett." She referred to her phone screen. "His real first name is Tegumetosa." She spelled it.

"For real?"

"Yeah, he's from someplace in central Africa."

"What else can you tell me about him?"

"He's from a warrior tribe in his home country, which explains the ritual scars, and he likes to work with a knife. He's cut some people pretty bad but nothing we can prove. The good news is he hasn't killed anybody—yet."

"Is he an illegal?" Tank asked. "If we catch him, will INS deport him?"

"You're out of date, Tank," I retorted. "INS is now ICE, Immigration and Customs Enforcement."

"Whatever. Can we find a three-letter agency of the U.S. government to deport him? Maybe CIA, NSA, DIA, IRS, or even FTC?"

"Nah," Kelly responded. "He has a green card. He's our problem to handle." She laid a hand on my forearm. "Watch your six with this guy."

Chapter 15

TEGUMETOSA "TEDDY" NGOMBO STUDIED THE SCREEN from the driver seat of a Jeep Grand Cherokee. He was tempted to throw the tablet computer out the window. It was no tool for a hunter, no tool for a warrior. Where the hell was Rice's car? He had stuck a GPS tracker under Rice's Toyota while Moffett smashed Rice's hand at the Tri-Patron facility. The GPS battery was supposed to last a week. Ngombo had checked the location of Rice's car every day. After a week, he used the tracker to find Rice's car, and he changed the tracker's battery. It should be good for another week, but nothing was showing. Nothing. He was a warrior, a hunter, and he had lost the trail. He slammed the steering wheel with his palm.

He had a backup—a special app he'd installed on Rice's phone in case the GPS tracker failed. Parents used the app to track their teenagers. He checked the tracker app. Nothing. That couldn't be unless Rice's phone battery was dead.

Moffett would be livid. He feared to confront his boss and tell him that he, Tegumetosa Ngombo of the most famous warrior clan in central Africa, had lost his quarry. In desperation he cruised the parking lot of the Orange Peel, but the Toyota was gone.

Ngombo double-parked and hauled an Atlantic County map from the glove compartment. He positioned one finger on the spot where he was now. Where could Rice be? Perhaps he went back to his apartment at the Albemarle Arms. Ngombo slammed the Cherokee into gear and squealed from the lot.

THE AFRICAN CLIMBED THE STAIRS TO THE THIRD FLOOR. He scanned both ways. No one in sight. He stopped at the door of apartment 3-H and knocked. Knocked again. He smashed his boot heel into the door next to the lock. The door slammed inward and splinters flew from the shattered jamb.

Crap! The apartment was empty. Rice had moved.

He trotted downstairs to the office, knocked twice, then called the phone number on the office sign.

"Albemarle Arms. This is Reggie speaking."

"I should like to speak to the manager."

"There ain't no manager; I'm the super."

"Then I should like to speak with you. Where can I find you please?"

"Here at the apartments. I'm always here; I live here. You wanna rent an apartment?"

"Yes, please. I am here at the apartments. I do not see you."

"I'm taking out the trash. Where are you?"

"At the office."

"Be right there."

Ngombo rotated in a circle. The nearest witnesses would be on the sidewalk next to the street, but many pedestrians used that walk. Too close. He needed to get the "super," whatever that was, out of sight. He waited.

Reggie appeared from around the corner. "Hey there. You the guy what called me?"

"Yes. What is a… 'super'?"

"Super. It's short for superintendent. I do the maintenance around here. Keep the place tidy and the like. What can I do for you?"

"I wish to rent an apartment."

"What size?"

"What size? I do not know. How big are your apartments?"

"One bedroom and two bedroom. Both our three bedrooms is rented. What size you want?"

"Uh, two bedroom please."

"C'mon. I'll show you a real beauty." He led Ngombo toward the front of the property.

"Do you have a unit further from the street? I like my privacy."

"Sure. I have another two bedroom in the rear, but it ain't so nice." He headed toward the back. "In here." Reggie unlocked the door and pushed it open. "See for yourself. Eight hundred a month, water included. You pay for electricity." He gestured Ngombo through the door.

Ngombo walked into the first bedroom and pivoted.

Reggie stopped near the front door.

That would never do; Ngombo needed to lure him away from the door. "Excuse me please, what is this here?" He pointed to something off to one side.

"What's what?" said Reggie, walking into the bedroom.

"I will show you. Wait here." He walked into the living room, closed the front door behind him, and pulled a knife. "Where is Al Rice?"

Reggie's eyes grew silver-dollar big. "What the hell? Who are you?"

The African warrior advanced toward Reggie, brandishing the knife. "Where is Al Rice?"

Reggie held his hands out in front. He backed up until his legs hit the bed, then lost his balance and fell backwards.

Ngombo stepped closer to the bed, held the knife where Reggie could see it. "Where is Al Rice?"

"How the hell should I know? I evicted that deadbeat bastard over a week ago. I ain't seen him since. You let me up; I'll tell you everything I know."

Ngombo stepped back and Reggie sat on the edge of the bed. "Why is everybody interested in Al Rice today?"

"What do you mean?"

"You the second guy come looking for Rice, but the other guy, he din't pull no knife on me."

Ngombo seized Reggie by the arm and waved the knife in his face. "What other guy? Who else is looking for Al Rice?"

Chapter 16

MY BLUETOOTH TOLD ME I HAD A CALL. "Chuck McCrary here." I curved my van to the curb. No point getting killed talking on the phone.

"This is Reggie Larkin, super at the Albemarle Arms."

"I remember you, Reggie. You got something for me?" I found a notepad in the console.

"You said if I learned anything else about Al Rice to call you."

"You learn anything else?"

"Bring another hundred over here, Chuck, 'cause I got some good stuff for you."

"What stuff?"

"Not until you give me the hundred you promised."

"Give me a teaser, Reggie. Convince me it's worth my trouble to drive all the way over there."

"You remember you told me that bad dudes were after Al Rice?"

"Yeah, I remember."

"Well, one of them bad dudes, he come by here. Said he was looking for Al Rice."

"Who?" I asked.

"A real scary-looking dude."

"This scary-looking dude got a name?"

"Gimme my hundred first."

I referred to the dashboard clock. "I'll be there in fifteen minutes."

I called Tank.

BACK IN THE CHEROKEE, NGOMBO CALLED MOFFETT. "This is Teddy Ngombo." The words caught in this throat like swallowing a burr. God, he hated the nickname "Teddy."

Tegumetosa meant "walks with lions" in his native language. "I can't pronounce Tegu—however the hell you say it," Moffett declared. "From now on, your name in my organization is Teddy." Ngombo salved his wounded pride somewhat by adding his surname whenever he identified himself.

"I have bad news," Ngombo continued. "Rice's GPS tracker stopped working. The battery must have died. I cannot find his car."

"Did you try the tracker app on his phone?"

"It is not working either. Rice must have let the battery die."

"Did you check his apartment?"

"Yes. He was evicted over a week ago. The apartment superintendent told me another man was there asking for Rice this morning. A private detective named Carlos McCrary. I have his business card. I shall give it to you when I see you next."

"McCrary? What did he want?"

"The super said McCrary was trying to protect Rice from the bad men who were after him." Ngombo laughed.

"The guy say who hired McCrary?"

"No. Only that McCrary wanted to find Rice."

"Go back to his mother's house and see if he's there. If that don't work, check out the Orange Peel club tonight. He can't stay away from Jennifer for long. He always crawls out from under a rock. Snatch him there."

Two minutes later, Ngombo accelerated up the ramp onto I-95 northbound. Three miles further, he slowed for the flashing yellow lights of a tow truck on the shoulder. The car beside the freeway might be Rice's. Could he be that lucky? He cut across two lanes of traffic, avoided a collision by a whisker, and jerked to a stop on the shoulder. He recognized the license plate of the car hooked to the tow truck. Thank the gods, the hunter was back on his quarry's trail.

He curved the Cherokee around the tow truck and got out. The operator had his hands on the control levers. "That car belongs to my friend Al Rice. Is he all right?"

The driver yanked a lever and the cable groaned as it hoisted the car up the tilted flat bed. "I never seen the driver, buddy. Cops reported this here abandoned car. Told me to impound it." He flipped another lever; the flat bed tilted forward. "That's all I know."

Ngombo about-faced without a word and returned to the Cherokee. He spread the Atlantic County map across the front seat. He traced the map to find Doraleen Rice's house. He studied the route from where he was to the house, deciding which way Rice would walk if he were headed home. He heard a rap on his window.

The tow truck driver stood at the window. "Hey, buddy, you wanna move your car so's I can get underway?"

"I am sorry. I shall move." Ngombo drove the Jeep to the next exit and parked at the curb of the access road while he studied the map, attempting to think like his prey.

Chapter 17

I KNOCKED ON THE ALBEMARLE ARMS OFFICE DOOR and Reggie opened it against the chain. He peered over my shoulder. "Good. The dude's gone." He closed the door and slid off the chain. "Come in, come in. Sit down."

I displayed a hundred-dollar bill for motivation. "What you got, Reggie?"

"Real scary dude. Black, but I mean real black, like maybe he was a real African from Africa. Talked real careful-like, like English weren't his first language."

I handed him the bill. "What was scary about him?"

"For one thing, the dude pulled a knife."

"Did he cut you? Are you okay?"

"No, I'm fine. He didn't cut me or nothing. He just threatened me. Mostly he waved it around."

"Describe him."

"Long dreadlocks in a ponytail held by a leather strap with fancy carving on it like maybe it come from Africa. I noticed it when he walked away. His hair come halfway down his back, like maybe he ain't cut it in years. Scars all over his face, but not from no accident. They looked like something I seen on the natives in an adventure film about Africa."

"Like scars from a tribal ritual?"

"Yeah, yeah, like that."

"Was there another scar on his cheek? Like from a knife fight?" I drew my finger down my right cheek.

"Yeah, now that you mention it, there was. How'd you know that?"

"This isn't the first time I've crossed his path. What did you tell him?"

"I told him everything, man. Dude threaten to cut me. I ain't keeping no secrets with a knife in my face, no sir."

"So you told him I came here this morning."

Reggie looked away.

"Don't worry Reggie. I would've done the same thing." That wasn't true but it did no good to make Reggie feel bad about water under the bridge.

"Yeah, I told him he was the second guy come looking for Al Rice today. I told him about Jasmine and the strip club and like that." He leaned back in his chair. "You have another hundred if I learn anything more?"

"Sure. Did you notice what kind of car he drove?"

"No. He jumped me in a vacant unit at the rear of the property. After he left, I waited five or ten minutes to make sure the dude was really *gone* gone. I don't never want to see that man again. Never."

"Okay. Thanks for the call."

"You better give me another card. Dude took the first one you give me."

I fished another business card from my pocket. "If this guy took my card, how did you know my phone number?"

Reggie grinned. "I memorized it while I handed the card over. Once the dude left, I wrote it down real quick like, before I forgot."

"I'll give you two cards this time. Hide one in case you have to give one away to anybody else who comes by."

Chapter 18

I STOPPED IN THE RIGHT LANE OF CHARLES BOULEVARD across the street from the Orange Peel Gentlemen's Club. Sunset colors blazed brightly in the sky over the club. The Orange Peel was smaller than the Crazy Lady and not well-maintained. Orange Peel was the right name in more ways than one. The orange paint had peeled off the front wall in patches and the rest had faded to a peach color. A scaffold at the left side wall marked where a new paint job was underway. The UB in "Club" was burned out on the neon sign. Why did a dancer like Jasmine with a lucrative gig at the Crazy Lady quit to work at a crummy joint like this? Something didn't add up.

I texted my researcher, Flamer21, *Flamer* for short:

Find out who owns the Crazy Lady strip joint. Also the Orange Peel, both on Charles Boulevard.

I surveyed the traffic, U-turned, and dodged a pothole as I bumped into the parking lot. I squeezed into a spot at the back, locked the van, and made my way around to the entrance.

A large canvas banner covered half the front wall. It announced *Under new management. Check us out!* A shiny new glass display box between the banner and the entrance featured photos of a half-dozen dancers. The name Jasmine caught my attention, but it wasn't the woman I was searching for. I examined the other photos. None were the correct Jasmine. I snapped a picture of each portrait in case it became important in the future. Rule Five: *You can never have too much information.*

I moved to the right of the entrance where there was another new display box. Bingo. The same picture I bought at the Crazy Lady. Each dancer must provide her own photo. I read somewhere that professional photographers call it a *glamour shot*. But at this club someone already used the name *Jasmine*. The former *Jasmine* became *Jennifer*. I wondered how many names she had used in her dancing career. I photographed all the portraits.

I circled the building on foot, searched the parking area for clues. Clues to what, I wasn't sure. But I photographed all the license plates in the half-full lot. If Jasmine/Jennifer was the key to finding Al, it might help to know which car was hers, and what name and address it was registered under. Rule Six: *You never know what you'll need to know.*

The back wall was painted matte black. A stinking dumpster sat askew to one side. Two freshly-painted orange doors opened onto the back parking lot. Both were locked from the outside. Fire code allowed anyone inside to hit a crash bar to exit, but those on the outside went around front to enter.

I stepped inside. Cheap tile floor, well-lit glass merchandise case selling X-rated DVDs. A bulky man in an orange-and-white striped muscle shirt and orange slacks stood by the case. I didn't think he was a cheerleader for the University of Tennessee. Nah, he must be a bouncer who doubled as the entrance cashier. No topless Erica here. His outfit was a twin of the one at the Crazy Lady except orange. Shaved heads must be fashionable for strip club doormen and bouncers.

Did I imagine a sharp intake of breath when the doorman saw me come in? It was subtle; his eyes and nostrils widened. Maybe they were expecting me. *Hmm.*

"There's a twenty-dollar cover charge." Orange Guy didn't smile like Purple Guy did.

"Twenty bucks. Hell, it's twenty bucks at the Crazy Lady." I had Tank's expense account, but I wanted to stay in character as a regular sucker off the street.

"Our cover includes two drinks."

I shrugged. Enough protest. I handed him a twenty. "Jennifer dancing tonight?"

Orange Guy sniffed. "She comes on about eight-thirty, quarter of nine. Maybe a half hour." He did not offer to stamp my hand with a purple heart or anything else. Just as well; I had to scrub to get the other stamp off my hand. "You need change for tips?"

"Sure." I handed him a hundred, and he counted out an assortment of ones and fives. "Remember: Don't touch the dancers or servers except to stick a tip in their bikini. Enjoy." He hauled back the orange curtain beside him for me to enter.

I moved into the darkened interior and stepped to the wall on the right. I backed up to it until my vision adapted to the darkness. Orange carpet in the showroom, threadbare at the entrance to the men's restroom. Foam soundproofing tiles spaced around the peach-colored walls were the sole decorations. A rectangular stage with two dance poles spaced twenty feet apart. Bars on either end butted up to the empty stage.

The stage lights dimmed. A disembodied voice came over the public address system. "And now, ladies and gentlemen, please join me in welcoming to the Orange Peel stage… from Gainesville, Florida… the one, the only… *Brandy!*" Scattered applause was audible above the throbbing music that roared from the speakers that bookended the stage. A dancer in a red sequined gown pushed aside an orange curtain and entered from the rear of the stage. The applause swelled when she unzipped the front of her gown and flashed her breasts with a sultry smile. She zipped the front again and commenced her dance. A handful of men at each end of the stage hooted and hollered their approval of each dip and gyration.

The front bar was set away from the stage to make room for the two bartenders, both male. One served the half dozen customers at the bar; the other made drinks for the servers. Four topless women with serving trays wandered among the tables. Two Asians, a white woman, and a woman of mixed race. They wore orange bikinis and an orange choker around their necks. I picked an empty table and slipped into a bench upholstered with fake orange leather that backed against the wall.

The white woman spotted me and paraded over on four-inch heels, swinging her hips. "Hello and welcome to the Orange

Peel. My name is Amber. What's yours?" Her professional smile seemed almost genuine.

"Chuck."

She held out her hand. "Nice to meet you, Chuck." She squeezed my hand. It was amazing how many topless women squeezed my hand.

"Nice to meet you too, Amber."

"What you want to drink?"

"Port City Amber."

"Amber like me?"

"That's right."

"We have it in bottles and draft. Would you like to tap Amber?" She winked and shimmied. "I'd like that."

I presumed she shimmied to display her assets, both of them. If so, it worked. "That's a good one, Amber. For now, I only want to tap the keg."

"This Amber will be back with your Amber on tap." She stoked my upper arm before she walked away. Maybe she wanted to feel my muscle. I often have that effect on women.

I studied the crowd and my vision adjusted further to the dim light. I'd never met Al Rice. I would recognize him from the family photo Doraleen loaned me, the picture Tank sent me, and the image I'd eyeballed on the no-fly list screen at the Crazy Lady. I studied every black face in the room. No Al Rice.

Amber returned with two mugs of beer. She laid a tab down. "That'll be ten dollars."

"The cover charge includes two drinks."

"It includes well drinks, house wines, and bottled or canned domestic beers. Draft beers are extra." She laid her hand on my arm again, gave it a squeeze. Yes, she definitely wanted to feel my muscle. "I'm sorry, Chuck. I thought you knew."

I dropped three fives on the tab. "Okay, Amber. Keep the change."

She scooped the bills into a pocket built into the tray. "Thanks, Chuck. I dance next. I'll come back to check on you in a little while. Oh, before I change, you wanna see a menu? We serve food." Amber lowered her voice conspiratorially. "And we have things that aren't on the menu also." She winked. And shimmied, of course.

"I'll pass for now, but I look forward to enjoying your dance."

Brandy finished her time on stage. She displayed little dance training, but made up in enthusiasm what she lacked in experience. Most tips were one-dollar bills in the waistband of her bikini. A big tip was two or three dollars. I didn't notice any fives. Her dances followed the same pattern the dancers at the Crazy Lady used—she finished nude and barefoot. She waved to good-natured laughter and whistles and exited through the curtain at the rear.

As I finished my first beer, Brandy returned to the showroom floor, entering through another orange curtain at floor level to the right of the stage. She appeared in her topless server outfit and began her route around the showroom floor to collect more tips. She reached my table and smiled. "Hello, I'm Brandy. Did you enjoy my dance?"

"Very much, Brandy." I extracted a fifty-dollar bill and held it in the air.

Brandy's gaze riveted on the bill.

"So you're from Gainesville?" I asked.

She dragged her focus off the fifty, reluctantly I thought. "Born and raised. You from Gainesville?"

"Not originally, but I went to the University of Florida."

"I attended Buchholz High School." Her attention moved to the bill again.

"I saw their band perform at a Gators football halftime show." I stuffed the fifty into her bikini. "Can I ask you a question?"

"You a cop?"

"No. I'm here to meet a friend."

"Since you ain't a cop, why you wearing a gun?"

"You're not supposed to spot my gun when it's clipped on the back. The doorman didn't object."

She scoffed. "That's Sammy. He's a dumbass. I don't miss much."

"I'm a private investigator."

"No shit?"

"For real." I handed her a business card, one without the crossed muskets logo.

She held the card to the light. "Carlos McCrary. What a strong, masculine name." She stuck the card down the front of her bikini.

"My friends call me Chuck."

"Chuck. Also a strong, masculine name. Since you're not a cop, we can be more than friends." She winked and shimmied. Of course. "I have a thing for Florida Gators. For fifty dollars, you ask me anything you want. And for two hundred fifty more, you can do more than that after I get off at two a.m."

"I'm tempted Brandy, but, like I said, I'm here to meet a friend. But I don't see him." I held out my phone with Al's picture. "His name's Al Rice. Have you seen him?"

Brandy's breasts rose with a sudden intake of breath. Her pupils widened in the dim light. She blinked twice. "Can't say as I have."

"Brandy, friends don't lie to each other. I really am a friend of Al's."

"Al don't have no friends."

"Al has friends. They just don't come here often."

"I ain't seen him tonight."

"You know Jennifer, of course."

"Of course."

I held up another fifty. "When's the last time you saw Al in here, maybe to watch Jennifer dance?"

She reached for the fifty and stopped. "You can stuff that one down my bikini too. I don't mind; really I don't."

I'd heard that phrase earlier today. The girls were encouraging customers to grope them. That struck me as indescribably sad. "That's okay, Brandy." I handed her the bill.

She shrugged and stuck it in her bikini.

"When did you last see Al?"

"Last night. He got real drunk and Billy—that's the head bartender—Billy threw him out."

"Do you know what happened after Billy threw him out?"

"Billy said he passed out on the sidewalk out front. A customer come in and told Sammy. Sammy and Guns, that's the bouncer, they drug him around back. That's all I know."

"Thanks, Brandy. Do all the dancers make the rounds down here following their performances?"

"Sure, you can't stuff no bills in a gal's bikini when she's stark naked, can you?"

"Good point." I smiled. "I have a favor to ask. Here's another fifty for you not to tell Jennifer that I'm looking for Al. I want her to come around to my table after she dances. Okay?"

"Don't see no harm in that, Chuck. You don't act like no pervert." She grabbed the fifty and winked. "Don't forget that offer for the other two hundred fifty. You look like you'd be a lot of fun."

The German strip joint I had visited in the army wasn't the only one that fronted for a brothel. The American ones I had visited were two for two.

Chapter 19

I NURSED THE SECOND BEER while I waited for Jennifer. The showroom filled.

The stage lights dimmed. A spotlight hit the stage and a man with slicked-back hair in an orange tuxedo entered with a cordless microphone. "And now, ladies and gentlemen, please join me in welcoming to the Orange Peel stage... formerly dancing with the Atlanta Ballet... the Georgia Peach... the star of our show... the one, the only... *Jennifer!*" He held back the orange curtain.

Jennifer, a/k/a Jasmine, a/k/a God-knows-who-else, pranced onto the stage in an orange and white ballet costume, complete with toe shoes, her red hair in a tight bun. A theme from Swan Lake wafted from the speakers. I had attended the Port City Ballet with Miyo, and I recognized many of Jennifer's movements, though I didn't know their names. She moved with swan-like grace. Jennifer didn't approach the edge of the stage during the first dance segment, so the patrons had no chance to slip bills into her costume. Just as well, since the ballet costume had no place to stuff bills.

As the crowd got restless with the Swan Lake dance, the music switched to the 1960s classic *The Stripper* by the David Rose Orchestra. I recognized it from the Oldies Channel on my satellite radio. The crowd went wild. Jennifer danced her way out of the ballet costume, slipped it behind the curtain, and moved close to the edge of the stage in her orange bikini and a white sequined halter top. Her skill level showed in the tips she collected—lots of two- and three-dollar tips and a few fives. She bent over and allowed the patrons to stuff bills into her top. Once both halves of her costume overflowed with bills, she danced near the curtain and expertly slipped the money from her costume and handed the stash behind the curtain. She danced out of the top, and I noticed that her breasts were artificially enhanced. She removed a hair pin and shook her long red hair loose with a shimmy so good that I stopped scanning the room and admired her performance. She circled both ends of the stage and collected more tips, filling her bikini to the brim again. She repeated the pass near the curtain, stashed the tips, and moved to the dance pole.

Every eye but mine, including the servers, focused on Jennifer at the pole. Another man in an orange-and-white muscle shirt and orange slacks stood against the wall. He wasn't there earlier. He must have been Guns, the bouncer Brandy mentioned. He didn't watch Jennifer; he watched me. *Hmm.*

As Jennifer exited the stage, Amber returned to my table. "She's really something, ain't she?"

"I've seen the Port City Ballet, and I recognize her classical dance education."

The server viewed my empty mug. "Would you like to tap Amber again, Chuck?" She winked. No shimmy this time. She didn't want to wear out the move.

"Yes, please."

She returned with the beer. The tab was still ten dollars. "Ten bucks for one beer?" I asked.

"Last time I gave you credit for your two well drinks." She touched my arm again. "I thought you knew."

All this touchy-feely stuff was making me uncomfortable. Her friendliness was sincere as a campaign promise. What type of desperation would drive a woman to do this?

"No problem." Tank could afford it, so I dropped fifteen dollars on her tray. "Brandy told me my friend Al Rice was here last night."

"Who?"

"Al Rice. Here, I have his picture on my phone." I held it up.

"Oh, him. I never knew his name. Yeah, he got sloppy drunk over Jennifer as usual."

"Did you notice where he went or know what happened to him?"

"Nah. He was his usual loser self. Lousy tipper, except with Jennifer. Her, he tips a lot. Can I bring you anything else?"

"I'm good."

Another dancer mounted the stage as Jennifer emerged from the curtain at floor level. She cut her eyes to Guns and he nodded. She stopped at two or three tables, working her way toward me. The music overpowered the conversation from the nearest table, but I read the body language. An enthusiastic fan stuffed another five in her bikini. She thanked him and paraded in my direction.

"Hi, I'm Jennifer. Did you enjoy my dance?"

Up close the tiny crow's feet were visible, the slight deepening of the creases that ran from the edges of her nostrils to the corners of her mouth. She appeared about the same age as Victoria Ramirez, my lawyer and occasional friend with benefits. Vicky was in her late thirties. How long was a stripper's career good for? I knew prostitutes who did business well into late middle-age; When I was a cop, I busted one who was over sixty.

I held a fifty-dollar bill where Jennifer would spot it. "You were wonderful. I've seen the Port City Ballet and you're as good as the dancers there."

"Thank you. I danced in the Atlanta ballet chorus line for five years."

"I've been to Atlanta on business a lot the last few years, and I often go to the ballet since we don't have much of one in Port City. What might I have seen you in?"

"*Swan Lake*. I danced part of it in my show, and I danced in *Carmina Burana* twice."

"I loved the *Carmina Burana*. That's why you looked familiar. Let's see, that was… what? Three or four years ago?"

"Five."

"Well, you were wonderful." I stuck the fifty in her bikini and produced another one. "May I ask you a question?"

She shrugged. Her breasts were bouncing punctuation marks. One more part of their customer service education: Jiggle your breasts whenever possible.

She hadn't taken the ask-a-question hint to offer to meet me after hours like the other dancers did. Was it because she was the star of the show? Or was she the exclusive property of someone else?

"Where did you study ballet?"

"The École Du Ballet Augustine in New York City."

I held up another fifty. "One more question?"

"Sure."

I slipped the fifty into her bikini. "Do you know where I can find Al Rice?"

Jennifer made a small step back. "I don't know any Al Rice."

I selected another fifty and held it in front of her. "Sure you do. You added him to the no-fly list at the Crazy Lady a couple weeks ago when your name was Jasmine."

She eyeballed the fifty like it might try to escape.

"Here, take it. There's plenty more where that came from. I just want information."

She grabbed the fifty and stuck it down her bikini. "You a cop?"

"Everybody asks me that. No, I'm a private investigator." I handed her a business card. "I'm also a friend of Al Rice. I'm not here to cause trouble for you or Al or anybody else. I'd like to ask a couple of questions. Is there someplace where we can talk? I'll pay you two hundred dollars for ten minutes of your time, and maybe a bonus if you have useful information."

"See that door back there on the side? Says *no admittance* on it?"

"Yeah."

"I gotta finish my rounds with the customers. After I finish and go backstage, give me fifteen minutes to change, then walk in that door. Don't bother to knock."

Chapter 20

THE *NO ADMITTANCE* DOOR LED TO THE CLUB'S OFFICE. "Jennifer asked me to meet her here," I told the man behind the desk. "I'm a private investigator." He was in his forties, receding hairline, in a golf shirt and blue jeans. He seemed pretty ordinary. I figured this guy for the bookkeeper maybe, or the office manager.

"I'm Pete, the bookkeeper," he said. "If she's expecting you, I'm sure she'll be here in a moment. Have a seat. May I see your identification?"

I displayed my credentials and gave him a business card. "People call me Chuck."

"A private detective. What brings you here, Chuck, if you don't mind my asking?"

"I'm looking for a man who comes here a lot."

"Who is he?"

"Al Rice." I showed the bookkeeper Al's picture on my phone.

"I remember him. He came here this morning before I opened up. He wanted his car keys."

Pete was the first person I'd met at either strip joint that didn't expect a bribe. Why was he so cooperative?

"What time was that?"

"I got here at 10:45, so it was about 10:50."

"You're here at 10:45 in the morning, and you're here twelve hours later?"

Pete smiled. "I work a split shift, four hours around the lunch crowd, and four hours from ten p.m. to two a.m. It lets me drive my kids to St. Rita's school in the morning and pick them up in the afternoon. I'm a single dad and I like to tuck them in bed before I come to work. We live with my mother. I know what you're thinking: What's a good Catholic who sends his kids to church school doing working in a strip joint?"

"It's not my place to judge."

"The pay is good. Church school isn't cheap. There aren't many jobs in my field where I can work a split shift."

"A man's gotta do what a man's gotta do. It's none of my business. Did Al seem okay this morning?"

Pete paused. "Don't take this the wrong way, but he smelled like he hadn't bathed in days. Also, he was rather, uh, adamant about getting his keys—like he was in a big hurry. He wouldn't wait until we opened. He threatened to break the door down if I didn't give him his keys immediately."

"Did he say anything else?"

"He asked to use the bathroom before he left."

"Anything else? Like maybe where he was going?"

Pete shrugged. "Sorry. I made fresh coffee. You want some?"

Again with the unprovoked friendliness. He needed the well-paying job, yet he hadn't asked for money. *Hmm.*

"Great, a little cream if you have it. Black if you don't."

Pete left through a door behind him.

I sat in a chair and studied the office. Glamour shots of dozens of dancers hung on the walls. A vintage Star Wars poster was incongruous in a joint that sold sex.

Pete returned with my coffee. "Did I add the right amount of milk?"

"It's fine, thanks."

"Make yourself comfortable; I need to get back to work."

Twenty minutes later, I'd finished my coffee. "Could you please check on Jennifer and make sure I understood her correctly?"

"Sure." The bookkeeper left.

I stood and paced back and forth. What was taking the guy so long?

Finally, Pete walked in. "I'm sorry, Chuck. Jennifer has left the building."

I LEFT THE BRIGHTLY LIT OFFICE and walked into the darkened showroom. I was nearly blind for the first few seconds.

An almost invisible black man in a black tee-shirt and black pants stepped from my right and grabbed my arm. Guns lunged from the left and grabbed at my other arm. He missed because I'd already thrown a left cross at the invisible man and caught him in the gut. That loosened his grip. My second punch to his gut did the trick. I swung my left elbow back and smashed Guns flush in the face. I felt the familiar pop of a broken nose.

The invisible man released my arm to clutch his stomach. I kicked Guns's knee and clubbed him with a karate chop to his thick neck on his way to the floor. I spun to the man in black, grabbed the back of his neck, and shoved his head down to meet my knee rising toward his face. I missed his nose and battered his forehead, and he dropped like a felled tree. Good enough. I pivoted and kicked Guns in the stomach. Another kick to the man in black's gut for a reminder. Nothing succeeds like excess.

The showroom was dark and the stage lights so bright that no one else in the club noticed the fracas. The loud music covered the sounds.

I walked from the showroom to the entrance foyer.

Sammy saw me and looked like he'd swallowed a frog. He started to make a move, then thought better of it. Smart guy. "Have a nice night, sir," he said.

"So far, so good," I retorted.

Chapter 21

TANK'S PHONE RANG, and he set his cup on Doraleen's coffee table. "Hey, Chuck. Where are you?"

"The parking lot at the Orange Peel Gentlemen's Club. I gotta be making progress; two hoods in the club tried to put the arm on me."

"Put the arm on you? What does that mean?"

"I waited in the club's office for Jennifer to come talk to me. She's the dancer Al is in love with. She never showed. After I left the office, two guys grabbed me."

Tank's heart skipped a beat. "What happened?"

"I left them both lying on the floor, contemplating the hazards of overconfidence. Are you at Doraleen's?"

"Yeah. I told Snoop I'd guard Momma Dora and I sent him home. It feels kinda good to be a bodyguard after sitting at a desk and talking about finance for the last few years. I feel like I'm helping the cause."

"You are helping the cause."

"Did you learn anything at Al's old apartment?" asked Tank.

"The same scarfaced thug who threatened Doraleen visited the super after I left. He was also asking about Al."

"So Moffett's crew is on the prowl for Al."

"We're in a race against time, Tank. I keep finding where Al was, not where he is."

"Did you look at those security cameras pointed at I-95?"

"Yeah, but I didn't find much. One company's camera caught a distant image of someone exiting the car and hiking off toward the north at 11:20 this morning. He was alone in the car. Probably Al, but I can't be sure. I suppose you haven't heard from him."

"Nope. I'm sitting here with my feet up, drinking decaf." Tank picked up his cup.

"The good news is Al was at the Orange Peel last night. He got drunk, had his car keys confiscated, and they threw him out. Al came back this morning to get his keys. I assume he was the one driving his car."

"But where was he headed?"

"Good question. Maybe he was on his way to Doraleen's house."

"Why did he stop on I-95?"

"The same reason anyone stops on I-95: He had car trouble. You plan to spend the night at Doraleen's again?"

"Yeah. I'll text Snoop that I'll drive her to school tomorrow. Wait a sec… I hear something at the door."

"Carry your gun, Tank. You know what happened to me, and it's after eleven. No friends would come visit Doraleen this late. Leave your phone on and slip it in your pocket so I can hear what's happening."

Tank's heart rate sped up. He set down his coffee and drew his pistol. He moved toward the door.

The door opened a few inches and clunked against the security bar. Whoever was there had used a key. The doorbell rang.

Doraleen came into the living room. "I heard the doorbell."

"Go back to bed, Momma Dora. Let me handle this."

"Tank, you're carrying a gun."

"Merely a precaution, Momma Dora. Please go to your room and close the door."

The door whacked against the security bar again. "Let me in. It's Al."

"Oh, thank God," said Doraleen as she hurried to the door.

Tank barred her way. "Let me make sure he's alone. You wait here." He padded to the door in his sock feet and stooped to put his eye to the viewer. "Step back, Al, and I'll open the door."

"Tank, is that you?"

Doraleen ran to the door. "Thank God, you're home."

I STOOD THREE FEET FROM THE DOOR so Tank could identify me through the peephole.

He opened the door. "Come on in. I made a fresh pot of real coffee."

"Good, we may be up for a while tonight."

Tank led the way to Doraleen's living room. "Al's in the shower. He smelled pretty rank when he got here. Have a seat, Chuck. I'll get coffee."

Doraleen hugged me and kissed me on the cheek. "Tank told me all you've done to find our Al and about those two men who attacked you. This is a happy day."

"In the end, nothing I did was necessary. Al came here on his own. I feel as useless as an elevator operator in a one-story building."

"Nonsense, Chuck. A Higher Power has guided this all along. I'm sure you were part of God's plan. I will celebrate His success."

Tank said, "Even if you were as worthless as tits on a boar hog."

Doraleen smacked him on the knee. "You watch your mouth, Thomas Tyler, or I'll turn you over my knee."

She stood. "Al's clothes should be ready for the dryer. I threw them in the washer while he showered. He smelled like a landfill, I do declare. I have a pot of chili on the stove. Al hasn't had a decent meal since I fed him breakfast a few days ago. I set the dining room table."

"I could do with a bowl of chili, Doraleen," I said. "I didn't have time for dinner, and Tank says you make great chili."

"Tank would eat road kill if I put it on a plate." She patted him on the shoulder.

Once Doraleen left, I lowered my voice. "This ain't over 'til it's over. Moffett is after Al, and we don't have a clue what to do now that we found him."

Al walked in wearing a bathrobe with a Miami Dolphins logo. "I heard the doorbell. I found Dad's old clothes. We wear the same size." He stuck out his hand. "You must be that private detective Tank hired to find me. I'm Al Rice."

I stood. "Chuck McCrary. Pleased to meet you, Al."

Al shook my hand then faced Tank. "I need a drink; I'll be right back."

Tank grabbed his arm. "Bro, what you need is coffee and lots of it."

Al shook his arm, struggling to dislodge Tank's giant hand. He would've had better luck opening a bear trap. "Lemme alone, Tank. I need a drink. A real drink."

Tank grabbed Al's other arm like a vise. "Alcohol and drugs is how you got into this mess in the first place, Al. Sit down while I bring you coffee."

Al wrenched his arms back and forth. He had as much chance to break Tank's grip as he did to escape a straightjacket. Al opened his mouth to speak as Doraleen walked into the room.

"Al, honey, your clothes are in the dryer. Oh good, I see you found your father's bath robe."

"The bath robe was all that fit over my cast."

"I'll check if the chili's ready. You boys sit in the dining room. I'll be right there."

Tank dropped Al's arms and gestured as if to say "after you."

Al glared at Tank and preceded us to the dining room.

Doraleen had set four formal places with her best China. Linen napkins in China napkin rings matched the tablecloth. A small bowl with Ixora blossoms floating in it decorated the center of the table. Four crystal goblets held ice water.

"Al, maybe you prefer iced tea to coffee," I said. "You might be dehydrated since last night. Coffee might upset your stomach."

"What do you know about last night?"

"I'm a private investigator, Al. It's my business to know things."

I gestured to Tank. "Better make it iced tea."

I sat in a chair across from Al. "Tank hired me to get you and Doraleen out of this mess with Moffett."

He scoffed. "I don't suppose you carry two hundred thousand dollars on you, do you?"

"That option is not on the table."

"Then I'm a dead man."

I shook my head. "Not yet you aren't. I need to ask you a few questions."

He made a noncommittal gesture which I assumed to be agreement.

"I watched a security video of you leaving your car on I-95 at 11:20 this morning. That was twelve hours ago. What have you been doing for the last twelve hours?"

Tank walked in with two crystal goblets of iced tea. He set one by Al and carried the other to the foot of the table, where he sat.

Al chugged a long drink and nodded his thanks to Tank. "I've been walking forever."

I waited.

Tank opened his mouth.

I raised a hand. Tank leaned back.

"Walking where?" I asked.

"Why, to here."

Tank pointed a finger at Al. "You mean you walked all the way from where you abandoned your car to here? That must be fifteen miles."

I frowned at Tank. "Let's you and I help Doraleen with the chili."

"I'll be back," I said to Al. I headed toward the hall door.

"Hey," said Al, gesturing. "Kitchen's through that door."

"I know. I need to talk to Tank for a minute."

I led Tank to the hallway and closed the dining room door. "Let me handle this interview alone. This is what I do for a living."

"Sorry, Chuck. I didn't realize it was important. I'll listen; I promise not to interrupt."

"Sorry, pal; that's not good enough. I may probe old wounds. It's like picking at a scab and it hurts. Al won't want his mother or his best friend to witness that, but he might tell me things he won't tell you or Doraleen. Come with me." I led him into the kitchen. "Doraleen, is the chili ready?"

She leaned over and sniffed the aroma. "It's almost finished simmering. I'll bring three bowls into the dining room in five minutes."

"If you don't mind, Doraleen, I'll talk to Al alone. You and Tank eat here in the kitchen. Once the chili is ready, please bring two bowls to the dining room for Al and me. You and Tank hang out here or in the living room. Anywhere but in the dining room."

Doraleen stirred the pot. "Al is my son. I have a right to know."

"Of course you do, but this type of interview is what I'm trained to do. Al will be more inclined to talk if you and Tank aren't there."

She regarded Tank. "Are you okay with this? He's your best friend."

"Momma Dora, I'd love to know what's going on too, but Chuck's the expert. That's why I hired him. He's the best in the business. Let's do what he says." Tank sat at the kitchen table and gestured for Doraleen to take another chair. He waved me on. "Go get 'em, bro."

Chapter 22

I RETURNED TO THE DINING ROOM AND SAT ON AL'S RIGHT. "So you left your car at 11:20 this morning. Walk me step by step from there to now."

Al had in fact walked the fifteen miles from his abandoned car to Doraleen's house. It took twelve hours because he was terrified Moffett would capture him. He stopped several times to rest. He hadn't eaten that day, but had drunk at water fountains in convenience stores and fast food stores on the way.

Doraleen backed through the swinging door, carrying two bowls of chili on a lacquered tray. "Here's a sleeve of saltines. You can't eat chili without crackers, fellows. I grated cheddar cheese on top but I left off the onions. Either of you want onions?" She opened the crackers and arrayed them on a China serving platter.

"I'm good, Momma."

"No thanks, Doraleen. Grated cheese is good enough."

"Chuck you want more coffee?"

"I'd like to switch to iced tea, Doraleen, if it's not too much trouble."

"No trouble. I'll be right back."

Al shoveled chili into his mouth. His cast let his fingers stick through, but he gripped the cracker awkwardly. He bit off half a saltine and washed it down with iced tea. He slipped a napkin from its ring and wiped a cheese string off his chin.

I waited until Doraleen let the door swing shut behind her. "How did you incur the debt to Moffett to begin with?"

Al swallowed. "I refinanced an earlier loan and added a new loan for another, uh, investment I wanted to make."

I ate a bite of chili. Tank was right. It was delicious. "How much was the earlier loan?"

"Eighty thousand plus twenty thousand interest."

"So the new loan was for one hundred thousand?"

"No, it was for sixty thousand." He wiped another cheese string off his chin.

"I got it: The principal was one hundred sixty, plus forty thousand more interest on the new loan."

"Yeah."

"What was the new investment you made?"

Al ate more chili, wiped more cheese from his chin. "I haven't eaten since yesterday. This is outstanding, in spite of the mess I make eating with one hand."

"Right. I'll repeat the question: What was this new investment?"

Al gazed down at his bowl. "That doesn't matter. It didn't pan out."

"Is that your way to tell me that you lost the money?"

He scooped another spoon of chili, held it above the bowl, and managed to scrape off the cheese strings with a cracker held in his left hand. His hand shook. "Yeah, I lost it. So what? It's ancient history. Can't turn back the clock."

"No, but maybe we keep history from repeating itself. What was the investment?"

He shoved the chili in his mouth. "The investment was, uh, illegal."

"I figured that." I swallowed another bite. "What was it? Cocaine?"

"Four kilos. Prime grade."

"How'd you lose it?"

Al didn't say anything, only gazed into his bowl and moved the pungent chili around with his spoon. His hand shook again, and he dropped the spoon on the edge of the bowl. His voice was so low I barely heard him. "I got ripped off, okay?"

Doraleen tapped twice on the door and carried in a goblet of iced tea. "Here you go, Chuck. Al, honey, you ready for more chili?"

"Yes, ma'am."

Doraleen grabbed the empty bowl. "How about you, Chuck?"

"Yes, please, and more iced tea if it's not too much trouble."

"Be right back."

I waited until she left. "Not the first time somebody got ripped off. How'd it happen?"

"One of the packages was cocaine—the only one I sampled. The bastards switched out the other three for packages of powdered sugar."

"And you didn't find out until later. After they ran off with your money."

Al nodded. "I sold the one package for fifty thousand. I paid Monster his interest on the loan with a little left over to live on."

"When was that?"

"Maybe six weeks ago."

"So, the loan was due again before Moffett smashed your hand."

Al stared at his bandaged hand.

I waited for a reaction.

He put both hands on the table. The cast clunked on the table top. He made smoothing motions on the already smooth tablecloth. Tears spilled down his cheeks.

Chapter 23

NGOMBO CALLED A NUMBER. "Teddy Ngombo is here. I have two license plate numbers for you, Bones. Please to get Monster's pet cop to run the plates." He recited the license numbers.

"It's past midnight," Bones answered.

"I need to know who owns these two vehicles. I do not care what time it is. The computers never sleep. Monster told me that."

"Where are you?"

"I am parked a hundred meters from Doraleen Rice's house. The vehicles of which I speak are parked in front. I need to know if either of them is connected to Al Rice."

"Keep your shirt on, Teddy. I'll get back to you."

While he waited, Ngombo checked the tracker app for Rice's phone. Still nothing. One more instance of Rice's irresponsibility. He had not yet charged his battery.

Ngombo's phone rang. "Teddy Ngombo is here."

"I got the info on those two cars."

"One is a minivan."

"Excuse my freaking ass. '...those two *vehicles*' you wanted, your freaking majesty."

"To communicate well, one must be precise."

"You want this shit or not?"

"To whom do they belong?"

"I emailed the info to your phone."

"Tell me the information," said Ngombo. "I have trouble with the features of this super phone that Monster gave me."

"I can relate to that, Teddy." Bones laughed. "The Porsche belongs to Tank Tyler. Lives at 96 Pink Coral Way. That's on a private island in the middle of Seeti Bay."

"I understand. And who is this Tank Tyler? Tank is an unusual name, even for America. Do you have any information on him?"

"Don't need it," Bones said. "He's famous."

"Then why do I not know of this man?"

"Cause you're from Africa and you don't know shit about football."

"I know a great deal about football, but here in America you misuse the word. Your barbaric sport should be called *American* football. I am not interested in this Tyler person's prowess at American football except as it relates to capturing Al Rice. Please tell me those relevant facts."

"His full name is Thomas Tyler. He played defensive end for the Port City Pelicans for years. The guy's bigger than Monster, if you can believe it. He's six-foot-six and weighs close to three hundred pounds. And he's rich. Not a little rich, you understand, but so freakin' rich that he paid cash to buy his new mansion last year."

"He is black, this rich American football player?"

"Yeah. Not as black as you, but he's black enough." Bones laughed. "I'd be real careful with this guy if I was you. Newspaper article I read in the sports section says he goes to a shooting range for fun. He's a dead shot with a rifle or a pistol, and he has a concealed weapon permit."

"I am afraid of no man. What about the license plate for the minivan?"

"The minivan is registered to a corporation. The address is a post office box. It's a dead end."

"Do you have any information on this Carlos McCrary whom I asked you about?" asked Ngombo.

"I sent that to your phone hours ago."

"As I told you, I have trouble accessing—"

"Yeah, yeah. Spare me the song and dance. I'll give you the abridged version: McCrary is trouble. Worse than Tank Tyler. He's a hotshot private detective who's solved enough high-profile cases to get his name on the news. He's former Special Forces."

"Special forces," said Ngombo. "What is that?"

"The freakin' Green Berets."

"McCrary wears a green beret?"

"Not any more, hot shot. You never watched a freakin' John Wayne movie in Africa?"

"Who is John Wayne?"

"Forget it. The Green Berets are the army guys who kick ass and take names. McCrary's got medals; guy's a freaking hero. If you come acrost him, don't mess around with a guy like that, Teddy. Not without backup."

"I am a warrior. My name, Tegumetosa, means 'walks with lions.' I have yet to meet my match."

"Yeah, sure. I'm just saying. Call me or Turk if you need backup."

"Could the minivan belong to this McCrary? Such a man might hide the ownership of his vehicles."

"Who knows?"

"Is there any connection between the American football player and the detective?"

"None that I found."

Chapter 24

DORALEEN CAME INTO THE LIVING ROOM. "He's asleep." She flopped onto the sofa and patted Tank on the knee. "You're so good to us, Tank. There's no way I can repay you."

Tank patted her tiny hand with his giant one. "Momma Dora, it's I who can never repay you." He faced me. "When I arrived at UAC, I was a farm boy from rural Alabama. I couldn't put two sentences together without three grammar mistakes. If I hadn't been a football player, the teachers at my dinky little high school wouldn't have made the time to tutor me so I could graduate."

"As long as I've known you," I said, "you've talked like a television news anchor."

"You've only known me a couple years." He pointed at Doraleen. "Momma Dora taught me how to speak proper English. She taught me the joy of reading for pleasure. She taught me how to study at a college level and apply myself to get good grades. I skated through high school on my football ability. Barely did enough to pass. I began the same way at UAC. Then Momma Dora saw my first test grades my freshman year…"

"I cracked the whip on him," Doraleen said, "that's what I did. Like I did for my own son." She stood. "Do either of you need more coffee or iced tea?"

"Please sit down, Momma Dora," Tank said. "I've had enough coffee."

I lifted my half-full cup. "I have some left."

Doraleen sat. "I'm glad. I'm tired. I'm too old for these late hours."

"As I was saying," Tank continued. "If it hadn't been for Momma Dora and Mr. William, I might've flunked out my first semester."

Doraleen raised her hand. "You're too modest, Tank. Your parents raised a bright God-fearing young man with the tools necessary to succeed." She smiled at me. "Tank was a little rough around the edges. He was in a college environment in which he had no experience. I pointed him in the right direction; he made the journey."

"You mean you can't make a silk purse from a sow's ear?"

She chuckled. "Right. Tank was raw silk that I helped make into a fancy purse."

"And here Tank is wants to do the same thing for Al."

Doraleen considered Tank. "When I see how you turned out, and I see how Albert wound up, at least so far..." Her eyes misted. "I could never say it to his face, but I wonder in my heart of hearts if Albert is really a sow's ear. My William used to ask my advice about the boys he coached and about the troubles these high-spirited kids got into. He'd carry on about some young man or other who made one bad decision after another. You remember what my William said?"

"It was unsuitable for tender young ears, but it got the point across." Tank grinned at me. "Mr. William said 'You can't shine shit.' But Mr. William never gave up on any of his players. I refuse to believe Al is irredeemable." Tank patted her hand. "That's why we're here, but we don't know how to do it. We have the will, and I have the financial resources if it were merely a matter of money... But neither Chuck nor I know how to cause a... a rebirth in Al to rekindle his self-respect. Maybe it takes a saint. I don't know. But we're here to make the attempt. Maybe you can give us some guidance?"

Doraleen tugged a handkerchief from a pocket and dabbed at her eyes. "Albert was all right until his father died. I know that he'd lost Janice, but I thought he'd recovered from that. Then, that day in New Orleans... It was a couple months later that he got kicked off the team. His life has spiraled downward ever since."

"What did he do to get kicked off the team?"

"That was over a decade ago," Tank said. "It doesn't matter anymore. For now, let's get Al into rehab. Maybe this time it will work." He stood. "First, we get rid of the alcohol in the house so Al doesn't get into it. Momma Dora, we should dispose of your sherry too. Can I pour it out with the other stuff?"

"If you think that's best, Tank, go ahead."

Tank left the room.

I finished my coffee. "Doraleen, every time I broach the subject of Al's getting kicked off the team, Tank changes the subject. Was Tank involved?"

"I don't think so."

"What did Al do to get kicked out?"

"I thought Tank told you." She twisted her handkerchief. "Albert was one of three UAC football players accused of gang-raping a freshman girl."

Chapter 25

NGOMBO PULLED HIS LAST GPS TRACKER and a magnetic case from his Cherokee's console. He strolled up the sidewalk across from the minivan, insuring the street was deserted. Two men, one black and one white, sat in the living room with the old woman. The black man was not Al Rice, therefore he must be Tank Tyler. He scanned both directions once more and darted across the street to click the magnetic tracker under the rear bumper. Who was the white man with Doraleen Rice?

He went back to his Cherokee, moved it a block further up the street. He plugged his tablet into the cigarette lighter to charge it.

A half hour later, the white minivan's dot moved on the tablet. Ngombo cranked the Jeep. He hung back three blocks. At two in the morning there was little traffic to hide him while he followed the vehicle, but there was no danger of losing the trail. The GPS dot glowed on the tablet screen.

Ngombo followed the white minivan onto the Beachline Causeway. His quarry headed across Seeti Bay to Port City Beach. The vehicle curved onto a residential street on the west side of the barrier islands. Ngombo closed the gap so he could see which address it drove into. The minivan jinked into the driveway of a high-rise condo building and ascended the ramp to the gated garage. He noted the address and returned to Doraleen Rice's house, stopping at an all-night coffee shop for a sandwich and coffee to go.

The Porsche was still there. Tank Tyler was spending the night. Was he there as a bodyguard for Rice? Or for the old woman?

Ngombo parked fifty yards down the block where he could watch the darkened windows. He unwrapped his sandwich and lowered the windows in the humid darkness.

He had finished his sandwich and coffee when the lights came on in the old woman's house. Ngombo sat straighter. Unconsciously, he fondled the handle of his knife. Maybe Tyler was about to leave. If so, no doubt Ngombo could break down the old woman's front door and search her home. If Rice were there, Ngombo the African warrior would find him and capture him like an animal.

Chapter 26

RICE WOKE IN A COLD SWEAT, his whole body shaking like leaves in a storm. He rolled out of bed and staggered toward the nightlight in the bathroom. He grabbed the door jamb to regain his balance. He swiped his hand at the light switch and lurched to the toilet. He threw up and collapsed on the tile floor. *I've gotta have a drink; I can't take this anymore.* He grabbed the countertop and heaved himself upright. His mouth tasted like bile. The tile felt cool against his bare feet. He leaned his forehead on the medicine cabinet beside the lavatory. The cool mirror made his head feel better. He leaned over to get a drink from the faucet but that made him nauseous again. He filled the bathroom glass to rinse the vomit taste from his mouth. *That's better.* He regarded his image in the mirror. His pajama top was stained with vomit. *Just like my freaking jacket.* He leaned both hands on the countertop and laughed at the irony.

He rinsed his mouth again. This time he swallowed a little water, learned he could keep it down. *Okay, that worked.* He stripped off his sodden top and tossed it in the corner. *I need a drink. Where the hell did I leave Dad's bathrobe?* He scanned the bathroom, then walked into the bedroom. He spotted the bathrobe on the bench at the foot of the bed and shrugged it on, working it over the bulky cast.

He eased open the bedroom door and tiptoed to the kitchen. Closing the door softly behind him, he switched on the light. *Where does Momma keep her booze? It's been so long since I lived here that I don't remember.* He started with the pantry and searched each shelf, pushing aside the canned goods, bottles, packages, and sacks of chips. Nothing. He left the pantry door open and moved to the cabinets. He opened the cabinet doors one by one and searched each shelf. Still nothing.

He moved to the dining room. A serving tray and six crystal sherry glasses sat on top of the sideboard. *God, I hate sherry, but right now, anything alcoholic is better than nothing.* He opened the sideboard doors, knelt, and scoured every shelf. *Why does Momma keep the tray and glasses on the sideboard and not keep the sherry near them?* He opened the bottom doors of the China cabinet. Nothing but more dishes. *This makes no sense.*

In a flash it hit him. Frantic, he ran to the kitchen and jerked open the doors beneath the sink. He hauled out the heavy trash bin and heard an ominous clank of glass. In panic, he peered into the bin at the empty liquor bottles. "Damn that Tank. He emptied them all down the sink." He threw the bin across the kitchen. Empty bottles flew out and smashed on the floor, their glass shards skittering across the floor.

A deep voice startled him from behind. "You're up early, aren't you, Al?" Tank stood inside the doorway in a tee-shirt and pajama pants, hands on hips, a scowl on his face.

Rice's mother stood in the doorway in fuzzy pink house shoes, unconsciously tying the sash of an embroidered Chinese housecoat while she searched his face. Her eyes were wide with fear.

Rice knew she was not afraid *of* him, but afraid *for* him. He wrenched his gaze from hers and gazed around the kitchen from one side to the other. His mind absorbed the tableau of his own destructive wretchedness: cabinet doors left open in his frantic search, cans and bottles in the pantry shoved aside, broken glass shattered and scattered near the far wall, the trash bin thrown without thinking against the same wall.

He fell to his knees, hands over his face. "No, no, no…"

Chapter 27

RICE DROPPED HIS HANDS FROM HIS FACE.

Doraleen skirted the broken glass and removed a dustpan and broom from the broom closet. "I'd better clean this up before somebody cuts their feet." She moved closer to Tank and began sweeping the floor around him.

Tank motioned her to stop. "I think it's time for Al to clean up after himself, don't you, Momma Dora?" Gently, he took the broom and dustpan from the old woman. In a soft voice, he said. "On your feet, Al. It's time to man up." He waited until Rice struggled to his feet. He extended the broom and dustpan toward his friend. "Come over here, bro. I can't walk in there barefooted until you clean up the broken glass."

Rice stared at the cleaning tools.

Doraleen stood there. Tears streamed down her cheeks.

Tank smiled at him. "I believe you know how to use these."

Rice wiped his tears with the bathrobe sleeve. "I believe I do." He grabbed the broom and dustpan. "You and Momma wait in the living room while I sweep up."

After Tank and his mother left, Rice swept the glass shards to the middle of the floor. The routine, repetitive motions calmed him. *Clean up my own mess*, he thought. At least that was a goal, any goal, for a man with no goals.

He righted the trash bin and set it next to the pile of glass shards. He bent over with the dustpan and fought off the nausea. Sweep, dump, sweep, dump, sweep, dump. *Any small goal is better for a man than no goals at all*. Hadn't he heard his father say that one time? He slid the trash bin under the sink.

He closed the cabinet doors, closed the drawers, and put the coffee maker back on the kitchen counter. After rolling the vacuum cleaner from the broom closet, he twisted the knob to *bare floor*, and vacuumed up the glass specks. He straightened the food items in the pantry and closed the door. *A goal, any goal, for a man with no goals.*

He washed his hands in the sink and surveyed the kitchen. Everything was in order. For the first time in a long time, he had accomplished something. Al felt pretty good. If only the other parts of his life were that easy.

Doraleen smiled from the kitchen door. "Would you like breakfast, honey? How about scrambled eggs and bacon?"

RICE FINISHED HIS MILK, set the glass beside his empty plate, and pushed back from the dining room table. "Thanks, Momma. I feel a little better."

"Did you get enough to eat, honey? There's more bacon and eggs." She pushed a plate of toast his direction. "You want more toast?"

"Better not push him, Momma Dora," said Tank. "Al hasn't been eating regularly. His stomach may need a while to adapt to real food. I, on the other hand, have no problem with real food. I'd love a couple more eggs and some toast."

Doraleen stood. "Scrambled well-done again?"

Rice sat straight. "Something's bothered me since I arrived last night, but I couldn't put my finger on it until now." He glanced around the room. "Where's Race Car, Momma? I haven't seen her since I got home."

Neither Doraleen nor Tank spoke.

"Is something wrong with Race Car? Did something happen to her?"

Tank glanced down at the table. "Race Car's not here, Al. She's at the vet's."

"Did she get sick? I know she's old, older than most cats ever get, but she's all we have left of Dad. What's wrong with her?"

"One of Moffett's men..." Tank lapsed into silence.

Rice stood. "What happened? Did Moffett send one of his thugs over here after I told him to stay away from Momma?" He pounded the table with his fist. "For God's sake, tell me what happened."

"Sit down, Al," said Tank, "and I'll tell you. Sunday afternoon Moffett's thug came by."

"Who came by?" Al asked. "Did you get a name, Momma?"

"No, honey. I assumed he was Moffett until Chuck told me Moffett was white."

"So, he was black?"

"Yes, with scars on his face and long dreadlocks. He spoke precise English, like it wasn't his first language."

Al hit the table with a fist. "Teddy Ngombo. I know that bastard. He's obsessed with knives. Fancies himself an African warrior." He rotated back to his mother. "What happened? What did he say?"

"I heard the doorbell. I went to the door, and this—what did you say his name was?"

"Teddy."

"This Teddy was holding Race Car. He handed her to me and... and he asked me who would care for her if I weren't there."

Al's heart hardened into a hot rock and fell into his gut. It burned like acid all the way down. "What else did he say, Momma?"

"He said you swore on my life that you would pay your debt to Moffett and that he took that oath seriously. He said you should take it seriously too."

"Oh my God, Momma. It was only a figure of speech after he smashed my hand with that hammer. I never meant that. You know I didn't."

"I know you didn't mean it, honey." Doraleen moved toward Rice and laid a hand on his shoulder. "But sometimes..." She drew her hand back.

"Sometimes what?"

Doraleen blinked back tears. "Sometimes you speak without thinking, and your actions have unintended consequences. Remember: The quality of our decisions determines the course of our lives." She plucked a handkerchief from her pocket and entwined it in her hands. "That Teddy person said I should make sure you pay the money you owe or I would regret it for the rest of my very short life. That's what he said, 'your very short life.'"

"I told Monster I'd kill him if he came near you."

She brought her palm to her son's cheek. "Once again, you spoke without thinking, honey. You may have created a blood feud with a ruthless monster who has thugs with guns and knives at his beck and call." She dropped her hand. "Who do you have? An old woman and a retired football player. You're no match for Moffett. Do you even know where to find him? He knows where I live."

Rice dropped his head. "What have I done? What have I done?"

"Al, whatever you've done, it's in the past," Tank said. "Nobody can change the past. We can plan for the future. I hate to call Chuck this early, but that's what I pay him for." He sent Chuck a text.

"What did Teddy do to Race Car? Why is she at the vet?"

"I'll get to that," she said. "Once that awful Teddy left, I didn't know what to do, so I called Tank. He rushed out here that afternoon and installed extra door locks on both my doors. Then he called Chuck McCrary. The next day—Monday evening—he and Chuck came here to discuss your situation at length. I let Race Car outside to do her business before Tank and Chuck arrived. While Chuck and I were talking, I realized Race Car hadn't come back and meowed at the door to be let in. You know how she does that."

Rice smiled. "She has the loudest meow in the neighborhood when she wants in or out."

Doraleen echoed his smile faintly. "Chuck volunteered to find her, but I wanted to come along. You know how nervous Race Car sometimes gets around strangers. Then we opened the front door…" She pushed the kitchen door open. "I can't relive that anymore; you tell him, Tank. I'll make your eggs and toast." She left.

Rice pivoted to Tank. "So what happened to Race Car?"

"She was lying in a puddle of blood on the front porch. Someone had cut off her ears and tail. She managed to drag herself up the steps and onto the porch. We drove her to vet. She's still there."

Rice was stunned. Without thinking, he grabbed a piece of toast and mopped his empty plate with it. He continued to mop the plate long after it had any effect.

Tank sipped his coffee while the silence grew.

Rice held the toast and stared at it like it held the key to the universe. He set it in the center of his plate and stared at it. "It's one thing to get into trouble on my own. But those bastards have involved Momma... even Race Car..." He pivoted to Tank. "This shit has to stop."

"And what shit is that, bro?" Tank jumped to his feet, knocked his chair over. He paced around the dining room. "Is it the shit where you gamble money you don't have? Is it the shit where you shoot or snort or swallow any goddamn drug you can get your hands on? Is it the shit where you borrow from loan sharks for a half-assed scheme that could never work in a million years? Or is it the shit where Monster Moffett puts a hit on an innocent cat? What shit you talking about? Tell me how the hell you're gonna stop *anything*. You're $200,000 in debt. You have no job, no money, and no prospects. You're a drug addict and an alcoholic to boot. How the *hell* you gonna stop any of that shit, huh? Hell, you have one good hand and you can barely feed yourself." He stopped pacing, eyes on fire, hands balled into fists at his sides.

Doraleen carried a plate of eggs through the swinging door. "What are you shouting about, Tank?"

Tank righted his chair. "Al said that when Monster Moffett touched you that this, uh, situation had to stop. I asked him how the hell he thought he could stop it." He stared at Al while he talked. "I knew this would happen sooner or later. I knew Al would get in deeper and deeper. I knew the wheels would come off on his life and he would suck you into his own personal swamp." He smacked his fist into his palm. "I knew it, I knew it, I knew it.

"You don't deserve this, Momma Dora. You don't deserve this." Tank tugged out a chair on the other side of the table. "God help me. I don't know how to fix this."

Tank's phone chirped. "It's Chuck. He'll be here in a half-hour."

Chapter 28

NGOMBO SLUMPED DOWN IN HIS SEAT after the headlights appeared in his mirror. Once the vehicle passed, he sat up. It was the white minivan. Something must have happened in the house when those lights came on. He finished his coffee and tossed the cup into the back seat.

The minivan parked and the same white man who was in the house earlier got out and trotted to the porch. In seconds, the porch light came on, the door opened, and the man disappeared inside.

"YOU THREE ARE UP EARLY." I sat in a chair across from Al and his mother on the living room couch. Tank filled the other easy chair to its capacity. "Your text interrupted my beauty sleep."

"You could sleep twelve hours a night and you wouldn't look any better, Chuck."

"So why the early rising?"

Tank gestured at Al. "You tell him."

Al clutched his hands in his lap. "I woke up with the shakes and I went looking for a drink. Momma and Tank caught me in the kitchen searching for booze."

I nodded. "Tank poured out all the alcohol in the house before I left last night. Or, I better say 'earlier this morning.' I'm glad he did, but I'm not glad that he was right to do it."

Al met my gaze. "I'm not proud of it either, and I'm determined to do better."

"And what brought on this determination?" I asked.

Al told me the rest of the conversation they'd had in the dining room. "When my, my, uh, irresponsibility gets Momma involved—and even Race Car—that's too much."

"That's good to hear. What exactly do you intend to do better?"

"I'm gonna stop drinking and doing drugs for one thing."

Doraleen and Tank glanced at each other. Neither said a word, but their expressions spoke volumes. I figured Al had made this promise before. Maybe lots of times.

MORE HEADLIGHTS FLASHED IN THE MIRROR and Ngombo slumped down again. A silver Toyota. At first, he thought it was Rice's Toyota, but this was a much newer model, shiny clean. The Toyota parked across the street. Ngombo wrote down the license plate before the headlights went out. A different white man, this one wearing a suit, got out of the car. The man glanced both ways and crossed the street. He mounted the front steps two at a time and stood on the porch. The light came on and Ngombo got a fair look at the man from fifty yards away. A middle-aged white man in a suit. Could he be a doctor? Perhaps Al Rice was injured or sick. Assuming Rice was there. The door opened and the man went inside.

Ngombo called the license plate in to Bones. He consulted the phone tracker app for Rice's phone again. Still nothing. When would that stupid bastard, Rice, charge his phone like a normal human?

The porch light went out. Was something about to happen? The door opened and the silhouettes of three men crossed the sliver of light from inside the house. In the streetlight's glow, Ngombo saw two black men and one white. The two black men got into the Porsche, the white man into the minivan. The middle-aged man stayed inside.

The two vehicles reached the freeway, and they drove in opposite directions. Ngombo followed the Porsche. He could find the minivan later with its GPS tracker. He hadn't had an extra tracker to stick on the sports car.

A half-hour later, the Porsche curved off the North Bay Causeway onto a bridge that led to Pink Coral Island, a gated community. Ngombo curved to the narrow shoulder and slammed the steering wheel with his fist when the Porsche drove through the guarded gate and the barrier dropped behind it. The elusive Rice was hiding in Tyler's mansion on his private island. Moffett needed to know that. Ngombo couldn't stake out the entire island from the shoulder of the causeway. That would attract attention Moffett didn't want.

Chapter 29

I MADE MY WAY TO MY CONDO ASSOCIATION'S SECURITY OFFICE. A thirtyish man sat at the desk, sipping from a Starbucks mug. He wore a familiar blue uniform and studied an array of monitors. I knew the face, but I couldn't recall his name. I cheated and read his nametag. "Jake, I'm Chuck McCrary. I live in 1423."

"Yes, Mr. McCrary, I recognize you. How can I help you?"

"When I drove into the garage at 2:15 this morning, someone followed me. A vehicle stopped in the street behind me after I rolled into the driveway. I'd like to review the security video of the street at that time. Can you help me out?"

"Sure thing, Mr. McCrary. Pull a chair up to that table, and I'll play it on the large monitor." Jake tapped his keyboard and a twenty-four-inch monitor on a nearby table came to life. "I'll fast-forward to your arrival… Is that your minivan there?"

"Yeah. Scroll back one minute and let's watch me drive into the frame."

Jake ran the video backward. "There you are. I'll run it in slow motion." The picture advanced and the white minivan inched its way down the street. It dipped through the shallow gutter, crept into the driveway, and scaled the parking ramp out of the frame.

"Okay, Jake, let it run in slow motion until I say stop." For a few seconds, the only motion in the picture was the languid sway of palm fronds. Then: "Stop there." Another vehicle eased its way into the frame. "Advance one frame at a time… Stop it. Can you zoom in? Great. Make a screen grab and crop it down to an eight-by-ten of that vehicle... Is that a Jeep? Yeah, it's a Grand Cherokee. Okay, run it and see if we have a shot of his license plate... Nope. He drove further down the street to U-turn. Yeah, there he is coming back... Can't make out his plate. Good job, Jake. Thanks." I grabbed the photo from the printer.

"What's this about?" Jake asked. "Someone stalking you again? Should we be alert for an attack or an attempt to breach security?"

"I hope not, Jake. The only people who know I live here are family and friends. It's not a matter of public record. Sit tight. If the situation changes, I'll let you know."

I returned to the garage and switched vehicles. Whoever followed me didn't know I owned a 1963 Avanti. I called Snoop from the garage. "How are things at Doraleen's?"

"She's fixing me breakfast... Thanks, Doraleen, black is fine... Sorry, Chuck, she needed to know how I liked my coffee. What did you find out about that Jeep Cherokee I saw parked out front?"

"It's a luxurious new Jeep Grand Cherokee with comfortable leather seating for five hoodlums and ample storage in back for their weapons and ammo. Plus, it has four-wheel drive in case they need to dispose of a body in a swamp. It's the same one that followed me home a few hours ago. He must have doubled back to Doraleen's. I believe he staked out her home expecting Al Rice to drop in."

"I knew there was something fishy when a guy sits in a car at zero-dark-thirty in the morning and slumps down in the seat so I won't spot him while I'm driving past. That guy ain't up to any good."

"It's a shame you couldn't read his license plate. I'd like to know who the car belongs to."

"Yeah, by the time I saw him move in the driver's seat, I was beside his car," Snoop said. "If I had gone back, it would have tipped him off that I'd made him."

"Whoever he was, he followed Tank and me after we left Doraleen's. We split up and he tailed Tank, probably all the way to Pink Coral Island. He's gotta know Al's staying with Tank. I assume he ran the plates on Tank's Porsche so he knows who Tank is. Did he show up back at Doraleen's?"

"Let me peek out the window, Chuck. I'll call you back."

I drove out of the garage and headed toward Tank's house. In a few minutes Snoop called back. "Yeah?"

"He's not out there. Too bad. If he'd come back here, you could roust him."

"There's more than one way to roust a stalker."

Chapter 30

I EASED THE AVANTI TO THE GATEHOUSE WINDOW and handed my driver's license over. "Carlos McCrary. He's expecting me."

"Mr. Tyler called, Mr. McCrary." The guard scanned the license and returned it. "Do you know the way?"

"There's one street. How hard can it be?"

The guard smiled. "Yeah, but the street is a horseshoe and this bridge hits it smack in the middle. Hang a left and follow it to the end." The gate rose.

I wound around the palm-lined curves of Pink Coral Way. The inland side of the horseshoe bordered the exclusive Pink Coral Golf Club, whose freshly-mown fairways, damp from the dew, glistened in the rising sun. I passed dazzling white bunkers and a myriad of flowers. The street ended at a circular turnaround fronted by four waterfront mansions that occupied a large peninsula on the island's southwest side. I stopped at the wrought-iron gates in front of Tank's house and started to text him. Before I could punch a single number, the ornate gates swung open. Tank must have been monitoring the security camera.

I drove fifty yards down a curved lane that led to a Mediterranean house large enough to house the population of a small Italian village. The lane of coral pavers ended in a circular driveway. A three-tiered fountain burbled in the center of the drive under century-old live oaks that overhung the lush tropical gardens. I parked at the coral steps fronting Tank's porch. The door swung open as I hit the top step. "Come in, Chuck. The guard called that you were on your way."

"Are you gonna add valet parking for hotel guests?"

Tank grinned. "Valet comes on at eight." He led the way across a circular foyer with a tiered crystal chandelier hanging in the middle of a twenty-foot ceiling. "Let's sit by the pool."

Tank hauled out a wrought-iron chair at a glass-topped patio table set for two under a closed Bimini-blue umbrella. The morning sun had not risen above the house, and the pool was still shaded. Seeti Bay sparkled at the edge of the manicured lawn that stretched down from the pool deck to the water's edge.

I sat and an elderly man in a pale blue guayabera carried over a large glass pitcher of orange juice in one hand and a coffee carafe in the other. A fringe of white hair surrounded his bald pate. He wore dark blue Bermuda shorts and sandals. "What would you like for breakfast, sir?"

"Whatever Tank's having."

"Very good, sir. A Western Omelet and coffee. Perhaps you'd like fresh-squeezed orange juice while Cook prepares your breakfast?" He poured the juice. "Coffee, sir?" He poured that too.

"Thanks." I picked up the orange juice and sipped until the butler left. "He reminds me of Bruce Wayne's butler Alfred."

"Except he doesn't drive the Batmobile in emergencies, and his name is Gregory."

"That his first name or his last name?"

"Does it make any difference?"

I laughed. "Right. Where's Al?"

"Upstairs, asleep in a guestroom." He pointed to a balcony trimmed with a wrought iron railing that overlooked the pool. "Al had a rough night. We all got up at three a.m. when he got the shakes. I figured sleep was the best thing for him while you and I figure out what to do next."

I stifled a yawn. "I could use a nap myself." I poured a little cream into my coffee.

"As could I. And I'll do that, once you tell me the plan and what I should do next." He threw me a mock salute. "Awaiting orders, sir."

"I thought you'd have a plan already. You're the egghead, the intellectual, the smartest guy in the room. Everybody knows that."

"Not me, *kemosabe*. I'm a poor ignorant Alabama pecan farmer. Ask me how to raise pecans and I'm your man. You city people, you're the ones with the plans." He drank a long pull of orange juice.

"First things first. Let's get Al healthy before you make him wealthy and wise."

"I don't know if anyone can make Al wealthy or wise, but I can surely help him get healthy. I'll bring a physical trainer and a nutritionist here this afternoon."

"Good idea," I agreed. "I don't know squat about how to unhook an addict from drugs or alcohol. Objective one was to find Al. Mission accomplished. Objective two was to bring him to a safe place."

"We have great security on Pink Coral Island."

"I hope so, because you may need it."

"That sounds ominous," Tank said. "What gives?"

"You remember a man in a Jeep Grand Cherokee followed us after we left Doraleen's house this morning."

"That's why we split."

"The Jeep followed you, not me."

"Did he follow me here?" Tank asked.

"That's what I would do in his place. Of course, he had to stop at the bridge to the island. But he could've gotten your license plate number while your Porsche was parked at Doraleen's last night. By now, he knows who you are and where you live."

"How did you spot him in the first place? I never saw anything."

"Snoop noticed him when he came to relieve us as Doraleen's bodyguard. Apparently, the Jeep was parked near Doraleen's house before I left the first time last night. I didn't notice him until he closed the gap to get my address after I drove into my parking garage. Wait a minute." I smacked the table with my palm. "Shit. He must've stuck a tracker on my van after I arrived at Doraleen's. That's why I didn't make him earlier when he followed me home from Doraleen's." I would find and remove the tracker the next time I used the minivan. "That's water under the bridge. Once he learned where I live, he returned to Doraleen's and staked the place out, waiting for Al. Then he followed your Porsche when you and Al left. He knows Al is here."

"Our gatehouse security is twenty-four/seven. How could Al be in danger here?"

Gregory served my breakfast. "Will there be anything else, sir?"

"Yes, Gregory. May I please have salsa?"

"Very good, sir. Anything else for you, Tank?"

"I'm good. Thanks."

I waited for Gregory to leave. "He calls you Tank?"

"I'm a pretty informal guy, despite the glitzy glamorous life of the rich and famous. He called me Mr. Tyler for a day or two before I told him to call me Tank."

"He called me *sir*."

"What did you expect? I've kept yours and Al's names under wraps. If you do tell him your name, he'll call you Mr. McCrary until you tell him to call you something else, like Carlos or Chuck." He grinned. "Or dipshit."

"You kept my name and Al's from your butler?"

"Yes, of course."

"Don't you trust him?"

Tank spread his hands. "I trust Gregory as far as I know. I have no reason to *dis*trust him or I'd fire him. But he doesn't need to know your name or Al's to do his job. I keep most things confidential. It comes with being a CPA and a financial advisor. I keep everything under my hat out of force of habit."

"That's a good habit."

"I hired Gregory six months ago. I bought this mausoleum of a mansion from an estate. Gregory kinda came with it. He'd worked for the previous owner for over thirty years. He lives in the servants' quarters over there." Tank gestured at a small bungalow half-hidden in the landscaping.

"Since you don't like this 'mausoleum'," I made air quotes, "why'd you buy it? I loved your old house."

"I like this place fine, but I don't let physical stuff go to my head. I bought this," he spread his arms in a broad gesture, "because it's good for business. Besides, I stole it; bought it for practically half-price."

"What was wrong with it?"

"Everything. The previous owner was an elderly widow who died intestate—that means 'without a will' for you illiterates. The house was built in 1928 and the last update was fifty years ago after she and her late husband bought it. After he died, she lived here as a recluse for ten years and let the maintenance go to hell. Her five children were scattered from New York to Hawaii, and they squabbled after she died. Nobody would move to Florida, and they couldn't agree on how to split the money once they sold the house. They neglected the house for three more years. In this climate you need constant maintenance on an old house like this. By the time I bought it, it was practically in ruins."

"But you said Gregory worked for the previous owner."

"When the old lady died, the heirs refused to hire Gregory. They basically abandoned the house. Gregory laid low, put the electricity for the bungalow in his name, and lived here below everyone's radar. He did a little maintenance, but he's an old man. When I first visited the house, the landscaping had run wild and I never noticed the servants' quarters hidden in the jungle. Once I had a contract and ordered a survey, I learned there was a bungalow. The surveyor told me somebody lived in it."

"Surprise, surprise," I said. "But you didn't need a butler, did you?"

"What was I gonna do, throw an old man out on the street? He needed a job."

Gregory came back with a dish of salsa. "Shall I serve, sir?"

"That's okay, Gregory," I said. "Leave me a spoon and I'll serve myself."

"Very good, sir." Gregory vanished like a ghost.

"So you stole this house?" I asked.

"Well, you could say that I found an exceptional bargain. I had to invest over a half-million bucks on repairs and renovations. I replaced the plumbing and re-wired the whole shebang to bring it up to code. That meant I replaced the walls too. But it cleaned up real nice, didn't it? It's worth twice what I have in it. Incidentally, I made a pot full of money selling my old house."

"Good for business, huh?"

"Yeah. My money management side is so big that Thomas Tyler Investments is under consideration to manage billion-dollar portfolios or more. Maybe even the University of Atlantic County endowment fund. My investment team has a couple dozen people to do the firm's heavy lifting. I mostly schmooze the clients and spearhead the marketing. I don't do much client work anymore."

"You do my work."

"That's different. You're a friend."

"Would you have taken my account if I weren't a friend of Bigs?"

"Of course I would. Who could resist your dimples?"

I spread my arms. "So, this is to impress clients?"

"It impressed you, didn't it? People like to do business with successful people. People at the billionaire level need to know I handle that kind of money. It doesn't help that I'm black and a former football player."

"President Gerald R. Ford was a football player."

"I rest my case. Thus, this place." He waved his hand vaguely. "Don't take it seriously, buddy. I sure don't. I'll flip this one too in five years and make another bundle."

I ladled salsa over my omelet. "Tank, it's none of my business, but I'm curious: How rich *are* you?"

"I'm not a billionaire—yet. If the good Lord's willing and the creek don't rise, I'll be there inside of ten years. This year I made the Forbes list of the four hundred richest people in the good old U. S. of A."

"And I thought you were simply a pretty smart jock who found a way not to blow his money." I tasted the omelet. Tank's cook was talented.

"That's what I am. Enough talk about Gregory and this mausoleum. Why do you think Al's in danger here?"

"Because of the golf club."

Tank scratched his chin. "Oh, yeah. The club has more than 300 members, and a lot of them don't live on the island. A guy with Moffett's contacts could find somebody to arrange an invite for a foursome to play golf. That would get a group of bad guys past the gatehouse. Then they hide out somewhere on the island—there are lots of places to hide in the landscaping—until dark."

"Or they come by boat. Lots of houses here are seasonal, and their owners have left for New York or Canada or Europe for the summer. I could find a dozen places to hole up within a quarter-mile of your house now that the season is over."

Tank drank orange juice. He stared at the half-empty glass. "We'll find another place to stash Al—and sooner rather than later. Too many hidey-holes on this island for a determined kidnapper. At least Moffett doesn't want to kill Al; he simply wants his money back."

I dabbed my mouth with a snow-white linen napkin with *TT* embroidered in the corner. "We hope that's what he's thinking, but if Moffett thinks his loan to Al is a lost cause, he might make an example of Al to keep his other customers in line."

Chapter 31

NGOMBO MADE SURE HE WASN'T FOLLOWED before he turned from NW Sixth Avenue onto NW 89th Street. For the next few blocks he watched his rearview mirror. He drove once around the block, following Moffett's strict protocol to keep his location secret. There was no tail. Moffett had more than his share of enemies on both sides of the law. The deadliest enemies were the ones who didn't follow rules like *due process*. Many of them would kill Moffett in a heartbeat. Or Ngombo for that matter.

Ngombo, Bones, and three other thugs had moved Moffett's furniture into the three-story concrete block building four months ago. When his presence there became known, he would move again. Ngombo dreaded moving Moffett's specially reinforced furniture again. The furniture was big, awkward, and heavy; moving it was beneath a warrior's dignity. He liked the current location. It had good parking for Moffett's organization.

Ngombo parked his Jeep in front. He counted five other cars in the lot. Glancing at a second story window, he waved to the sentry. He walked the narrow passage between Moffett's building and the next one to the rear alley and banged on a rusted metal freight door. The access door opened and Ngombo regarded the man who let him in. "Is he up?"

"He's eating breakfast. Again."

Ngombo clanged up the metal stairs two at a time to the second floor.

Moffett's bulk dwarfed the kitchen chair in the converted warehouse loft that was his current home. His butt draped so far over the chair that the seat was hidden. He slid the large platter

"What are you?" snarled Moffett. "A goddamn expert on the Geneva Convention?"

"I do not wish to attack a woman. It is not honorable for a warrior. I prefer you to send someone else."

Moffett heaved himself ponderously to his feet and stalked toward Ngombo until he stood six inches away. He stared down at the shorter man. Ngombo smelled the pancakes and sweet syrup on his breath.

"Teddy, you question my orders again, and I will cut off your black balls and stuff them in your mouth. I will take your own knife and slit your throat from ear to ear. I will dump your worthless body in the Atlantic Ocean where the sharks will eat it." He paused and glared at Bones.

Ngombo swallowed. His mouth was dry; his palms wet. "Yes, I understand, Monster."

Moffett returned to the table and cut another bite of pancakes. He peered at Ngombo. "Why are you still here, Teddy?"

"Monster, there is a further complication."

"What complication?"

"Tyler is not the only man connected to Rice and his mother. I reported yesterday that a second man named Carlos McCrary was searching for Rice. He might be the one in the white minivan. Now a third man is involved, Raymond Snopolski. Bones looked up his license plate. He arrived at the mother's house before Tyler and the man in the white minivan left with Al Rice. He may be an additional bodyguard for the old woman."

Moffett pivoted to Bones. "Tell me about this Snopolski."

Bones referred to a laptop. "Raymond Snopolski… Yeah, I got him, boss. Lots of items on Google. Let's see… Okay, he's connected with this Carlos McCrary guy. They're both licensed Private Eyes and Snopolski works for McCrary sometimes. Oh yeah, his nickname is 'Snoop.' Former detective with the Port City cops. Won the PCPD pistol competition three years in a row. He stopped competing so someone else could win." He raised his gaze. "Sounds like a dangerous guy, boss."

Moffett crammed another wad of pancakes in his mouth and swigged more chocolate milk. He wiped his mouth on his sleeve.

"Okay, Teddy, take three guys. Bones, find out who's available, but tell them Teddy's in charge." He sneered at Ngombo. "After all, he's a freaking African warrior."

NGOMBO DROVE PAST DORALEEN'S HOUSE. He'd had no sleep the previous night. He called Bones. "No cars were parked at the old woman's curb and none in her driveway. She is not home I think. Where could she be?" He hoped she had left town so he would not demean himself with the dishonor of attacking a woman.

"Lemme Google her. I'll get back to you. Hang loose."

Ngombo checked the other Jeep in his mirror. He accelerated and drove to a neighborhood café. He waited for the other three men to join him. "We shall eat lunch while we wait to hear from Bones." Ngombo needed coffee to stay awake.

The driver of the second Jeep said, "No sense kidnapping an old woman on an empty stomach." Ngombo was not amused.

Lunches for the men had arrived after Bones called Teddy. "The old woman teaches English at Carver High School. They dismiss at 2:25 on Wednesday. She should be back home by three o'clock."

The gods had conspired to force Ngombo to behave dishonorably. Perhaps the gods planned a larger goal for him. He sighed and finished his second cup of coffee. The gods were hard to understand.

Chapter 32

TANK SHOWED AL INTO THE ROOM.

Al followed him inside and spun in a circle. "What did you do, Tank, buy your own freaking health club?"

"Pretty much. This new house has rooms I'll never need. I made this ballroom into a home gym."

"I thought you worked out at Jerry's Gym?"

"I do. I usually meet Chuck or my gym rat friends. But sometimes I'm too busy to drive to the mainland." Tank waved a hand. "This was the solution. Now you can use it too."

Rice spread his arms and circled in a gesture that included the crown molding, the Cuban tile floor covered with protective pads around the equipment, the three crystal chandeliers, and the faux-finished walls. "I don't understand you, Tank. You pay cash for a multi-million-dollar mansion and you can't afford to loan me a crummy two hundred thou to save my life."

Tank sighed. "We need to talk, Al. The trainer won't be here for another ten or fifteen minutes. Let's go outside."

Once the two men were seated by the pool, Gregory approached. "May I get you gentlemen anything?"

"Gimme a Bloody Mary," Al said.

Tank raised a hand. "Nothing alcoholic for my friend as long as he's here. Nothing for me, Gregory." He waited until the butler withdrew out of earshot. "You swore to Momma Dora and me at five o'clock this morning you had quit drinking."

"One Bloody Mary isn't drinking. It's mostly tomato juice."

Tank scoffed. He gestured Gregory over. "Bring my friend tomato juice, please. Coffee for me."

"Very good, sir." The old man went inside.

"Al, I never loaned you any money after that first twenty thousand over ten years ago."

"Of course you did, bro. You loaned me lots of money."

"After you didn't pay back that twenty thousand, the rest of the money hasn't been loans; it's been gifts. I never expected you to pay me back. I still don't.""Then why cut me off this time, bro?" He waved at the swimming pool and gardens. "It's not like you can't afford it."

"Bro, after you approached me a few days ago and asked me to bail you out of this latest mess, I added it up: I've given you $795,000 over the last thirteen years. Seven-hundred-ninety-five thousand hard-earned dollars. And what do either one of us have to show for it?"

"Not much, bro." Rice shrugged. "I've had a run of bad luck."

"Bad luck for sixteen years? That's what you call it: bad luck?" Tank stopped when Gregory approached with a serving tray.

"Yeah, man," Rice said, "Anyone can have—"

Tank made a cutting motion with his hand. "Wait."

They waited while the butler served the drinks. Gregory retreated out of earshot again, and Tank continued. "Al, you exhibit what my friend Chuck calls a *convenient memory*. You remember facts that are convenient for you, and you forget the rest. Luck is distributed randomly. Believe me, I know; I minored in math at UAC. Everybody gets their fair share of both kinds of luck, good and bad. You gotta face reality—the *real* reality; what you've done for the last sixteen years ain't working, bro."

Rice lifted his tomato juice and stared at it. "Ain't working, huh?"

"Look around, Al. You and I both started broke. You even had a head start of one year in school and middle-class parents. My parents were dirt poor until I made it to the NFL. You had a first-class high school education. My little bitty country school taught the Three R's and that's about it. You and I made different decisions on which way to go with our lives. Momma Dora always says the quality of our decisions determines the course of our lives. How does the quality of your decisions compares with the quality of mine?"

"Not very well, I suppose." Rice set his juice glass down.

"Al, I didn't say you should be like me. I didn't say you ought to make the same decisions I make. You're you, and I'm me. But your decisions to this point steered you *precisely* where you are. And the decisions you make today and tomorrow will determine the course of your life." Tank leaned forward. "Wake up, bro, before it's too late. You're almost dead right now. Keep going this way, and you'll die before your time."

Rice scoffed. "You sound like Momma."

"I take that as a compliment. Buddy, we both made a big mistake in college. I moved on from it; you didn't."

Rice's gaze flicked to Tank. "Don't forget: You got away clean with that mistake, and I got caught."

Chapter 33

SNOOP WATCHED A JEEP GRAND CHEROKEE STOP at the curb fifty yards down the street. He punched Chuck's number into his phone and stared out the window again. A black man with long dreadlocks exited the Jeep. Even from that distance, Snoop knew it was Scarface, the African Chuck had warned him about. Another Grand Cherokee jerked to a stop behind the first one. Three more men got out. Though it was a warm Florida spring day, all wore bulky jackets.

Snoop had planned for this. He spoke into his phone: "Eleven ninety-nine. Four men. Scarface is one of them." He hit *send* and ran into the kitchen.

Doraleen glanced up from the stove. "I'm baking a chocolate cake, Snoop. Would you prefer chocolate icing or pink strawberry?"

"Doraleen, you remember we talked about an emergency plan while we drove home from school? A plan where you would hide by the canal behind your house? The emergency is here right now. Four men have stopped up the street who are here to kill or kidnap us. We need to run *now*."

Doraleen stopped dead. "But I'm wearing house shoes."

Snoop appraised her pink fuzzy house shoes. "You don't have time to change shoes. Those men will break down your door in ten seconds. Scarface is with them. We gotta get out of here *now*." He flicked off the stove, jerked the mixing spoon from her hand, and dropped it in the sink. "Run out that back door this instant, Doraleen. Your life depends on it. Let's move." He grabbed her arm and led her toward the door. *Two dead bolts and a security bar, like the front. I'll say this for Tank; he's consistent.* He twisted both bolts open, slammed back the security bar, and jerked the door open. He stuck his head out. "Coast is clear, Doraleen. Let's go. You'll hide behind your garage while I call 9-1-1."

He crossed the porch and unlocked the screen door. Doraleen stood in the doorway, bewildered. *Civilians,* he thought. He grabbed the old woman's arm and yanked her from the kitchen. A crash sounded from inside the house. Snoop drew the kitchen door closed and shoved Doraleen toward the screened door. "Hurry, Doraleen, or we both die here. Hide behind the garage. I'll hold them up."

Doraleen came around. "Right, right." She grabbed the hand rail and descended the concrete steps from the screened porch.

A dilapidated chainlink fence stretched the six feet between the front of garage and the wooden privacy fence that separated Doraleen's yard from the one next door. Behind the fence was an abandoned dog run that stretched to the wooden fence at the back of the lot. Doraleen fought to open the gate, but it jammed against the thick St. Augustine grass.

Snoop ran over and dragged the gate open. He helped Doraleen through and shoved the gate closed behind her. "There's a gate in the wooden fence at the back that leads to the canal. They won't see you back there. You wait by the canal until I come get you. Don't make a sound. I'll hold off the bad guys until help arrives. You got your phone?"

Doraleen pulled it from a pocket of her skirt. "Right here."

"Good. Call 9-1-1. Tell them we have a home invasion in progress at this address."

A concrete turn-around apron branched at right angles to the driveway. Snoop stood on the apron and watched the house, gun at the ready. He shifted his attention between the driveway and the screened porch. He hoped they didn't attack from both directions; he had one pistol. He called 9-1-1 in case Doraleen was too flustered to make the call.

Chapter 34

"CALL KELLY CONTRERAS," I yelled at my dashboard. I accelerated the minivan from the office parking lot. The Bluetooth activated the radio speaker and I heard the detective's phone ring.

She responded on the second ring. "What's up, Chuck?"

"Snoop texted me an *11-99*. Scarface is there with three other men. I'm on my way to Doraleen Rice's house. You know the address."

"Dispatch received two 9-1-1 calls about a home invasion in progress at the same address. The calls came from Doraleen Rice's number and Snoop's. A response team is underway. I recognized the address and figured it could involve our boy Moffett. Bigs and I are on our way."

"I'll be there in… damn, it's gonna be twenty minutes." *People can get killed in a lot less than twenty minutes.* I punched the accelerator harder and prayed the cops got to Doraleen's house in time; I knew I wouldn't.

AN AMBULANCE, A FIRE TRUCK, THREE SQUAD CARS, and Kelly and Bigs's unmarked car blocked the street in front of Doraleen's house. Red, blue, and amber emergency lights danced across the fronts of the houses on both sides of the street. I parked three doors down and ran up the front steps. The door was open. The jamb had splintered when the invaders kicked in the two dead bolts. Two black footprints marred the door.

Bigs was standing in the living room. "House is empty. No sign of her or Snoop. Neighbors reported they heard at least a dozen gunshots."

"Snoop's car is in the driveway," I said. "They've been kidnapped."

Kelly entered from the bedroom. "I searched every closet, under every bed, inside every cabinet. They're not here. I don't see any bullet holes inside."

"They ran out the back after Snoop saw them coming. You searched the garage?"

"Of course. There were four bullet holes in the garage, but no one inside. We found one body on the screened porch and another in the driveway. I figure Snoop shot two of them. Doraleen Rice's car is in the garage. I searched the car and even in her trunk."

"What about the canal behind the back fence?"

"There's a canal back there?" asked Kelly.

I bolted through the hallway, across the kitchen, and threw open the back door. I jerked to a halt on the back porch and stepped carefully around the body. I scanned the six-foot-tall privacy fence that enclosed the backyard. The wooden wall at the back stretched from the side fence to the back corner of the garage, unbroken by a gate. That made no sense; there had to be a back gate.

I ran down the back steps to the old fence on the right of the garage. I jerked the metal gate open and ran to the back of the old dog run. The enclosure was longer than the garage, and the extra three feet concealed a wooden gate that wasn't visible from the back porch.

I thumbed the latch and tugged the gate open. "Oh my God."

Snoop's body lay half in the canal, his midsection covered in blood that made pink swirls in the tea-colored canal water. More blood covered the side of his head. Still more painted his right shoulder.

Chapter 35

I JUMPED IN THE BACK OF THE AMBULANCE TO RIDE WITH SNOOP. My heart pounded like it was the engine. I squeezed Snoop's hand while the attendant did chest compressions. With the other hand I applied pressure to Snoop's stomach like the EMT instructed me. "Hang in there, Snoop. Don't you dare die; you'd ruin my whole day."

Snoop didn't respond.

The bag of saline drip swung wildly from its hook while the ambulance swerved from lane to lane. It screamed down I-95 toward the nearest trauma center, Cedars of Lebanon Hospital. I glanced out the windshield and chewed on my lower lip while a dilapidated pickup truck drove unperturbed in the fast lane at fifty miles per hour. I yelled at the ambulance driver, "Why don't they move over? He hears the siren. Why the hell doesn't he pull over?"

The driver spoke over her shoulder. "Happens more often than you'd think. Might be deaf. Might be panicked and doesn't know what to do. Might simply be an asshole. It doesn't matter; I'll pass him on the right." And she did. The truck faded from view. "Don't worry, buddy. We'll get your pal to Cedars inside two minutes. Hang on."

The ambulance screamed down the exit ramp, cut across three lanes of the access road, and bounced up the emergency room driveway. I released Snoop's hand and pressed both hands on the blood-soaked pad on his stomach.

The driver cut the siren and the vehicle slammed to a stop. The EMT climbed onto the gurney, one knee on each side of

Snoop's hips. Both back doors flew open. He leaned over my hands and continued CPR. Two green-gowned doctors grabbed the gurney and rolled it to the door, snapped its folded wheels into place. The attendant said, "Three GSWs to the abdomen, through-and-through to the shoulder, and a head wound." He reported Snoop's vital signs.

I walked beside the gurney and kept pressure on Snoop's wounds, or at least the ones I could reach, while the doctors wheeled him inside. Inside the glass double doors, a doctor put his hands next to mine. "We'll take it from here, sir. He's headed straight into surgery." The doctors shoved the gurney across the tile floor and through another set of double doors, metal this time.

I found the ambulance driver who had followed the gurney inside. "What happens now?"

She shook her head. "This was the worst I've seen since Iraq. Surgery will require hours. Make yourself comfortable in the waiting room. Oh, wait. Your shirt is bloody. I have an extra scrub top in the ambulance that'll fit you. I'll get it."

I felt lost and useless. I surveyed the ER, hoped for something I could do to help. Admission desk, interview kiosks, triage nurse's station, dozens of chairs in the waiting area, most of them occupied. Two empty wheelchairs waited off to one side. Not a person noticed me; they had troubles of their own.

The driver came back carrying a green scrub top. I noticed she had changed her own bloody top. "Let's step out of the way." She handed me the clean top.

I peeled off my bloody shirt, tossed it in a trash bin, and slipped on the clean one. "Thanks for the shirt."

"I notice you've got scars," she observed. "Iraq?"

"And Afghanistan. Snoop's in worse shape than I ever saw over there. I never got a chance to ask you in the ambulance. What are Snoop's chances?"

"Let's sit down over there." The driver led me to an unoccupied corner of the seating area. "I know where they keep the coffee in this joint. You want some?"

"You didn't answer me. That means it's worse than I thought."

She shrugged. "Let me get you coffee; we'll talk. How you take it?"

"Little cream, no sugar."

The EMT left and I called Snoop's wife. "Janet, this is Chuck. Where are you?"

"On my way to Cedars emergency room. Kelly Contreras called me. How bad is it?"

Break it to her gently. "Don't know how bad yet. They wheeled the gurney straight into surgery. You're not driving are you?"

"Of course I'm driving. How the hell do you think I'm going to get there?"

"Janet, you should hang up. Don't drive when you're upset and distracted. We'll talk once you get here."

Her voice broke. "I'll... I'll... oh hell, you're right. Doesn't do Snoop any good if I wreck the car on my way there. I'll talk to you soon." She hung up.

Kelly and Bigs walked through the glass doors. "How is he?" she asked.

I shook my head. "I asked the ambulance driver. She changed the subject and went to get me coffee, so it can't be good. Three GSWs to the abdomen, one to the shoulder, and a head wound. He'll be in surgery for the next few hours. Thanks for calling Janet. She's on her way down."

The two detectives grabbed chairs in the waiting room.

The ambulance driver came back through the metal double doors carrying two cups of coffee. She handed one to me. "Hello, detectives." She sat down with us and set her coffee on an end table. "Are you friends of the injured man too?"

"More like family. Snoop's an ex-cop like this one here." Bigs gestured at me. "What can you tell us?"

The ambulance driver spread her hands. "Since the victim's a civilian and not a cop, and since you aren't technically family members, I'm not allowed to tell you doodly-squat—officially. But unofficially, he has three GSWs to the abdomen, a through-and-through in the shoulder, and a head wound that might be a graze. Head wounds bleed like crazy, and he'll have a concussion from that, but it's no biggie long-term. The abdominal injuries are touchy—lots of bacteria and shit like that—both literally and figuratively." She frowned. "You saw him when we wheeled him down that driveway. His wounds are bad as any I've treated. I'd prepare for the worst. That's all I know." She picked up her coffee. "I gotta move the ambulance and get ready for another run once my partner comes back. Detectives." She shook hands around and left.

"Somebody needs to be here when Janet arrives, but it doesn't have to be you. Bigs and I will wait for Janet. She won't have to sit here alone. Did anybody call Snoop's daughters?"

"I know I didn't," said Bigs. "I don't have their numbers. We'll wait for Janet to get here."

"I'm torn. On the one hand, I want to sit with Janet until we hear news on Snoop. On the other hand, the bastards who shot him are out there, and they have Doraleen Rice."

Kelly said, "Snoop's text said he saw four. One neighbor swore she saw four, maybe five men get out of two cars. The description of the cars both sounded like Jeep Grand Cherokees."

"Tank Tyler is the only person the kidnappers will know to contact. I'll tell him to expect a call." I carried my phone outside and away from curious ears.

Chapter 36

TANK WAS ASLEEP WHEN HIS PHONE RANG. He fought to wake up. "Hey, Chuck. I was catching a catnap while Al is with the physical trainer. That crazy stuff last night and this morning messed up my internal clock."

"Tank, I have bad news. Have you heard about Doraleen?"

Tank jumped from the bed. "Is something wrong with Momma Dora?"

"Four gunmen stormed Doraleen's house two hours ago and kidnapped her. They shot Snoop, but not before he killed two of them."

Tank's stomach tied in knots. "Oh, geez. Tell me everything."

Chuck told what he knew about the attack. "You're the logical person for the kidnappers to contact. We didn't find Doraleen's cell phone at her house. We figure they snatched it. Your number will be in her contact list."

"So will yours; I added it to her phone."

"Good point. Don't be surprised if they wait until tomorrow to make contact. They might let us stew for a while. If they contact you first, give them my number and hang up. Don't answer any questions, and for God's sake, don't tell them anything about Al. Refer them to me, then hang up."

"Got it." Tank glanced at the clock beside his bed. "I've had Al with a physical trainer and a nutritionist for the last couple hours. That's why I could sneak off for a nap. With Momma Dora kidnapped, we need to find a safer place for Al. Any ideas?"

"Yeah, let's kill two birds with one stone and hide him in a rehab facility. There's a good one out near the Everglades. It's called Sunny Place. Tell the trainer to sneak Al out in his car and deliver him out there. Register him under the name John C. Calhoun."

"Who?"

"John C. Calhoun, the first vice president of the United States to resign. He was elected with John Quincy Adams and reelected with Andrew Jackson. He didn't like Jackson, so he resigned as VP. Also he was a slave owner. It's the last false identity anyone would expect a black man to assume."

"What if I need to go there to make payment arrangements?"

"You still own that Mercedes, don't you?" asked Chuck. "They know the Porsche, and I don't want them following you."

"Yeah. I'll head out there now and have the trainer follow once Al finishes his exercises."

"Don't go unless necessary. Even in the Mercedes, somebody might follow you. Moffett probably staked out the bridge to your island. Try to register Al by phone first. Use your landline, not your cell. No unnecessary chances."

"Okay. What will you do without Snoop for backup? Can I fill in?"

"Why do you ask? You plan to kill someone?"

Tank paused. "Yeah, if it comes to that."

"It might. These are not nice people who grabbed Doraleen, and Snoop killed two of their men. They probably aren't happy about that. Neighbors reported hearing over a dozen gunshots of which at least five hit Snoop, and he's a trained professional. If I were you, I'd think long and hard before I dealt myself into the muscle end of this thing. I get paid to risk my life; you don't."

"I told you: Momma Dora is a second mother to me. I want in."

"Tank, you're personally involved with Al and Doraleen, and that leads to emotional decisions. Emotional decisions could make you very dead. Worse, they could make *me* dead, and that would ruin my whole day. Snoop and I've been tested under fire together; you and I haven't."

"There's always a first time. You need another set of eyes and hands, and you've watched me shoot, if it comes to that."

"Tank, it's good that you can shoot a paper target fifty feet away, but a paper target doesn't shoot back. It's a whole other thing to shoot at a hired killer who's shooting back from twenty feet away."

"I can't sit around and be a bystander, Chuck. If I promise to keep my cool, can I help?"

"Let me sleep on it, Tank. I'll get back to you on that. In the meantime, get Al to Sunny Place."

Tank pictured the last time he shot a paper target. He remembered the sound of the rapid-fire *bang, bang, bang,* hushed through the earmuffs. He had placed five of six shots in the five ring and missed the target with his sixth. Chuck hit five in the seven ring and one in the five. Snoop planted all six in the eight ring. Tank was a better than average shooter, but not in the same league with Chuck and Snoop. How good did he have to be as a backup, even if Chuck did take him? He could never replace Snoop, but no one could. The question wasn't whether he could be as good as Snoop. The question was whether he was good enough to cover Chuck's back.

Tank pictured an armed man twenty feet away, shooting at him. He shuddered. He pictured it again, more vividly. He imagined the man aiming a gun at him, muzzle flashes shooting like fiery suns from the barrel. He shuddered again, but not as much.

He remembered that he wore ear protection at the shooting range. If he were Chuck's backup, there would be no hearing protection. He imagined the gunfire assaulting his unprotected ears—deafening, sharp, and explosive. How would the sheer volume of noise affect his aim, let along another man doing his best to kill him? Would he panic? Would he freeze?

For six years in the NFL, he challenged three-hundred-plus-pound linemen, sometimes two or three at a time, trying to level him. That prospect never fazed him.

This possibility was something else entirely. The offensive linemen had not wanted to kill him.

Chapter 37

I WALKED BACK INSIDE. Janet Snopolski had arrived and was sitting with Kelly. Janet stood and wrapped her arms around me. "Chuck, tell me he'll be all right." Tears streamed down her cheeks.

I didn't know if it were true or not, but I did what she asked. "He'll be all right." I patted her on the back. "Where are the girls?"

"Bigs went to pick them up at home." She smiled a little and sat down. Kelly grasped her hand.

I sat on the other side. "Janet, I'd like to wait here with you until we get word on Snoop's condition, but…"

"You go find the bastards who shot my husband." She waved a dismissive hand at me. "Go. Go. You men are no good in hospital waiting rooms. Go do something useful." She smiled again. "Kelly will keep me company until the girls arrive. Find those dirtbags for me—for Snoop."

"Kelly," I asked, "did you find an address for Scarface?"

"Scarface?" said Janet.

"Teddy Ngombo. Easier to remember than his real name. Snoop texted me that Scarface was one of the shooters."

THE TAXI LET ME OFF AT DORALEEN'S HOUSE. I ducked under the crime scene tape and went inside.

Frank Bennett stowed his fingerprint kit. "Hey, Chuck. I got good prints, but it'll be tomorrow before I have results. We found a bullet that hit the dirt in the yard. Should get decent ballistics from that for at least one shooter, and we got the guns of the two stiffs."

"Snoop's text said there were four shooters. How many were there really?"

"Witnesses said they saw at least four men, maybe five. They came in two cars, possibly Jeep Grand Cherokees. After they lost two men, they left one of the Jeeps here because they only had two still alive to kidnap Doraleen Rice. If there were two men to a car, there were four. It's not clear. You know how eyewitnesses are."

"Did you get the bullets that hit the garage?"

"We dug four bullets from the concrete wall. They were so damaged that I doubt we'll get any useful ballistic markers. There were three more bullet holes in the rear fence, but the slugs would have fallen in the canal. We do know from the weight of the slugs that they came from at least two different weapons. Don't know how many more shooters fired. We'll analyze everything. Kelly said to keep you in the loop."

I held up the keys to Snoop's car that Janet insisted I use. "Okay if I take Snoop's car?"

"Sure. It's not part of the crime scene."

I had parked my car three houses away a few hours before. I retrieved a few crime-fighter/super-detective tools out of it and paired both my cell phones to Snoop's Bluetooth.

Chapter 38

T<small>ANK ENTERED THE HOME GYM</small>.

Al Rice stood amidst the equipment as if undecided where to start. "Tank, I want to see Race Car. I *need* to see Race Car."

That's all Tank needed—a delay getting his pal safely to the rehab center. "Chuck said to get you to Sunny Place, ASAP. You're not safe here. Moffett has Momma Dora. We don't want him to grab you too."

Rice dropped his head. His shoulders shook. He clenched and unclenched his fists. When he looked up, his eyes brimmed with tears. "Tank, you and Chuck are doing things, taking action, and making things happen. I'm bouncing around like a balloon in a tornado. I'm not a cop. I don't know how to find Momma. Even if I did, I've never held a gun in my life. I wouldn't know the first thing about how to rescue her."

He gestured with his hands like he was trying to grasp something. "I feel really helpless right now, okay? I can't help my own mother for crissakes. At least let me comfort our cat. Think of her as an inadequate surrogate for Momma."

Tanks hugged his friend. "Okay, buddy."

Al wiped his cheeks. "Bro, you know how much that cat means to Momma and me. You were with us in the cemetery when she came to us. She's all we have left of Dad. I'll ride with Carson, the physical trainer, right? They don't know his car. We can swing by the vet's clinic on the way to that rehab facility."

Tank smiled. Al was right. "Lie down in the back of Carson's car until you get well away from the island, in case they staked out the entrance."

"No problem. I'll tell Carson I'm ready to go."

Once they reached the mainland, Carson bumped into a convenience store parking lot. "You can move up here now."

Rice got out of the back seat and opened the passenger door. "You have a phone charger? My battery's dead."

Chapter 39

THE ADDRESS KELLY GAVE ME FOR SCARFACE was on the second floor of an eight-story apartment house built in Port City Beach's fashionable Art Deco District. The apartments were built in the 1930s as the tony Franklin Apartment Hotel. New Yorkers and Bostonians whose money survived the Great Depression would spend all winter at the Franklin and similar hotels. Lifestyles of the rich and frozen. Refugees from northern climes have wintered in sunny South Florida for over a hundred year, ever since the railroad reached Palm Beach. The Franklin Hotel was a pre-War favorite. Following World War II, the Franklin fell out of favor when newer hotels were built on the beach. The Franklin commenced a decades-long decline and ended as a flophouse in the late twentieth century. A wealthy gay couple bought it out of foreclosure and converted it to a twenty-first century cozy hideaway for upwardly horny young professionals and wannabee fashionistas to live fulltime.

The wages of sin must be pretty good for Scarface to afford to live there.

I circled the block searching for his Jeep Cherokee. I found one Cherokee parked a block away. It was the wrong color, but I called in the plate. Couldn't hurt. It belonged to a young couple who rented an apartment elsewhere on the block. Wrong vehicle.

Entering from the alley, I parked in a visitor's spot in the rear parking lot. No Jeep Cherokee anywhere in the lot and a Mazda Miata occupied the spot for unit 2-G, not a Jeep. I called in the license plate. The Mazda was registered to Helena

Hopkins at this address. Maybe Kelly had the apartment number wrong.

I climbed the stairs to the second floor. The apartments fronted on an exterior walkway that stretched in a semi-circle both directions from the outdoor elevator lobby. The walkway was deserted except for the potted plants and hanging baskets that decorated the walk from one end to the other. It reminded me of an old-fashioned Fern Bar from a 1980s movie. Boy meets girl meets jungle.

A light shone behind the window for Unit 2-G. I drew my Glock, held it alongside my right leg, and backed against the wall on the far side of the door. If he shot through the door, he'd miss me. I hoped. I reached across the door and knocked with my left hand. Nothing. I waited a minute and knocked again.

The door opened a crack and a young woman's eyes appeared over the chain. Brown eyes, brown hair, light makeup. "Yes."

Perfume wafted from inside. "Is Teddy here?"

"Who?"

"Teddy Ngombo. This is his address."

"No, it's not. I've lived here over a year and the man who lived here before was named Rostow. You must be mistaken." The door began to close.

"Are you Helena Hopkins?"

"Yes, do I know you?"

"No, ma'am. I found your car in spot 2-G in the lot out back. I called in the license number and the Port City Police Department gave me your name."

"Are you a police officer?"

"I'm a private investigator working with the police. We're searching for a man named Teddy Ngombo. But my contact with the police gave me the wrong apartment number. Perhaps you've seen this man around. Goes by the name Teddy, but his full name is Tegumetosa Ngombo. He's from central Africa. Six-one, one hundred-eighty-five pounds, speaks good English with a slight British accent. He has long dreadlocks tied into a ponytail and tribal scars around his face. A rather jagged scar marks his right cheek like this." I dragged a finger down my cheek at an angle. "If you've seen him, you'd remember."

"I remember a guy with scars like that. I saw him around the pool once or twice. I think he lives somewhere on the top floor."

"Thanks. Sorry to bother you."

I returned to the walkway between the parking lot and the elevator. I had seen the mailboxes there. *T. Ngombo* was listed in 8-G. *Y. Nilsson* occupied 8-F. The nameplate for mailbox 8-H was blank. Kelly had the wrong apartment number. The parking spot reserved for 8-G was empty.

I rode the elevator to the eighth floor.

Unit 8-G's front window was dark, its curtains drawn tight as a Scotsman's purse. Scarface wouldn't be home, but I had to verify. I drew my Glock, held it beside my leg. I was at the right door this time and I felt tense as a guitar string. I stood against the wall next to the door. I reached across and knocked with my left hand again. Nothing. I knocked again. Still nothing. Either he was not in or he slept the sleep of the dead. The thought wasn't that far-fetched if he'd been awake all night like I had.

I needed somewhere to stake out his apartment. He might spot me on the walkway or the passage from the parking lot. If I hung out near the pool, I would stick out like a skunk at a cat show—particularly at night. The sightlines were lousy to Scarface's door anyway, what with the jungle plants that decorated the walkways. I couldn't wait in the parking lot because I'd never see him if he parked on the street and entered from the front.

The window for unit 8-F was lit and the blinds were raised enough for me to see gauzy curtains moving in the evening breeze. The window was open four inches. Anyone glancing out that window could see Scarface come and go from his apartment. The open window meant Y. Nilsson might be a nature-lover or it could be a signal of a newcomer to South Florida. Most Port Citians who lived here more than twenty minutes ran the air conditioning pretty much twenty-four/seven. I holstered my weapon and knocked. A wireless video and audio doorbell mounted on the door replaced the peephole from the last century.

A woman's voice that sounded like music came from the speaker. "Who is it?"

"Carlos McCrary."

"What do you want?" She had a slight accent. Nilsson was a common name in Sweden and Norway.

"I'll show you my identification." I held my PI license up for the camera. "Can you read this on your screen?"

"Is that a private investigator license?" Her accented voice sounded sexy in spite of my tiredness.

"Yes, ma'am."

"What do you want?" she repeated.

I couldn't tell her I wanted to use her apartment for a stakeout, so I told a different version of the truth. "I need to locate your next door neighbor, Tegumetosa Ngombo. Do you know where he is or when he'll be home?"

A few seconds passed while she checked me out with the monitor. I smiled for the camera. Maybe the dimples would do their magic.

The door opened until the chain stopped it. Her expertly frosted blonde hair looked like she was born with it. She had pale blue eyes and wore subtle pink lipstick and green eye shadow. A knockout, maybe twenty-five years old. Five-foot-ten in her bare feet with pink pedicured toenails. A gold robe highlighted her cleavage by framing it with the lapels of the white satin shawl collar. A matching white satin sash cinched around her waist and accentuated her breasts. She wasn't wearing a bra. The robe stopped above her knees, revealing well-tanned, flawless calves. "What did you say is my neighbor's name?"

"Tegumetosa Ngombo. He goes by Teddy. Tall, black African. Six-one, one hundred-eighty-five pounds. Speaks good English with a slight accent. Long dreadlocks tied into a ponytail, tribal scars on his face."

"Yes, I know this man Teddy. We had one date. He has strange ideas about women."

"When was the last time you saw him?"

She appraised me through the crack in the doorway. Apparently she liked what she saw because she smiled. "May I see your ID again?"

I'll show you mine if you'll show me yours.

"Sure." I held my credentials to the gap in the door.

"What is that other thing?" She pointed a finger with a professional manicure.

"That's my concealed weapon permit."

Her cheeks flushed, her eyebrows lifted. "A concealed weapon permit? Let me see it again."

I recognized the look and the tone of voice. She was a gun groupie. I'd met women like her before, women fascinated by a man who carries a lethal weapon. Some are afraid of guns; others carry pistols in their purses. Their common trait was that all were intrigued by the idea of lethal violence in the hands of a man. And if the man were young and handsome, that was even better. As a foreigner, she might be fascinated by the gun culture of the United States. I'd met many Europeans of both sexes who were. "You carry a gun?"

"Yes," then playing to her fetish, I added, "a Glock 19." Maybe she'd let me wait inside for a stakeout. The company was pretty nice also.

"You are a private detective?"

Now the accent sounded Swedish. That accounted for the blue eyes and blonde hair. Maybe she was a natural blonde.

"In the flesh." I smiled then realized she might not know that idiom. She smiled back; the dimples get them every time.

"Please come in." She closed the door, slipped off the chain, and opened it again. She held a glass of white wine in her left hand. Her pink manicured nails matched her toes. "I never met a real private detective before." Big smile. "Of course, I am new to America."

"Then this must be a real treat for you." I returned her smile, but I didn't wink; that would be overkill.

She stepped back and swung the door open. "Would you like a drink?"

That I didn't expect.

Chapter 40

THE BLONDE LOCKED THE DOOR BEHIND ME and slipped the brass chain into its holder. I didn't expect that either. Was I a fly she had lured into her web? Or maybe it was her habit to chain the door.

"I am Yvet Nilssen." That musical voice again. "From Stockholm." She offered her hand, fingers down, wrist up, like she expected me to bow and kiss it. Maybe they did it that way in Stockholm. If she'd been American, I would suspect she saw the gesture in a French-language film at a Port City Beach art theatre.

I grasped her fingers in mine. "I'm Chuck McCrary." I resisted the urge to click my heels together.

"May I call you Carlos?" She must have paid attention when she read my creds. "It seems more... more appropriate for you."

Also more European, I thought. "Please do, Yvet." Since we were best buddies, I gave her another dose of the dimples. I handed her a business card without the logo of the Lone Ranger atop Silver. I didn't want to give her ideas about "Save a horse; ride a cowboy." She held the card for a heartbeat and dropped it on a side table near the window.

"I drink Chardonnay, but I have Merlot and, uh, Tequila, I think. I'm sure I'll find *something* you'd like." Another smile, this time with fluttering eyelids. *Oh boy.*

Yvet and I played parts in a script written long ago by a Hollywood screenwriter. Or maybe Shakespeare.

All the world's a stage,
And all the men and women merely players;

They have their exits and their entrances,
And one man in his time plays many parts...
Or maybe it wasn't play, but a mating dance. I could deal with that. "Chardonnay is fine." I wondered what part I'd be called on to play.

For the first time I was glad my girlfriend Miyo had not agreed to an exclusive relationship. Sexuality simmered beneath Yvet's silken robe. I was ready to take one for the team. She exuded a vibe of inevitability. That and an expensive perfume. I'd bet she called it *Parfum*. I remembered an old joke: What's the difference between perfume and *Parfum*? Three hundred dollars an ounce.

I was willing to bed a beautiful single woman who made the first move, but this immediate physical magnetism that Yvet displayed struck me as shallow and superficial. She loved me only for my dimples and my Glock. Maybe just my Glock. At least the attraction helped my case.

"May I hang your jacket, Carlos?" She reached to hang my coat in the closet, and her robe hiked higher at the back of her thighs. The silk draped smoothly over her hips with no hint of a panty line.

Is she completely naked underneath?

I picked a seat on a fashionable over-stuffed couch that faced the window. I kept an eye on the space below the Venetian blinds in case Scarface strolled past. The other eye I kept on Yvet.

She moved like a dancer as she brought my Chardonnay from the kitchen. Her fingers brushed mine when she handed me the glass—a classic mating dance move.

Act One had begun.

She walked across the living room to an easy chair near the window and fine-tuned her robe's sash to expose more cleavage. It felt like she'd danced this dance before.

She sat sideways on the chair and tucked her legs up under her. The silk bowed to gravity and revealed one thigh. *Brava!*

I wasn't sure about the choreography or our respective roles, but I wanted to remain in her living room. Yvet assumed she was entertaining a new gentleman friend, but I was on a stakeout. I didn't want to dance in the bedroom.

I made small talk, which I'm not good at. In fact, I'm lousy at it. Beautiful women make me tongue-tied, but this time I couldn't be my normal goofball self. Instead, I recalled the way my maternal grandmother entertained at her home near Mexico City when I was a child. I recalled the conversations she had at a ladies' tea to make everyone feel at ease. Chit chat, chit chat.

Yvet was a swimsuit and leisurewear model who'd arrived in America less than a year ago. Yes, she loved the warm South Florida winter, but she missed the snow and the white Christmas in Sweden. Oh how she envied my dark tan. I didn't tell her I was born with it, courtesy of my Mexican mother. She was a blonde and a model, so she must be careful of the sun. Yes, her skin tanned. "See my legs?" She lifted her robe a little in another well-crafted dance move.

I wondered again if she was naked underneath. Of course, she was naked underneath; that was the whole point of her move. If our roles played out the way I expected, I'd find out soon enough. I had been awake since three that morning and I hoped I was up for the task—pun intended.

She noticed me glance out the window behind her. I snapped my focus back to her face. Well, mostly to her face.

She straightened her leg and pointed her pedicured toes toward the ceiling, letting the robe fall farther to expose her bare hip. Important to make sure her tan was smooth and even with no tan lines except for her bikini bottom. "This is my only tan line." Such a bother that she must wear SPF 50 sunblock to go to North Beach.

Her North Beach reference was my cue to perform my next dance step. "That's the topless beach." I smiled and sipped my wine. *Your move, Yvet.*

She smiled back. "In Europe, all beaches are topless beaches. Or nude." She gulped another generous portion of wine.

Once she finished her Chardonnay, she would want our mating dance to move to the bedroom for Act Two. Her glass was almost empty.

I improvised my own Act Two to get back on task. I had forgotten to keep my eyes on the prize. No, not *that* prize, the other one. "So, about Teddy Ngombo, do you know where I might find him? Or when he'll be back?"

She frowned as if I'd missed a step or maybe missed my cue. "Not really." Resuming the dance, she finished her wine and rose from her chair as gracefully as a lioness commencing her hunt. Her golden robe fell open all the way, her cleavage converted to a full-frontal flash.

She was a natural blonde. The lioness had spotted her prey, and she moved in for the kill.

She carried her empty glass across the room to an end table next to the couch. She leaned over to set it down, and the robe fell open to expose her left breast, perfectly shaped and perfectly tanned. No tan lines. I was confident her right breast matched; after all, she was a swimsuit model. The sash on her robe had magically slipped loose by the time she sat next to me on the couch. She lifted my half-full glass of wine from my fingers. "You won't need this." She downed my wine in a heartbeat. I figured she'd done that once or twice before.

I snuck another peek out the front window when she leaned across my body to set the empty glass on the lamp table. She noticed the glance and laughed. "I have an idea, Chuck. If we switch off this lamp," she touched the lamp's brass base and it dimmed, "we shall sit here in the dark and you will see my neighbor when he comes home." She winked at me. "I know that's what you came for; I'm a bonus." She extinguished the lamp and threw the room into darkness.

Chapter 41

A COUPLE MORE DANCE MOVES AND YVET WHISPERED in my ear, "Why don't we move this party to the bedroom? We will be more comfortable there."

"Let's stay here on the couch. I need to know when Ngombo comes home. I know a way we can easily manage right here. I'll demonstrate." I lifted her onto my lap.

"Ooh, you are so strong." She wiggled into a more comfortable position on my lap and her robe fell to the floor. She wrapped one arm around my neck. She tugged at my belt with her other hand, then stopped. "May I unclip your holster?"

"I thought you'd never ask."

RUBBER-SOLED SHOES SQUEAKED ON THE WALK outside Yvet's partially-open window.

I came alert, which was not easy with Yvet still astride my lap.

The footsteps grew louder.

I laid a finger across her lips. "He's coming."

She giggled and whispered back, "Why should we be the only ones?" She wiggled her hips and I nearly lost focus.

A silhouette passed across the bottom of her window and the steps grew fainter. They stopped and I heard Scarface's key in the lock.

I slid her off my lap. "He's gone inside. I doubt if he'll come out again tonight."

"You are investigating Teddy, are you not?"

"Yes, I am."

"After we had our date, he gave me his phone number. It is in my phone's contacts. Would you like it?"

Would I ever.

I reached to the floor and fished my phone from my pants pocket. I handed it to her. She entered Ngombo's number in my contact list. "I shall enter my number also." She brushed her lips on my ear and whispered, "I did a favor for you. You will now do a favor for me, yes?"

"What did you have in mind?"

"Let's move to the bedroom. There are certain things we cannot do on this couch."

LATER YVET WALKED ME TO HER FRONT DOOR and slipped off the chain. "Don't worry, Carlos. You don't need to call me tomorrow to tell me what a wonderful time you had. I don't expect you to send flowers. We Swedes have a more, uh, more… I think the English word is 'nonchalant,' yes, *nonchalant* attitude toward sex than you Americans. I had a lovely time. It would be lovely to meet again. If not, that is okay too."

She kissed me goodbye and closed the door behind me. I heard the chain slide into place, punctuating the success of the lioness's hunt. Game over. We both won.

As I expected, a black Jeep Grand Cherokee was in the space reserved for unit 8-G. I surveyed the lot for any other Grand Cherokee that had arrived while Yvet entertained me. Or did I entertain her? There were none. It was Scarface's. I called in the license plate to a contact in the Port City PD. It was registered to *TCL Enterprises, Inc.* with an address of a post office box at the Port City North Shore Branch. I texted Flamer to investigate TCL Enterprises.

Now that I knew where Scarface lived, and what he drove, I changed my plan. I didn't need to confront him. Besides, a bullet could shoot through the wall between his apartment and Yvet's. I got a GPS tracker from Snoop's Toyota and fastened it underneath Scarface's bumper.

I called Kelly. "It's too late for me to call Janet in case she's sleeping. How's Snoop?"

"Not good. He was in surgery for several hours. Lost a lot of blood. His condition is 'grave.' Oh god, I hate that word *grave*; it reminds me of death. I'm sorry, Chuck. He may not make it. Bigs and I stayed with Janet until her daughters got there. I'm home now, but I called the nurse in the ICU a few minutes ago. No change. You have any luck with Scarface?"

"He lives in apartment 8-G, not 2-G. Someone screwed your file up. He's at home now. Has anyone heard from the kidnappers?"

"Don't you ever sleep?"

"Soon. I've been busy as a busker juggling five balls. Have they called?"

"Like I said, I'm off duty. Haven't you heard? With the kidnapping, this is an FBI case. Special Agent Eugenio Lopez is in charge."

"I hadn't heard, but kidnapping is a federal crime. I'm sure with the FBI on the case we can relax; the world is in good hands."

"You remember what happened to Pinocchio's nose when he lied?"

"Seriously, I'm beat. I'll talk to Gene Lopez in the morning."

Chapter 42

NGOMBO LOCKED THE DOOR BEHIND HIM. He rotated the dead bolt and slipped the door chain into its slot. That accursed white devil in the suit and tie had killed Bud and Hambone. Ngombo didn't even know the real names of the two dead men, but they had been under his orders, so he said a prayer to his gods for their spirits.

He dragged himself to a chair and unlaced his boots. He had bruised his heel kicking down that old woman's front door. The door was sturdier than he expected. He'd kicked it twice before the jamb splintered. He rubbed his heel gingerly. He considered soaking it in ice water, but he needed sleep more.

He leaned his head back on the chair, tempted to fall asleep right there. He had been up all the previous night. Then Moffett sent him to kidnap the old woman. He had caught a short nap in the car between lunch and when the old woman arrived home after school, but he'd had almost no sleep for forty hours.

He noticed his phone. If he switched it off, he assured himself a few hours uninterrupted sleep. No, Moffett insisted he be available 24/7. He'd better leave it on. He scrolled to the next screen and tapped the tracker app he'd installed to follow Rice's phone. The wait symbol flashed. Ngombo perked up. Maybe the idiot Rice had charged his phone. The map lit with an arrow on Rice's location, or at least the location of the bastard's phone. Thank the gods, Rice had charged his phone. Ngombo glanced at his watch. Oh, God, it was late and he was too tired to search for Rice. He noted the phone's location, closed the app, and fell asleep in the chair.

Chapter 43

FBI SPECIAL AGENT IN CHARGE EUGENIO LOPEZ TOLERATED ME as well as he tolerated anyone who wasn't a Fed, but that wasn't much. Even after the genius way I had handled a nasty bit of business for him in Chicago some weeks before, he didn't seem happy to see me. Or course, Lopez never seemed happy. "Are you here as a witness to the Doraleen Rice kidnapping?"

"Nope."

"How about the attempted murder of Raymond Snopolski a/k/a Snoop?"

"Since when is attempted murder a federal crime?"

"Since it was in connection with a kidnapping. Were you a witness?"

"Can't say that I was."

"Then why are you here?"

"I need to find Doraleen Rice."

"So do a bunch of us professionals whose job that is. Butt out. You can read about it in the paper once we find her." Gene had known me long enough to know I wasn't a butt-out kind of guy, but he went through the motions.

"What does the FBI know about TCL Enterprises, Inc.?" I read my notes. "Registered address Box 2277, Port City Post Office north branch?"

Gene slid his keyboard out. "*Hmm*. That is interesting. The name has come up before."

"In connection with what?"

"You know I can't discuss an ongoing investigation with a civilian."

"Perish the thought," I said. "What would the neighbors think?"

"How do you like your coffee?"

"Thanks, Gene, but I had a cup on the way here."

"You didn't hear me, Chuck. How do you like your coffee?"

Oh... sometimes I'm a little slow on the uptake. "A little cream, no sugar."

"It will take me three minutes to get coffee." He closed his office door behind him.

I spun the screen where I could read it. *Human trafficking?* I made notes.

FLAMER CALLED.

"Stand by," I said, "Let me pull over." I did. "What have you found?"

"You sent me on a real scavenger hunt, you know that? This was like finding the *Titanic*. Really deep diving."

I have never known Flamer's real name, only his email address and the *Flamer21* handle. He's never told me the significance of the *21* either.

"What kind of researcher doesn't like a challenge, Flamer?"

"Yeah, well, this is gonna cost you extra, big guy."

Flamer would be a bargain at twice the price, but I'd never tell him that. "Okay. What did you learn about the Crazy Lady and the Orange Peel?"

"The owners use three different legal entities: the club building, the land it sits on, and the liquor license. The Crazy Lady building belongs to CL Operations Ltd., a Caymanian corporation registered with a lawyer in Grand Cayman, but CL Operations Ltd. doesn't own the land that the building sits on. CL Operations Ltd. leases the land under a ninety-nine-year lease at a pretty cheap rent. That land belongs to the CL Land Trust, a Florida Land Trust controlled by a Tallahassee lawyer named Leonard Satin. The Crazy Lady's liquor license belongs to a guy named Bernard Prevossi. It's in the email I sent."

"How cheap is the rent?"

"Real cheap. Barely enough to cover the property taxes."

"Why so cheap?"

"Ask your CPA."

"Good idea. Copy Tank on the emails after we hang up. How long has this screwball ownership arrangement been around?"

"Satin arranged the Crazy Lady ground lease three years ago, when the club building was first built. That's right after the CL Land Trust acquired the land."

"Let me get this straight, Flamer. The Tallahassee attorney, Leonard Satin, had this CL Land Trust buy the vacant land and lease it to CL Operations Ltd. in Grand Cayman, which then built the building?"

"Right. Construction lasted six months. The club has been open a little over two years. Bernard Prevossi owns the liquor license, but he had no official connection to the Florida Land Trust, nor the Caymanian corporation."

"Great. What about the Orange Peel?"

"It's a similar scheme, but different. The Orange Peel building is eleven years old. The land and building were purchased by the OP Land Trust, another Florida Land Trust set up by Leonard Satin. The same day, the OP Land Trust sold the building and leased the land to OP Operations Ltd., a different Caymanian corporation registered with the same law firm in Grand Cayman. Another ninety-nine-year land lease with rent high enough to pay the property taxes."

"So, the same lawyers set up different legal entities to do the same deal."

"Right."

"When did this round-robin deal occur?"

"Two weeks ago."

I knew the answer to the next question, but I had to ask. "And the liquor license?"

"Also belongs to Bernard Prevossi."

Bingo. "Have you researched Prevossi?"

"Working on it now."

Rule Seven: *There is no such thing as a coincidence—except when there is*. The Crazy Lady and the Orange Peel belonged to the same person, but was the owner Leonard Satin, Bernard Prevossi, or someone else whose name hadn't popped up yet? I had another idea. "Check out the Fuzzy

Bare strip club, spelled B-A-R-E, three or four blocks up the same street."

"I'm not into strip clubs, Chuck. Unless they're tranny or gay."

"Very funny. Find out who owns it, smart guy, and send a copy to Tank."

"I will, Chuck. I'm pulling your chain."

Banker Lady told me the dancers were independent contractors. But suppose Jennifer was *transferred*, for lack of a better word, by the mysterious club owner, whoever he was, from the Crazy Lady to the Orange Peel to improve the new club he recently bought. She was a star dancer, no doubt, and the showroom had filled for her performance.

I called Tank and explained the complicated legal structures used to acquire and operate the strip clubs. "Flamer's copying you on the emails. Read them and tell me what you think. Charge your professional consultation fee to me."

"If I do that," Tank said, "you'll add ten percent to cover your overhead and charge it back to me for out-of-pocket expenses on the case."

"What makes you think my overhead is only ten percent?" We shared a laugh.

"I'll look into it," Tank said, "no charge. But I practically guarantee you it's done to avoid U.S. taxes while accumulating tax-free money offshore."

"Thanks. On another subject, have the kidnappers contacted you?"

"Nope. Where are you?"

"Downtown near the Federal Building. I visited the FBI agent handling Doraleen's kidnapping case."

"And…?"

"And the two men Snoop killed had long criminal records. Did you get Al registered at the Sunny Place as John C. Calhoun?"

"Yeah, last night. I was about to visit and see how he's settling in."

"Remember to drive the Mercedes," I reminded him.

"Yes, Mother."

"I also need to pursue Scarface." I said. "I stuck a GPS tracker under his Cherokee last night."

"That's good news. Maybe he'll lead you to Momma Dora."

Chapter 44

NGOMBO BOLTED UPRIGHT AND CRICKED HIS NECK. Damn, he had fallen asleep in his chair and his back was killing him. His phone played a jungle drums ringtone he'd found on the internet to remind him of his homeland. That had awakened him. He tried to rub the back of his painful neck and discovered his right arm was asleep.

He checked his watch and swore in his native language. He had slept the clock around. Moffett would not be happy. His phone lay where he dropped it the previous night. He grabbed it, clumsy with his left hand, and wrenched his back. "Yes, Bones, this is Teddy Ngombo." He flexed his arm to restore the blood flow.

"Where the fuck are you, Teddy?"

Bones must be angry. He never used language like that. "I am at home, Bones. I had not slept in forty hours."

"What are you gonna do, sleep the whole fucking day? We're short two men, what with Bud and Hambone being gone. Get your ass over here." Bones disconnected.

THE GPS TRACKER I HAD STUCK UNDER SCARFACE'S JEEP was on the move. I called Gene Lopez. "Teddy Ngombo's not home. He's driving west on the North Bay Causeway as we speak. You can serve that search warrant on his apartment without spooking him."

"How do you know?"

"You don't want to know. Just serve the warrant."

"Already tried. We went to the address in the PCPD file and he didn't live there."

"He doesn't live in apartment 2-G; he lives in 8-G."

"How did you learn that?"

"Masterful detective work. Change the address and get a new warrant. His apartment is empty."

"Did you find him and follow him out without telling me?"

"Not exactly. I was in the right place at the right time."

"What the hell does 'not exactly' mean?"

"I had an impromptu date with Ngombo's next door neighbor last night. I watched him through her window when he came home."

"Chuck, I could haul you in for obstructing a federal investigation. What else do you know that you haven't told me?"

"Hey, I gave you Ngombo's license number. I presume you have a BOLO on it. He's crossing North Bay Causeway. Maybe he's on his way to where they're holding Doraleen Rice."

North Bay Causeway connected Port City's northern half to the beach. Snoop was in Cedars of Lebanon Hospital which was in the same general direction Scarface was headed.

I debated the ethics of continuing to use Snoop's Toyota. Janet asked me to drive it, but Snoop had gotten the Toyota shot full of bullet holes a few weeks before working another case for me. I'd feel guilty as hell if the bad guys shot more bullet holes in his new paint job. I decided to return to Doraleen's house and swap the Toyota for my minivan. Scarface had seen the minivan, but there were thousands like it. He hadn't seen my 1963 Avanti, and there was no way I would risk the antique car. My grandfather, Magnus McCrary, gave it to me for a college graduation gift.

Before I got on the freeway, I called Janet. "How's Snoop?"

"There's no change in his condition," she said. "The doctor said the longer he survives, the more likely he'll recover. I thought, '*Duh*, Dr. Obvious.' The doctor said his heart wasn't beating when the EMTs got him in the ambulance. He hasn't regained consciousness and they say there might be some deficits from oxygen deprivation to his brain before you found him. God, how I hate that word."

"What word?"

"Deficits." She cried out. "It means my husband might be a vegetable."

When I'd found Snoop and felt for a pulse, there wasn't one. I started CPR immediately, but I hadn't told Janet about his stopped heart. It would have served no purpose but to worry her more. "Are the girls with you?"

"Yes. We've been here all night. We're going to lunch."

"I have good news about my hunt for the bad guys."

"I need good news," Janet said.

"Last night, I found where the guy who shot Snoop lives. I mounted a GPS tracker under his car. He's on the move. I hope he'll lead me to where they have Doraleen."

"That's good to hear. If Snoop wakes up—no, *after* Snoop wakes up, I'll tell him."

"Should I bring Snoop's car back so you and the girls will have a second car at the hospital?"

"My car's here; we don't need a second one. You keep Snoop's car. It makes me feel like he's on the job, even when he's at death's door in a hospital bed."

I prayed she was wrong about the death's door part. "After I find Scarface, things might get rough. I'd hate to get Snoop's car shot up again."

"That's why God invented insurance, Chuck. Although, I imagine the insurance company will cancel us if it happens again."

"Tell you what, Janet, if the bad guys shoot Snoop's car again, I'll buy him a new one and add it to my expense account with the client. Tank can afford it." I checked Scarface's location again. He had reached the mainland and drove north on NW Sixth Avenue. I had a hunch where he was headed, and it was in the same neighborhood where I liked to have lunch.

I hit the Day and Night Diner at their lunch rush. I bought a pre-packaged sub and went searching for Scarface's Jeep.

Chapter 45

NGOMBO BOUNCED THE JEEP UP THE DRIVEWAY and slammed it into a parking spot. He waved at the sentry in the upstairs window, jogged around to the rear entrance, and climbed the stairs two at a time to Moffett's loft.

Moffett sat before a large platter with the scraps of a paella meal. Sauce drippings and food crumbs spattered the cloth napkin tucked in his shirt collar. "You're late, Teddy," he mumbled around a mouthful of food. "I intended to move our guest this morning. We're two men short and you made us behind schedule."

"I am sorry, Monster. I went forty hours without sleep—" He halted when the boss lifted a hand.

Moffett set his fork down. "Forget it, Teddy, it's water over the dam. We'll discuss it later if it happens again. For now, I gotta assume that someone in the neighborhood saw both the Jeeps at the old woman's house. Maybe a neighbor's surveillance camera, maybe a nosy teenager with a cell phone video. Who knows? If that happened, the cops are searching for your Jeep."

Bones asked, "You want we should dump the car, boss?"

"Don't be an idiot, Bones. Those things are worth thirty thousand apiece, and we already lost one at the Rice woman's house. We don't know that Teddy's Jeep has been made. We won't use it until we find out for sure one way or the other. We won't dump it; we'll simply… ignore it a few days. Park it with its back bumper toward the building so no one reads the license plates from the street. In fact, do that for a couple of the other vehicles in the lot." He waved dismissively. "In any event, we're gonna leave those vehicles where they are for a while. Teddy and Bones and Turk, go get the old woman and put her in a different SUV, maybe the Denali. Yeah, drive the Denali. Bones knows where to stash her."

"Monster," Ngombo said, "the cell phone of Al Rice came back online last night and I received a hit on the tracking app."

"Why didn't you say so in the first place? Where is the bum?"

"At a rehabilitation facility out near the Everglades named the Sunny Place."

"After you move the old lady, check the place out. I need to know how good their security is. If it's a big institutional building, we can't force our way in and grab him like we did the old lady."

Ngombo had dodged a bullet. Moffett overlooked his oversleeping, at least for now. But he was still ordered to dishonor himself with this woman. He hoped the gods knew what they were doing. He went down the hall and unlocked the door.

"Mrs. Rice, we are leaving in two minutes. If you wish to relieve yourself before a long journey, I shall be back in two minutes."

"I need five minutes," Doraleen said.

"Very well, five minutes." That was the honorable thing for a warrior to do.

Chapter 46

I FOUND SCARFACE'S CHEROKEE TWO BLOCKS AWAY in a parking lot on NW Fourth Avenue between 88th and 89th Streets. A figure in the second-floor window told me there was a sentry. I kept moving and videoed the lot to capture what license plates I could, but Ngombo's and one other vehicle pointed the wrong way.

I stopped at the curb in the next block and called Gene Lopez. "I found Ngombo's Jeep at 8823 NW Fourth Avenue. He has company."

"How so?"

"There are four SUVs in the front lot and possibly more in the alley. Moffett must like to send his thugs around in big vehicles with room for cement bags, ammo, and bodies in the rear."

"Very funny."

"I've texted you the video of two vehicles' license plates I spotted when I drove past. I didn't move close enough to video the other two because Moffett posted a sentry in the second-floor window. I'll be interested to know if either one is registered to TCL Enterprises."

"Have you found any evidence Doraleen Rice is inside?"

"Ngombo's Jeep is parked there. Does that help?"

"Might be enough to get a warrant to hit the site. Never hurts to ask. Could take a couple hours to get the judge's signature. Four agents are on the way there to make sure they don't move her."

"I know this neighborhood; I worked another case a few blocks from here. There's an alley behind the building for truck access. You might send two guys back there and the other two to the front. Give them my number. I'll keep an eye on the front entrance and parking lot until they get here. I can't do anything about the back."

"No sense crying over what we can't change. I'll have my guy call you."

The feds arrived in fifteen minutes. Barry Barocca was in charge. He'd called me after Lopez hung up and arranged to meet me down the block from the target building. He shook hands and introduced ourselves. "Special Agent Lopez said you were the guy who spotted Ngombo's vehicle. Nice work, what with its license plate facing the wrong way."

"Thanks. No one entered or left the parking lot since I talked to SAIC Lopez." Gene's whole title was a mouthful, but most feds are picky about titles. I didn't know if Barocca was that way, and it never hurts to be my usual charming self. "Moffett likely posts a sentry in back, so I'd suggest that your agents in the alley stay out of sight."

"I stationed one at each end to seal the alley. Now we wait for the warrant and the assault team."

"Okay. You don't need me anymore." I had places to go and people to see. "Call me if you need me."

Chapter 47

NGOMBO CURVED THE DENALI TO THE CURB across the six-lane boulevard from the Sunny Place, the hunter assessing the landscape where his quarry was hidden. Lush flowers, bushes, and trees grew between the boulevard and the six-foot wall around the facility. No security gate. A two-lane driveway of ornamental pavers began at the street and led between ornamental pillars with carriage lamps on top. He drove ahead and peered through the entrance. The driveway wound between two large parking lots and disappeared at the back. The facility could have been a luxury resort.

He drove up the driveway. It ended at a circular turnaround with an ornamental fountain in the center. A one story entrance building had a green tile roof over coral-colored walls. The six-story tower adjacent had balconies for each room. Lodgings for the patients? *Patients?* Or were they *residents?* It didn't matter to Ngombo. Maybe *customers* was the right word. A white-columned porte-cochere led from the turnaround to double glass entrance doors. The parking areas on either side of the curved driveway were half full of cars, mostly shiny new ones. The place was expensive and extensive, designed for high-end customers. He continued around the circle and returned to the boulevard.

Rice had no money. Perhaps his rich friend, the American football player, was paying. If so, that was one more link between Rice and a big money source. The *leverage* that Moffett wanted.

The building was too big and too rich to invade like Doraleen Rice's house. They must lure Rice to come to them.

Chapter 48

FLAMER SENT ME A REPORT ON WALTER WELLINGTON. Wellington managed a franchised hardware store in Fort Lauderdale. Like many college football players, he didn't complete enough coursework to earn a degree before his athletic scholarship ran out. At least he had a job.

The entrance door rang a bell when I opened it.

"Can I help you?" Wellington was a little shorter than I was and a lot heavier. Many normal-sized men add fifty pounds of muscle to play NCAA football, except for wide receivers, cornerbacks, and safeties. They burn three or four thousand calories a day in practice, and they handle the weight as useful muscle. Once they stop playing, they either lose the weight or it turns to fat. Wellington's muscle had turned to fat. His red cheeks indicated he suffered from high blood pressure too. Nice souvenirs of his UAC college career. If I had been fast enough to play NCAA football, my life would have taken a far different path.

"I'm Chuck McCrary. I called you yesterday."

We shook hands and Wellington told a clerk he was going on break. We walked across the street to a coffee shop. "Yeah, I remember Al Rice. He played left side linebacker; I played right. Gosh, that was fifteen years ago."

"Sixteen, actually. That's the time you and Bob Barnabas and Al Rice were kicked off the football team."

Wellington's mouth tightened. "Oh crap. This is about Bettina Becker, isn't it?"

"Yeah. I need information."

"You work for the DA?"

"I'm not a police detective. I'm a private investigator." I handed him a business card. "I work for Al Rice."

"So you're not a cop?"

"Nope. I couldn't get you into trouble if I wanted to, and I don't want to. I want information to help Al out of a tough spot."

"What? Did that bitch sue Al? Hasn't the statute of limitations run by now? Let me tell you, the whole gang-bang thing was her idea from the get-go. If anything, Al could sue her for harassment."

"No, Bettina is not suing Al. I need information for another reason."

"What reason?"

"That's confidential, but I can assure you it has nothing to do with you."

He seemed relieved. "What do you need to know?"

"What happened that night?"

Wellington sighed. He studied his coffee cup.

I waited. Maybe his mind was revisiting the past, or at least the repercussions.

Finally, he leaned across the table and lowered his voice. "I remember it like it was yesterday. Or maybe last night. It wasn't rape; I guarantee you that. It was consensual all around. I know it's not politically correct to say a woman asked for it, but in this case it's true. Bettina Becker literally asked for it." He leaned back and spread his hands. "From all four of us."

Doraleen said there were three players involved. *Hmm*. "Tell me about it."

"Al and me and a couple other football players, we heard about this keg party at somebody's apartment off campus. Small cover charge for all the beer you could drink. I think it was like fifteen bucks or something. We figured what the hell? We were big football players. We could drink a hell of a lot more than fifteen bucks' worth of beer. It was as much a joke as it was anything else. Football season was over and spring training didn't start for several weeks. We paid our fifteen bucks and downed a lot of beer. Lots more than we should have." He sighed. "Big, big mistake."

"Who all was with you?"

"Me and Al and Bullet and Tank."

I got a sick sensation in my stomach when he mentioned Tank. "How many other people?"

"Bettina was one of maybe twenty girls there. Must have been forty guys."

"Sounds like a big party," I said to continue the conversation.

"Oh, it was. People filled the living room, the dining room, the kitchen, and spilled out onto the pool deck. Everywhere you looked, there were students drinking beer."

"Including Bettina?"

"Especially Bettina. She was German. Did you know that?"

"No, I didn't."

"An exchange student from a little German town I never heard of." He smiled a faraway smile. "She had this real cute accent, like in the movies, except with her it was for real. She talked about how much she missed German beer. Said she could drink our weak American beer all night, and she wouldn't feel it." He scoffed. "She was wrong about that. Pretty soon she couldn't hardly walk straight, and she stumbled into the deep end of the pool. Me and Bullet were pretty drunk by that time, but we jumped in after her. We lugged her to the shallow end. She called us her heroes and said we'd saved her life. Hell, the pool was maybe six feet deep. She was so tall, she could stand on her tiptoes and keep her face out of the water.

"She's wasn't in any danger; she was playing a drunken game and we were too. Then she kissed us both, and it wasn't a peck on the cheek. She throws her arms around my neck and sticks her tongue down my throat. She kisses Bullet the same way. Like I said, the whole thing was her idea. We didn't even come on to her and she was hot to trot."

"But you didn't have sex with her in the pool, did you?"

"Nah, there were fifteen or twenty people around the pool for crissakes. The three of us climbed out sopping wet. It was pretty funny really. Al and Tank were standing near the pool to enjoy the show. Bettina wore a white UAC Falcons tee-shirt with no bra, like in a wet tee-shirt contest. Swear to God, except for the Falcons logo on the front, she coulda been topless. Her tits were spectacular. Bettina noticed Al and Tank staring at her and asked if they had been ready to rescue her. They said yes and she gave each of them a passionate kiss like she did me and Bullet. She called them her handsome black heroes. Bettina says 'Let's all go upstairs and take off these wet clothes.' She leads us back inside—including Al and Tank—up the stairs, and into a bedroom."

"All five of you were in the bedroom?"

"Yeah. Bettina strips off her clothes and stands there stark naked and dripping wet. Man, she was fine." He smiled at the memory. "She kicks her clothes into a corner. She says, 'I will fuck all four of my handsome heroes, one at a time. I will do the wet ones first.' She tells me and Bullet to strip off our wet clothes. She grins and whistles and claps while we do it. Of course, we're smashed out of our minds." Wellington drank coffee.

"She grabs me and Bullet around our necks and she rubs against us and she says, 'So who wants to come first? You two handsome black ones, you can watch until it is your turn.' She pushes me onto the bed, climbs on top, and she says, 'You will come first.' The whole thing was her idea, honest to God. She literally asked for it."

He shook his head. "Biggest, stupidest mistake I ever made. I should have run like hell, wet clothes and all."

"So Al and Tank were in the room?"

"Them and Bullet. Frankly, it was a little distracting having three men watching me and Bettina humping our brains out. What with that and all the beer I'd drunk, she had to work a little to, ah… get me across the goal line, so to speak. But she managed. Then after she finished with me, she rolled off and said, 'Now the other white hero.' She shoved me over and I fell onto the floor. She lay down on the bed and told Bullet she wanted on the bottom this time. She told him to climb on top. I felt a little sick from so much beer, so I pulled my wet clothes back on and took off."

"Where were Tank and Al?"

"They were standing to one side. Before I closed the door behind me, I saw Bullet a-humping up and down like one of those oil well pumps. He didn't seem to mind anybody watching. Of course, Bullet was always a showoff." He finished his coffee and crushed the cup in his hand. "And I never saw the bitch again until the school disciplinary hearing."

"So what happened with Al and Tank? Did they have sex with her too?"

Wellington shrugged. "Beats the shit outta me, man. You'd have to ask them."

Chapter 49

FBI AGENT BARRY BAROCCA CALLED while I fought rush hour traffic on my way back to Port City. I told the Bluetooth to accept the call, slowed down, and eased over to the right lane of I-95. "Please tell me you rescued Doraleen Rice."

"Sorry, Chuck. She wasn't there."

"Did you arrest Teddy Ngombo?"

"He wasn't there either. Neither was Monster Moffett. We caught the two goombahs who were sentries at the front and back windows and two other guys. Fortunately, all four had outstanding warrants. We can hold them as long as we need to. We found something you might clear up for us. Could you come by the crime scene?"

Twenty minutes later. I parked on the street and walked to the yellow crime scene tape. A local Port City cop stopped me. "Sorry, sir, you can't enter here."

"Special Agent Barocca asked me to come down. Call him please."

He did. "Yes, sir, go right in." He lifted the yellow tape for me to duck under.

Barocca waited at the top of the stairs on the second floor. "Come on up, Chuck. We found where the victim may have been held." He led me to a windowless room that held a cot, a camp toilet, a folding card table, and two metal chairs.

I breathed deeply. "Doraleen was here. I recognize her scent. Unless one of the kidnappers wears Shalimar perfume." I surveyed the room. One word was scraped into the faded paint on the wall: *Galahad*. "She wrote that word as a message to me."

I glanced at Barocca. "She calls me her Sir Galahad. How do you think she wrote that?"

"Near as we can figure, she yanked off the rubber caster from that chair leg and used the bottom of the leg to gouge letters on the wall. Pretty clever."

"She's a smart lady. Have you received any message from the kidnappers?" I asked.

"No, and that's unusual."

"This is an unusual kidnapping. We know who did it, and they know that we know. At least we needn't worry that they'll kill her because she can identify them. They're not holding her for ransom so much as for collateral."

"Collateral?" asked Barocca.

I explained the situation. "So Al owns Moffett two hundred thousand dollars. All Moffett wants is his money. He must figure Al will convince Doraleen not to press charges once she's released."

Barocca said, "Doesn't work that way. Doraleen doesn't have to press charges. He's a federal case."

I shook my head. "He was already a federal case. Maybe a mental case too. Moffett's not rational."

Chapter 50

I MET TANK AND AL IN THE FOYER OF THE SUNNY PLACE. Twelve-foot ceiling with white crown molding, peaceful green walls with white picture frame molding. A deep green carpet absorbed most sounds. In the early evening following dinner, it was peaceful, serene, and deserted except for the receptionist.

"Did you have dinner, Chuck?" Tank glanced at his watch. "I ate here with Al. They have great food, and they're open for ten more minutes."

"I stopped at the Day and Night Diner on the way out. Thanks anyway. Though I could use that coffee I smell." I spotted an elegant sitting room across from the receptionist. A mahogany sideboard held a coffee urn and service items.

The three of us fixed coffee and found seats in a private corner.

"How are you doing, Al?" I asked.

He shrugged. "I don't know. Earlier I had the shakes so bad that I sat down a few times. I can't hold this coffee cup for more than a few seconds or my hand shakes." He set the cup down. "I got the sweats so bad that I mopped my brow with a towel. I had the chills so bad that I got in bed under a blanket. But at least I'm sober." He smiled a thin smile. "Of course, between this place and Tank, I didn't have much choice."

"The key question is what will you do when you do have a choice?" I asked. "Tank's not going to be your nanny forever."

Al's smile faded. "One day at a time. Isn't that what they say: Take it one day at a time."

We were alone. "I met with Walter Wellington today."

Al said, "Who?" Tank frowned. He knew.

"Wally Wellington. He played right side linebacker at UAC. You played left." I studied his expression while I sipped my coffee.

"Oh… yeah." Al acted even more uncomfortable than when I'd first arrived.

"He told me his role in the Bettina Becker situation."

Tank set his cup down with a bang. "Chuck, I told you that whole thing was ancient history. It has no relevance to Al's current problems."

"I believe it does, Tank. I think Al hasn't recovered to this day from the Bettina Becker fiasco. When something bad happens, it throws anyone for a loop. I know it does me. It takes time to recover, if you ever do. If it's a physical injury, like the wounds I got in Iraq and Afghanistan, then you can be antsy about things for a long time. I still feel a physical reaction where my worst scars are. You follow me?"

Tank rubbed his right knee. I don't think he realized he did it. His knee surgery in his second year in the NFL had cost him half a season. "Tank, does your knee ever bother you?"

He smiled. "You've got me there, bro."

"And Al," I said, "you lost the love of your life, Janice Jackson. That's got to leave a scar. I've had my heart broken four times. It hurts like hell every time. Am I right?"

Al flashed two or three different expressions so fast I couldn't follow them. I had struck a nerve that had been raw for sixteen years.

And I knew why. "When did you find her again?" I asked.

"What do you mean?"

"When did you learn that Janice Jackson was dancing at the Crazy Lady under the name Jasmine?"

"You know about that, huh?"

I nodded. "When did you find out she'd come back to Port City?"

"How'd you know that, Chuck?"

"I'm the world's greatest detective; I have magical powers. Tell me how long you've known she was Janice Jackson."

"Three, maybe four, months. It was a fluke that I found her. I was drinking in the Crazy Lady one night and she comes on stage and dances. At first, I didn't pay much attention. You seen one stripper, you seen 'em all, right? But this girl danced to Swan Lake. Strippers don't dance to Swan Lake."

"But Janice did," I said.

"Yeah. She was exquisite. I even stopped drinking long enough to enjoy her performance. I didn't recognize her at first."

"No surprise after sixteen years," I said. "The last you heard, she was studying ballet in New York, and now she was a redhead."

"Mainly I didn't recognize her because I was drunk. I studied her for the longest time and couldn't remember where I knew her from." He lifted his cup. "After her show, she came out into the audience like they do and made the rounds to collect more tips. I told her how much I enjoyed her dancing, and asked her if we'd met before."

"She didn't recognize you, either?"

"Not then. I mean, I'd changed, y'know. I was sixty pounds lighter, and I'd lost a little hair." He rubbed his receding hairline with his palm. "I haven't taken very good care of myself, you know."

"That's all changed, buddy," Tank said. "You'll get better and better every day from now on."

Al smiled at his friend and benefactor. "Chuck, you've been to the Crazy Lady and the Orange Peel. You know how the dancers moonlight as hookers. They come on to you after their dances."

"I thought they came on to me because I'm irresistible to women."

"Sorry to break your bubble, Chuck. It's their job to flirt with the customers and book dates for sex following their shift."

"I'm crushed and heartbroken."

Al sipped his coffee. "I thought it strange that she didn't pick up on my 'haven't we met' line and offer to meet me later. But she didn't. I went back the next night, and that's when I recognized her."

"Did she recognize you?"

"She came to my table following her show. I said, 'I remember where we met. It was at Carver High. Hello, Janice.' She stared at me. 'I don't know you,' she said and walked away real fast. But I know she knew it was me. The next night after her dance, she walked past my table without stopping. I followed her and told her I still loved her. She was frightened. 'I don't know you,' she said. 'Leave me alone, Al.' You get that? She called me 'Al.' She knew who I was."

"Why do you think she denied it?" I asked.

Al shrugged. "Who knows? Maybe she felt bad asking me for money since we'd been so close. But I noticed that she didn't proposition any other customers either."

"Maybe she belongs to the boss," I offered.

"Oh, God, I hope not," said Al. "That's when I borrowed that extra money from Monster. I needed to make a pile of money on the drug deal. With money, maybe Janice would come back to me."

Tank said, "And we know how well that worked out."

I wished Tank wouldn't interrupt, but I continued. "So you lost Janice sixteen years ago; that was strike one. I'll come back to that in a little while. Let's talk about your father. You lost your father at the happiest time in your life, right after you won the Sugar Bowl. You have the biggest smile in the world on your face as you and Tank come out of the locker room after winning the game. Then you see Tank's father standing there with the worst news you could imagine."

Tears welled in Al's eyes. "No, you're wrong there. It wasn't the worst news I could imagine. I could never, ever imagine news that bad."

Tank's eyes were wet too.

Al smiled a rueful smile. Tears ran into the creases around his mouth. "Shoulda, woulda, coulda, that's the story of my life, bro."

"So your Dad passes away unexpectedly and unfairly. That's strike two. Then Bettina Becker comes along…"

"She accused Bullet and Wally and me of rape."

I noticed he didn't mention Tank.

"And you got thrown off the team even though you were innocent."

Al smiled a rueful smile. "That's not it, Chuck. I wasn't innocent."

Chapter 51

TANK PICKED UP HIS COFFEE AND STARED INTO THE CUP. He didn't look at either one of us.

"That's not what Wally Wellington told me. He said the whole gang-bang thing was Bettina's idea."

"Oh, it was her idea all right."

Tank nodded his head unconsciously.

"Since it was her idea, why do you say you're not innocent?"

Al lifted his coffee and stared at his hand. It didn't shake. He set the cup down. "When Bullet and Wally screwed their brains out with Bettina, she was already bombed. Today, we'd say she was incapable of consent." He clasped his hands in his lap. "And I fucked her anyway." More tears ran down his cheeks. "So I am definitely not *innocent*, even if a jury might say I'm not guilty."

"And you've dragged that guilt around with you like an anchor for the last sixteen years."

Al regarded me through tears. He shrugged, said nothing.

"Strike three," Tank said softly.

Tank squeezed his friend's shoulder. "Al, I never knew..." He halted for a second. "I never figured... No, I never *thought* that way. I thought that whatever hits you, you shake it off. You man up and carry on. That's what a man's supposed to do."

"Not all men, Tank. I'm not strong like you. I never was. You looked up to me because I was a year ahead of you, but you shouldn't have. I was never strong emotionally like you are. I never had my shit together like you."

I drank my coffee and waited for something to happen. Neither of the other men spoke, so I said, "That's not all Wally told me."

Tank lifted his coffee again and stared into the cup.

"He said there was a fourth football player in the room that night." I waited. No one spoke. The denial hung like a thick fog in the air, so thick I could practically squeeze it between my fingers.

I drank my coffee and eyeballed Tank.

Finally, he spoke. "What am I supposed to say, Chuck?"

"I want the truth'"

"For crissakes, why? What does it matter now?"

I set my coffee cup down with a clatter. "'What difference, at this point, does it make?' You remember who said that, Tank? Who the hell do you think you are, Hillary Clinton? It matters because people were harmed. It matters because the truth always matters. It matters because you're carrying around a terrible secret about Bettina Becker like Al is. That secret made you both into victims."

Tank glared at me. "Those were self-inflicted wounds."

"A self-inflicted wound is still a wound," I said. "Bettina wasn't the only victim that night. You and Al and Wally and Bullet were victims too. Tank, you remember the cliché *the truth hurts*? Well, that's not true. The truth only hurts if it *should*. I want the truth, and I'm staying right here until I get it."

Chapter 52

TANK LEANED BACK. "The truth. To paraphrase Jack Nicholson: Maybe I can't handle the truth. God knows I've been avoiding it for sixteen years." *Al has known the truth for sixteen years and he can't handle it. It ruined his life. That secret is the deceitful glue that has held our dubious relationship together all these years.*

Tank knew that Chuck could handle the truth. Hell, Chuck handled Taliban and Al Qaida fighters in battles to the death.

The question was could he, Tank, handle the truth he had pushed aside and refused to think about for sixteen years? He closed his eyes and thought back...

HE COULD SEE BETTINA BECKER stripping off her wet clothes. It had been sixteen years, but it seemed like it was happening now. Omigod, she was beautiful. And stacked. And hot. And available. She called him her black hero and promised to thank him for saving her life. He didn't do anything but admire her tits through a wet tee-shirt, and she kissed him like he was the last man on earth. Then she led the four of them into the bedroom and promised to have sex with them all.

Bettina said something to Wally and Bullet that Tank didn't even hear. They started stripping their clothes off. She laughed and clapped and danced up and down and her breasts bounced and jiggled like a child's toy.

Tank had trouble standing while Wally, then Bullet, then Al took their turns on the bed with Bettina. He stared, entranced, enthralled, and enraptured by her body.

Al finished and rolled off the woman, dragging himself to his feet. He struggled to pull on his wet clothes.

Bettina rose from the bed and teetered to keep her balance. She stumbled over and wrapped her arms around Tank's neck. She was nearly six feet tall. "You, handsome black giant, I saved the biggest for last."

Tank stared at her, not moving. He wanted her so bad he would have died right then to have sex with her one time.

She kissed him warmly, and he tasted the beer from her tongue. He smelled the swimming pool chlorine in her damp hair. It made him queasy.

Bettina fell backwards onto the bed, laughing and chanting, "I want German beer. I want German beer," over and over.

"Have fun, dude," said Al. He closed the door behind him.

Bettina and Tank were alone in the bedroom.

Bettina giggled. "There he is, my beau… my beautiful black giant. My big… my big black hero. Take off your clothes, and I will thank you properly." She hiccupped once and passed out.

Tank stood wavering near the door until she began to snore. She didn't act sexy now. She was pitiful. Suddenly, like switching off a light, he didn't want to have sex with her. It would have been sex with a body, not a woman. He shuddered at the thought.

He spun toward the door, then stopped. He couldn't abandon her while she lay naked and unconscious on the bed. He considered trying to dress her, but her clothes were still wet. She was limp as a rag doll. There was no way to get her into that tee-shirt. And the tight blue jeans? Forget it. But if he abandoned her unconscious, another man could stumble into the room and do what Tank refused to do.

He peered around the room, grabbed the bedspread off the floor, and covered the girl. That would keep her warm while she slept it off. He stuck a pillow under her head. He made one last survey of the room and thought about what else he should do.

Tank locked the bedroom door from the inside, switched off the light, and went into the hall. He shut the door behind him and jiggled the handle to make sure it locked.

I HARDLY BELIEVED WHAT I WAS HEARING. "So after all that, you didn't have sex with her?" I asked.

"When it came down to it and she passed out, I couldn't do it."

Al set down his coffee cup. "So you didn't bang her?"

"Nope."

"Why the hell not?" he asked. "You knew she wanted us both. She told the whole goddamn world what she wanted, called us her black heroes, begged us for it."

Tank shrugged. "She passed out, man. It didn't feel right."

"She wasn't passed out when I screwed her," Al said.

"Al, I'm not pointing fingers. If she hadn't passed out when I was in the room, God knows what I might've done. Maybe it was dumb luck that I didn't screw her. That rape kit she did the next morning would have found my DNA as well as yours and the other guys. I could have been kicked off the team too."

"So that's the guilty secret you held onto for sixteen years—that you *didn't* take unfair advantage of a girl who was too drunk to consent?"

"No, no, Chuck. That's not why I feel guilty."

"Explain it to me, big guy, because I don't get it."

"It wasn't that I didn't take advantage of her after she passed out," Tank said. "That was the *only* honorable thing I did that whole goddamn night. Everything else I did was dishonorable."

"Such as?" Al asked.

"I knew Bettina was snockered the minute she led four horny football players into a bedroom and said she wanted all of us." Tank spread his hands. "My crime is that I let you three have sex with a woman who was in no condition to consent. I stood by, literally, while you three raped her."

Chapter 53

N GOMBO TAPPED THE TRACKER APP FOR R ICE'S PHONE. "Monster, his phone is still off."

"I don't give a crap; call it. I'll leave the loser a voicemail."

Ngombo punched the number for Rice's phone. "It went to voicemail." He handed the phone to Moffett.

Moffett waited for the beep. "Listen to me, you lousy loser rat bastard. We have something precious to you, and it's not your stupid cat. This is the collateral for your loan. I want my money by tomorrow at five o'clock. Your buddy Tank Tyler can't hide you out west in the boondocks forever. Have my money by five o'clock tomorrow afternoon, or else I want your sorry, no-good ass in exchange. I'll swap you for this, uh, other item. Your choice. Five o'clock tomorrow. I'll call you at four-thirty with instructions, dumbass. You'd better answer the damned phone, if you know what's good for you—or her." He disconnected.

"D ID YOU GET IT, G ENE?" I ASKED.

The FBI had tapped all the phones involved: Al Rice's, his mother's, mine, even Tank's in case they called him. The warrant covered Moffett and his known associates like Scarface, but that was worthless when they used burner phones. I'd given Lopez Scarface's number from Yvet's contact list, but Scarface was too smart to use that phone for anything criminal.

Lopez answered, "He called from Doraleen Rice's phone, then he switched it off and removed the battery so we can't trace it. Voiceprint analysis will prove Moffett made the call." He studied the screen. "He called from a moving vehicle on I-95. There's no way for us to tell where they're holding Mrs. Rice."

"Maybe there's another way," I suggested. "He wants to lure Al to come to him. Maybe we can reverse that and lure him to come to Al."

Lopez raised a hand. "Al Rice is a civilian, and he's a victim too. The FBI doesn't put civilians at risk."

I didn't argue. Instead I stood to leave. "Okay, Gene. I'm sure you know best."

"Okay, smart guy, I know you don't give up on anything that easy. I'm warning you: Don't put Al Rice at risk. We use Al Rice's phone to return Moffett's call. Once he answers, we trace the location."

"Won't work. You said he switched Doraleen's phone off and removed the battery. He won't know if Al's phone returned the call. Moffett won't use Doraleen's phone to call Rice tomorrow. I wouldn't use it if I were him, since we're primed to trace it the instant he switches it on. He'll call with another burner phone from another moving vehicle."

Lopez frowned. He'd lost the argument. "When Moffett calls to gives Rice his instructions, we can catch him that way."

"Sure you will." I left.

I CALLED TANK FROM MY CAR and brought him up to date. "I considered your offer to be my backup. You still want to lay your life on the line?"

"I thought about it a lot, Chuck. I could have prevented this whole thing with Al if I had stopped them from gang-banging that girl. If Al hadn't been kicked off the team, he might have recovered from those other two losses. If I'd come forward and done the right thing then, his life would be different. So would Wally's and Bullet's. So, yeah, I'll step up even though I'm sixteen years late."

"Don't cry over spilt milk, Tank. But you're right about one thing: It's never too late to do the right thing. Meet me in the Sunny Place parking lot tomorrow at nine a.m."

"Okay. I cleared my calendar for this."

"Bring two Glocks and four or five extra magazines for each. You'll need a shoulder holster for one and a belt clip holster for the other. You own a Browning .380 don't you?"

"Yeah."

"Bring it. We'll strap it into an ankle holster."

"I don't own an ankle holster."

"I'll bring an extra one."

"Okay, Chuck."

"And, Tank," I added. "Don't tell Al we're coming."

Chapter 54

I PARKED NEAR THE ENTRANCE TO SUNNY PLACE and called Tank. "I'm parked in the second spot to the right after you pass the entrance. Park beside me. We'll drive my van."

"Where we going?" asked Tank.

"You'll see."

Three minutes later, Tank slid his Mercedes into the space two slots over from mine and got in my passenger seat. "I feel twenty pounds heavier carrying this arsenal. If we need this much firepower, we're gonna be in a truckload of trouble."

"Uh-uh. Carrying this much firepower may keep us out of trouble in the first place. Remember Rule Nine: *You can never carry too much firepower.*"

"Rule Nine? What's that?" Tank fastened his seatbelt.

"I made a couple dozen rules on how to be the world's best Private Eye. Rule Nine is *You can never carry too much firepower.* By the way, you already broke Rule Seventeen: *Never get personally involved in a case.*" I saw Tank's abashed expression. "Don't worry about it, buddy. I break that rule a lot myself."

"Are these rules written down anywhere?"

"Nope. Stick around long enough, and you'll learn them." I slipped the van in gear and drove out to the boulevard.

"Where we going?"

"To my private shooting range."

THE LAST TIME I'D DRIVEN THIS FAR OUT Atlantic County Road 888a, I had led a hit squad into an ambush at the abandoned phosphate mine in the Everglades. Four mobsters against Snoop and me. We won; they lost. That gunfight was at sunset. This time it was morning when we arrived at the end of the sandy road.

The old mine didn't look like the O.K. Corral. The abandoned machinery reminded me more of the aftermath of a battle of alien war machines from a *Star Wars* movie. Vines climbed from the sandy ground to claim their green empire on the rusty steel, overwhelming the creepy behemoths. The tracks churned up by Snoop's rented Jeep were still visible where it had shredded the wild grasses and vines that Mother Nature used to reclaim her domain.

I parked between the three sand hills. My van's dust trail followed us, drifting on the ocean breeze, and enveloping the van. "Don't open the door. Wait for our dust cloud to dissipate." It did and we popped our doors. The silence was broken by a distant bird call I didn't recognize. I knew it wasn't a Sandhill Crane, since that was the one bird call I did recognize. No outdoorsperson, I.

"See that?" I pointed. "The perfect berm to catch our bullets. Our own shooting range, miles from any habitation."

"Where are the targets?" Tank asked.

"Don't need 'em. Pick a tuft of grass. Fire off ten or twelve rounds to get a feel for shooting in the real world."

"I didn't bring my earmuffs."

"You ever fired a gun without ear protection?"

"Nope. Every shooting range I've used requires earmuffs or earplugs or they don't let you shoot."

"That's what I thought. If we get into a gunfight, we won't have time to put on earmuffs, even if we carried any. Gunfire is noisier than you think. When you don't expect them, loud noises can disorient the hell out of you. That's why assault teams use flashbang grenades. Your life—and more importantly, my life—might depend on you not getting surprised by gunfire."

Tank smirked. "It would be bad form to put good ol' Chuck at risk, wouldn't it?" Tank drew his Glock 19.

"I brought you here for a baptism of live gunfire in the real world, not the controlled environment of a shooting range." I aimed my own Glock and rapid-fired six rounds.

Tank jumped. "Geez. I see what you mean. That's louder than a NASCAR race."

"And we're outdoors. Imagine how bad it sounds indoors, which is where we'll find Doraleen." I stepped back. "Okay, congratulations; you're my backup. Let's see you shoot."

Tank rapid-fired five rounds, then five more. "My ears are ringing."

"They'll ring for a while. That's enough. I don't want to damage our hearing. Mission accomplished."

Chapter 55

AL MET US IN THE LOBBY. "What's up, guys? Any developments? They won't let us keep cell phones here."

"Let's sit down. I need coffee." I led Al and Tank to the coffee station in the sitting room where we had had our deep discussion about self-inflicted wounds. Was it really the night before?

We fixed our coffees and found a quiet corner in a separate smaller sitting room where we were alone. I briefed Al on Moffett's call to his phone. "So Moffett plans to call your phone at 4:30 this afternoon to give you instructions on how to surrender to him."

"Then he'll turn Momma loose. I gave this whole freaking' mess a lot of thought. Everything that's happened to Momma, to Race Car, even to your friend Snoop—all this is my fault. It's time for me to accept responsibility for my bad decisions. I'll surrender to Monster, if he'll release Momma. Let's do it. My life isn't any great loss. I can be a better son to Momma dead that I ever was alive."

I raised both hands. "Not so fast, Surrender Man. There's no way in hell that Moffett will release Doraleen. He's in too deep. Kidnapping is a federal crime with the death penalty. And with the other crap Moffett has done, the U.S. Attorney is sure to go for the needle. Moffett will be lucky to get a plea bargain for life without parole. He won't release the star prosecution witness for his kidnaping trial, that's for sure."

"One other thing," said Tank. "You owe Momma Dora more than sacrificing your life for nothing. If you get yourself killed, how is she gonna feel? What will she have to live for?"

Al looked from Tank to me. "I gotta find a way to make this right."

"That's why we're here," I said. "Tell me about the time Moffett and his thugs kidnaped you and beat up your hand."

Al regarded his bandaged hand. "Sure, anything to get Momma out of trouble. What do you want to know?"

"Everything."

WE CRUISED ANOTHER STREET in the two-mile square industrial district in western Port City. Al had remembered enough to narrow the search to that large neighborhood. Block after block of office-warehouse combinations lined both sides of the streets behind wide parking lots with room for loading docks for each unit. The differences lay in the paint jobs and the landscaping between the street and the parking lots. The buildings themselves came in two types: Large freestanding units and long strips designed for several small businesses. We'd searched a couple hours, scouring parking lots for SUVs that looked familiar, or buildings Al recognized. We stopped once and bought sandwiches to eat in the van while we cruised the district. The buildings all looked alike.

My theory was that Moffett had a stronghold in the district. That was why he felt safe hauling Al there to work him over. Maybe that was where he had transferred Doraleen. It was the best idea I could think of.

"Anything seem familiar, Al?" I asked.

"That's the problem, Chuck; they *all* seem familiar. I'm ashamed to say that I was drunk at the time Bones and Turk grabbed me. They threw me in the rear of an SUV, drove me to this industrial district, and the next thing I knew they were dragging me into this big warehouse. Every memory is blurry." He stared at his injured hand. "I hope I live long enough to get this cast removed."

"What kind of stuff was in the warehouse?" I asked.

"There were tall metal racks or shelves like you'd see at a Home Depot or a Lowes. Must have been thirty feet tall. Row after row of boxes and crap on the shelves."

"What was in the boxes?" I asked. "What were they selling?"

"Beats me. I was scared shitless and half drunk. I'm lucky to remember the gray metal racks."

"When they dragged you into the warehouse, did you enter through a front office or through a loading dock?"

"A loading dock. There were steps at one side that we climbed from the parking lot to the warehouse floor."

"Which side of the dock were they on, the right or the left?"

He closed his eyes. "The right, I think, but don't hold me to that."

"That's good, Al," I said. "We didn't know about the steps before."

Tank rode in the second row of my minivan. "What kind of SUV did they put you in?"

"It had two rows of seats and a cargo area in the back."

"Was it a Jeep Grand Cherokee?" asked Tank.

"Maybe."

I drove into a half-empty parking lot and studied my video of the vehicles at Moffett's building on NW Fourth Avenue. All were some type of SUV or van, but not all were Grand Cherokees. If Moffett owned a fleet, they were not the same model vehicle. I called SAIC Lopez. "Gene, do you have the registrations on those other vehicles I videoed in the lot on NW Fourth Avenue?"

"They all belonged to TCL Enterprises registered at the same post office box."

"Y'all find out anything about the post office box? Like a street address for the renter?"

Lopez sighed. "It takes time to work through the post office. Lots of red tape and regulations to protect privacy. Gotta get warrants. You know how it is."

"But you're the FBI, the good guys," I said. "I thought y'all walked on water."

"Don't start with me, McCrary. This is a kidnapping and we do the best we can. I'm not in the mood for your so-called humor."

Lopez was pissed when he called me *McCrary*. "Okay, next best thing. What other vehicles that were not there might belong to TCL Enterprises?"

"You have a lead on something, Chuck?"

"So I'm not McCrary anymore; I'm good ol' Chuck again. Were there any other vehicles registered to TCL Enterprises?"

"Hold on a sec… Yeah, I got four more here. There's a 2013 silver Dodge Caravan, a 2014 black Jeep Grand Caravan, a 2013 blue Honda Pilot, and a 2015 white GMC Denali. You want the license plates?"

He read them to me while I wrote them on a notepad. "Thanks, Gene."

"Wait a sec, Chuck. What are you up to?"

"Moffett drove Doraleen away in a different vehicle. If we find the vehicle, maybe we'll find Doraleen. Issue a BOLO on those four vehicles, Gene. Let me know if you find one. Gotta go. Talk to you later."

I couldn't tell Lopez I was searching for Doraleen without him. He would demand that I not go around him. Then he would threaten to arrest me for interference with a federal investigation. At least, that's what he usually did. Then I would do it anyway, and there would be a big kerfuffle. Lopez was so picky that way.

Lopez operated under a handicap: He followed due process rules, search warrants, Miranda warnings, and such. The FBI was concerned, and rightly so, with the Bill of Rights. I was concerned with right and wrong. Lopez followed the rules; I made my own rules. If I let Lopez get involved, he would slow me down. Doraleen might wind up dead.

I called Flamer. "You're on speaker. I'm here with two friends, Tank Tyler and Al Rice."

"Tank Tyler as in NFL Hall of Famer Tank Tyler?" asked Flamer.

I gestured for Tank to speak. "Hello, Flamer. This is Tank Tyler, former Port City Pelicans defensive end."

"It's an honor, Tank. I've always been a big fan."

"Thanks, Flamer. Chuck tells me you're the best researcher in the known universe. We need your help to save a woman's life. I'll give you back to Chuck to tell you what we need." He gestured for me to go ahead.

"Who owns the building at 8823 NW Fourth Avenue? We'll hold."

Flamer answered within seconds. "It belongs to Fifth Avenue Venture Number 27, Ltd. with an address on Fifth Avenue, where else, in New York City. Why?"

"Montgomery 'Monster' Moffett lived there until yesterday, and a bunch of SUVs registered to TCL Enterprises were parked there. He kidnaped Doraleen Rice, Al's mother, and held her there overnight. Now he's moved her, and we need to find out where. How long has this New York outfit owned the building?"

"Seventeen years."

"Okay. Do they own any other property in Atlantic County?"

A short pause. "Three auto parts stores, two office supply stores, and three drug stores. Looks like a real estate investment company organized as a partnership for tax purposes."

"Then Moffett rented the building short term and they're not part of his mob. What did you learn about TCL Enterprises?"

"You remember Leonard Satin, the Tallahassee lawyer who controls the land under the strip clubs?"

"Yeah."

"He is the registered agent for TCL Enterprises, Inc. That's not all. I researched the Fuzzy Bare like you said. Same deal as the Crazy Lady and the Orange Peel. A Florida Land Trust owns the land, and a Caymanian corporation owns the building. Same lawyers involved."

"Good job. Who owns the Fuzzy Bare's liquor license?"

"You get three guesses and the first two don't count." Flamer said.

"Mickey Mouse," I retorted.

Flamer made a buzzer sound with his mouth. "Wrong."

"Superman."

Another buzzer. "Wrong again. Last chance."

"Bernard Prevossi."

"Bingo. Give that man the prize."

"And what did you learn about Prevossi?"

"He's got two more liquor licenses in Orange County and three in Duval County. All strip clubs."

"You got a file on him you could send me?"

"Yeah, it's on its way, but I didn't tell you the most surprising part."

"What's that?"

"He's got two more liquor licenses in Miami Beach and one in Key West."

"Why is that a surprise?"

"Those licenses are for gay bars. In fact, I've partied at the one in Key West. Pretty cool place."

"Okay, thanks."

I slipped the van in gear. "Gentlemen, we are searching for a silver Dodge Caravan, a black Jeep Grand Caravan, a blue Honda Pilot, or a white GMC Denali. We scan every vehicle near every three-story building we pass with steps for the loading dock."

"So we've eliminated the smaller buildings?"

"You heard Al. The gray storage shelves were thirty feet tall. We didn't know that before, and we didn't know about the steps. Now that we do, we'll move faster."

Chapter 56

Bones walked over to where Ngombo was eating his sandwich. "You been watching the boss lately, Teddy?" Moffett had gone into the restroom.

Ngombo swallowed. "I always watch Monster. He is the boss."

"No, that ain't what I mean. I mean, like, does he seem, like *normal* to you?"

Ngombo regarded Bones suspiciously. "What do you mean?"

Bones glanced at the restroom door. "This kidnapping thing. Does that seem rational to you?"

"I do not know. In my country, we often take hostages and exchange them between tribes. But never an old woman. That would be... unwarrior-like."

"It's different over here. Kidnapping is almost as big a deal as murder. And it's a federal offense, *federal*. That means the FBI. Those guys, those feds, they got long arms, y'know?"

"No, I do not know. What is long arms?"

"They reach a long ways and they never forget. Not *ever*. They got agents, and money, and informants, and shit like that." He flicked his gaze at the bathroom door again. "They ain't so easy to fool as the local cops."

"What do you propose?" asked Ngombo.

Bones shrugged. "I dunno. I feel real creepy holding an old woman. Nothing good's gonna come from this."

"Do you wish to free her?"

Bones heard a click and glanced to one side. The bathroom door was opening. "So, how's the sandwich, Teddy?"

Chapter 57

TANK SPOTTED THE WHITE DENALI FIRST. It was parked at a long four-unit building on NW 108th Street between NW 103rd and 104th Avenue. I slowed down for him to read the license plate. "That's it."

"And there's the black Jeep Grand Caravan," said Al. "I don't see the silver Caravan or the blue Honda Pilot."

The office-warehouse was the second unit in the block-long structure. A discreet sign said *Tri-Patron Imports*. I hung a right at the next corner and drove down the alley behind the building. The silver Caravan had parked between a truck door and a regular steel door with a wire-reinforced window fronting the alley.

"No access back here, guys," I said.

I called Lopez. "We have a lead on where they have Doraleen Rice." I gave him the address. "Three of the four TCL-owned vehicles that were not at the lot on Fourth Avenue are here. I'd bet they'll leave in one before 4:30 to call Al Rice."

"We'll have a SWAT team and a hostage negotiator there within thirty minutes," Lopez replied.

"I'll post a man in back to make sure they don't leave that way. I'll wait in front with Al Rice until your team arrives."

"McCrary, I warned you not to put Rice in danger."

"See you when you get here, Gene." I disconnected. Lopez would be pissed. It wouldn't be the first time. He'd probably call me *McCrary* again.

I parked fifty yards down the alley in a slot on the opposite side from Moffett's unit. I'd picked a spot between two other cars parked behind the same building. Anyone coming out Moffett's back door wouldn't notice me wedged between the other vehicles. I turned to Tank. "Let's get you into a vest." We popped our doors and walked to the back. I opened the rear hatch and handed Tank an armored vest.

Thunder rumbled in the distance. Rainy season had begun, with its typical late afternoon showers.

"Is that vest bulletproof?" he asked.

"If the balloon goes up, you'd better hope so," I replied. I adjusted the straps on the vest. It was barely large enough for his XXXL body. "You stay here and mind the back door. If anybody comes out, hide behind that dumpster and call me. I'll stick a GPS tracker on that van so we won't lose them. Got it?"

"Got it."

I sneaked back down the alley, staying close to the wall where no one could spot me from Moffett's rear door. I fastened the tracker underneath the Caravan and returned to my van. "Test your phone, Tank. Call me."

"Is that necessary?"

"Watch and learn, Tank. Rule Ten: *Always test your equipment; your life could depend on it.*"

He called me. Both our phones worked. Thunder boomed again, louder this time. I glanced at the thunderheads rolling in from the Everglades.

"Al and I will park around front where we can wait for Gene Lopez's crew. Remember, if anybody exits from that back door, call me. Don't be a hero. Heroes can wind up dead."

"Is that a rule too?"

I clapped him on the shoulder. "Nah. That's basic survival advice."

Chapter 58

AT THE END OF THE ALLEY, I CURVED RIGHT AGAIN and stopped at the curb. "Let's suit up." I helped Al into an armored vest, buckled on my own, and drove back to Moffett's street. I parked between two cars in the lot next door to Tri-Patron Imports. We could watch both the cargo door and the people door.

I texted Flamer the street address.

> Complete report on Tri-Patron Imports and building ownership. Call with results.

"Now we wait."

Al felt his coffee cup we'd brought from the sandwich shop and made a *meh* expression. "Room temperature."

I lifted my cup. "Cold coffee is better than no coffee at all."

He smiled. "Chuck, why are you helping me?"

"The simple answer is that Tank is paying me," I replied. "This is what I do for a living."

"This is a dangerous business. Tank told me two hoods tried to kidnap you at the Orange Peel. Hell, we're both sporting bulletproof vests, for crissakes."

"At least, we hope they're bulletproof." I grinned. "Let's hope we never find out."

Al smiled back, but it was a conditioned reflex. "That's what I mean. A guy could get killed in your profession. Surely it doesn't pay *that* well. Private detectives also find lost children, catch wayward husbands, and investigate bogus insurance claims. That kind of project won't get you killed, and it pays pretty well. What's the real reason?" He waved his injured hand. "I'm sure as hell not worth dying for."

"Maybe not yet, but someday you could be, Al. You could be."

"How the hell would I do that?"

"Start by making the right choices from now on."

Al stared out the windshield, but I don't think he saw anything but his own memories. "I don't have much practice making good choices, do I?"

"Doraleen says you're like a sheep without a shepherd, like an old-fashioned bumper car at an amusement park. The other cars push you around. She said you don't take control of your own life."

"How do I take control?" he asked.

"Be less like a sheep and more like a tiger."

Chapter 59

"I'LL HAVE TO GIVE THAT A LITTLE THOUGHT," Al said. "Right now, I'm not worth shit, and I don't want you risking your life for me."

"I'm not doing it for you. I'm doing it for Doraleen." I laughed. "Besides, this job beats hanging around a cheap motel with a low-light video camera to catch a cheating husband." I laughed. "This is what I do, and I don't want to do anything else. I knew in grade school that I was the knight on the white horse. Your sweet mother calls me her Sir Galahad."

"Yeah, I know the poem. Did you know my full name is Alfred Lord Tennyson Rice?"

"Yeah. That's a pretty cool name."

Al scoffed. "You wouldn't think so if you were in grade school and the other kids were bigger than you. They'd call me 'your lordship' and steal my lunch money. At least that stopped in middle school."

"How so?"

"That's when I got my growth. In seventh grade, I was the biggest kid in middle school. No more teasing and no more stolen lunch money. How about you? Were you Sir Galahad in school?"

"I was in third grade, and three fourth-graders tried to steal lunch money from a new kid in my class. I lit into all three of them."

"Fourth-graders? Three boys a year older than you?"

"Yeah."

"What happened?"

"They beat the crap out of me." I laughed. "But they let the other kid alone. Don't get me wrong, it wasn't a one-sided fight. I bloodied all three noses and kicked two bullies in the balls. I gave better than I got, but they outnumbered me and they were bigger. I was sore for a week."

"But you did it regardless. Why?"

I shrugged. "I never considered *not* doing it. The new kid was scared and he was the underdog. It wasn't right for those bullies to steal his lunch money. By the way, they never tried that again, so getting my ass kicked was worth it." I lifted my cold coffee again. "Hey, I do other stuff. I've found lost children—at least a lost teenager who got in with the wrong crowd. I've caught wayward husbands, and I've uncovered my share of bogus insurance claims. It's not like I go from one gunfight to another. Mostly my days are pretty tame."

"Whether or not you get paid, I appreciate what you're doing for me and for Momma."

"Don't be so serious, Al. You'll make me all teary-eyed." I grinned. "I hate it when that happens. Not good for my tough-guy image."

My phone rang. The screen said it was Tank. "Oh crap," I said as I answered. "This can't be good."

Chapter 60

NGOMBO HELD DORALEEN RICE'S ARM while Bones glanced both ways down the alley. "All clear," said Bones. He pointed the remote at the Caravan and both rear doors glided open. "Load her up, Teddy." Ngombo muscled Doraleen down the metal steps and shoved her into the left rear seat.

Moffett wobbled his bulk down the steps.

Lightning split the sky. Thunder boomed, the ground shook, and several car alarms yowled.

Bones closed the rear door with the remote while Ngombo hurried around and took the right rear seat. Locking the steel warehouse door behind him, Bones slid behind the steering wheel. He engaged the child locks so no one could unlock the rear doors from inside.

Moffett reached inside the other front door and made sure the passenger seat was shoved all way the back. The rain hit, pelting him with large drops. Thunder rolled again. "Shit," he said. He shoehorned his bulk into the seat and buckled his seat belt with great difficulty. "You shoulda parked the Denali back here, Teddy. It's got wider seats than this damned Dodge."

Ngombo knew the seats were the same size, but he didn't argue. Moffett had trouble squeezing his immense body into any vehicle except maybe the trailer of an eighteen-wheeler, but Ngombo didn't dare say that. "Next time, Monster."

Bones switched on the windshield wipers and slipped the van in gear. "We going to the Tuscan site, boss?"

Moffett ignored him. "Head out to the Loop. We'll make the call from there this time."

As the van passed the dumpster where Tank was hidden, no one in the Caravan saw him call Chuck.

I DISCONNECTED TANK'S CALL. "Call Gene Lopez," I told Snoop's Bluetooth. I squealed away from the parking place.

The speaker rang once and Lopez answered. "Gene, this is Chuck McCrary. Moffett and two other men are on the move with Doraleen Rice. They're in the Caravan. We're following. I'll call you once I know where they're headed."

"Don't endanger any civilians, Chuck. Stay back. We're fifteen minutes out," Lopez said. "Keep me posted."

I didn't tell him that I was so far back I was out of sight. GPS trackers are illegal without a warrant. Lopez was picky like that.

I bounced the van out the driveway and fishtailed down the street on the wet pavement. I squealed around the corner and headed toward the alley. Tank had run from the dumpster to the street. I jammed to a stop and popped the door locks.

Tank slammed open the door and leapt into the rear seat. "Damn, you'd think the rain could wait five minutes longer."

"Mother Nature can be so inconsiderate," I said. "Did you see Doraleen?"

"She looked scared but otherwise okay. Her and three other men. One was Scarface; I recognized his dreadlocks. The second man was so huge it must be Moffett. The driver was an average sized white man." He clicked his seatbelt.

"The driver is Bones," said Al. "He's Monster's right-hand man. He's the one who knew to remove the battery on Momma's phone so you couldn't track it. He's pretty tech-savvy for a high school dropout."

Now that I'd picked up Tank, I slowed the van down. "Al, hand the tablet to Tank. Tank, boot that tracker app. Let's see where they're headed."

"They're headed west," Tank said, "Maybe they're aiming for Loop 495." He handed the tablet to Al in the front seat. "Hold the screen where Chuck can see it."

I-495 looped around Port City from I-95 near the north end of Atlantic County, west toward the Everglades, south about two miles away from the Everglades, and back to I-95 near Atlantic County's southern border. It was a good place for Moffett to make his 4:30 call to Al. The Loop has good cell service and fast-moving traffic. The cell signal would be impossible to triangulate, and there were ample exits to escape on after he made the call.

"Call Gene Lopez," I said. The Bluetooth rang him.

"Where are they headed, Chuck?" Lopez asked.

"They're headed straight west on NW 115th Street. If they go five miles, they'll hit Loop 495."

"They'll go either north or south from that entrance," Lopez said. "Which way would you go if it was you?"

"Beats the hell outta me. Six of one, half a dozen of the other. I'll let you know when he turns."

"We're on 45th Street. I'm headed straight west to the Loop to throw up a roadblock ahead of him if he goes south."

"Too many exits. He'll jump off at 63rd once he finishes the call."

"Maybe, but I got nothing to lose by trying," Lopez replied. "There's a fifty-fifty chance he'll pick south regardless."

"And if he goes north?" I asked.

"I didn't tell you this since you're a civilian, but if he heads north, stay on his ass. We'll catch up soon as we can."

NGOMBO ACCESSED THE TRACKER APP AGAIN. Rice's phone was on and revealed its location by an arrow on the screen. He studied it for a minute. He reached over Moffett's shoulder and held the phone where his boss could see the screen. "Something is wrong, Monster. Rice's phone is on 115th Street two miles behind us. It is following us. How can this be? The last time we saw it, it was at the rehab facility."

Moffett grabbed the phone and zoomed in on the map. "The crazy bastard is following us. He's following *me* for crissakes. Stop the car." He showed Ngombo's phone to Bones. "Bones, how could Al Rice follow us? He's two miles back."

Bones frowned at the screen. "McCrary must have hid a tracking device on this car." He drove into the next convenience store lot and parked on the back side, away from the other cars. "Don't let her signal anybody."

Ngombo drew his knife and held it to the woman's neck below her ear. "Do not make one sound, not one wave, not one false move."

Doraleen nodded.

Bones peered out the windshield. "Goddam rain. Wait here." He opened the door, scurried to the back bumper, and squatted out of sight. A minute later he stood with a small black box in his hand. He jogged around to the front of the store, feet splashing in the puddles. In a minute he came back and slid into the driver's seat.

"What did you do?" asked Moffett.

"I move his tracker to another car. Let McCrary follow *them* for a while."

Chapter 61

"THEY'VE STOPPED AHEAD," said Al. "You better hang back. What the hell? They pulled off the road."

I hit my turn signal, dropped my speed to thirty, and slipped into the right lane. Other traffic flowed past us. A half-mile further, I asked, "They still stopped?"

"Yeah. You better slow down."

I did. "Where did they stop?"

"The intersection at 158th Avenue. Must be a store or something there," said Al.

Tank said, "That doesn't make any sense. They have a kidnaped woman in the car. If someone sees her or she manages to get out, they're screwed."

"Not necessarily," I said. "The van has tinted windows. It's difficult for someone on the outside to see in. With this rain, nobody's gonna hang around a parking lot. They put her in the back seat, and Scarface is there to keep her under control. Still, it's unusual." I risked a quick glance at the screen. "There, they're moving again." I increased the pace to the speed limit.

"Wait a minute," Al exclaimed, "they U-turn; they're headed east. They're coming back this way. Maybe they forgot something back at the warehouse."

I shook my head, then realized Al was studying the screen. "Not hardly. It's gotta be something else. They changed their plans." I had a bad feeling, but I kept it to myself. No sense making Al and Tank feel worse than they did already.

"Remember," Tank said, "we're searching for a silver Caravan, not a Jeep Grand Cherokee this time. Al, with you in front, you see better than me. The rain spoils my view through this side window. Hand me the tablet and I'll monitor the tracker. You two watch for Momma Dora's van."

Al handed Tank the tablet.

"Tank," I said, "tell us when they get two blocks away. I'll drift over to the left lane so we can watch the eastbound traffic better." I accelerated and slipped into the left lane.

"Here it comes," Tank said a minute later. "They're two blocks ahead and headed this way."

I split my attention between the pickup truck ahead of me and the vehicles eastbound on the other side of 115th Street. Cars, delivery vans, eighteen-wheelers, and minivans. I hoped a big truck didn't block our vision when the Caravan passed. My gut told me something was haywire. I needed visual confirmation. Once the van passed, I intended to let them get two blocks away, make a U-turn, and drop in behind. I studied each minivan that came at us. There were a lot. Also a lot of big trucks. "Is that it?"

"No," said Al. That's white, not silver. There." He pointed. "No, that's an older model."

"The map on the screen says they passed us," said Tank. "Did you spot them? Did you see Momma Dora?"

"I didn't see a damned thing," I replied. "I missed them. How about you, Al? Anything?"

"Nothing, and I watched every damned minivan. Maybe they were in the far lane hidden by a big truck."

"Turn around, Chuck," Tank said from the back. "They're three blocks behind us."

I slipped into the left lane and pulled a U-turn. "I want visual confirmation." The traffic got heavy as we approached the rush hour, and the rain didn't help. I needed two miles to catch up.

"They're a half-block ahead," Tank said. "You must be able to see them."

"All I see is that white Caravan that passed us before we turned." I closed the gap. "Even if we got the color wrong, it's the wrong license number."

"Let's follow from the tracker," Al said. "Tank, give me the tablet. I have to be doing something." He took it from Tank. "Okay, we're behind them. They have to be there."

"I don't see them, Al. I think we've been had."

"Don't give up, Chuck," said Al, his voice breaking. "That's Momma up there."

I drove east in silence. The rain stopped.

My Bluetooth flashed an incoming call, Gene Lopez. "Accept call."

"Which way did they go, Chuck?" he asked.

"Something's fishy, Gene. Stand by." I glanced at the tablet in Al's lap. The red arrow slowed as if it intended to turn. Ahead, the white Caravan moved into the right lane. Its turn signal flashed. It splashed through a gutter and parked at a big box electronics store. So did the red arrow on the tablet. "Gene, I have bad news."

Chapter 62

I PULLED INTO A JAVA JENNY'S FOR A SKULL SESSION. God knows I needed coffee. Maybe a chocolate chip cookie or two? Or a dozen? Maybe a new brain? I'd been had, and I didn't feel like the world's greatest private investigator. "It's time for Plan B, gentlemen."

Tank munched on a chocolate chip cookie. "What's Plan B?"

"Pay the money—"

Both men started to object, and I raised both hands. "Hold on, gentlemen. Let me finish. Pay the money, follow the money, free Doraleen, and capture Moffett. Oh, yeah, and retrieve the money. That's Plan B." I bit off half my cookie. "Unless either of you can think of something better?"

Al said, "This is above my pay grade, Chuck."

"You're the expert, bro," said Tank. "That's why you make the big bucks. What do we tell Gene Lopez?"

"Gene will be a problem," I answered. "He has warrants to tap every phone we own: yours, mine, Doraleen's, and Al's. We need to operate under Gene's radar."

"Why? Kidnapping is a federal crime," said Tank. "Aren't these guys the experts in hostage situations?"

My phone rang; it was Flamer. "Tri-Patron Imports is a corporation whose registered agent is Leonard Satin."

"Surprise, surprise," I said.

"And he's the registered agent for the Florida Land Trust that owns the building."

"Aha," I said.

"I can't believe you said that."

"That's what the cool private investigators say when they find a clue."

"Geez," Flamer said and disconnected.

"I was asking about the FBI," Tank said. "Don't we want them involved in this?"

"Usually, yeah, but not this time. The FBI obeys the Fourth Amendment to the Constitution, even with scumbags; I don't."

Al selected another cookie. "Which amendment is the fourth?"

"That's the one against unreasonable searches and seizures," Tank responded. "It requires search warrants, probable cause. Stuff like that."

"But we three are private citizens," I said. "All we care about is getting Doraleen back safe and sound. We don't need no stinkin' search warrants. We do what's best for Doraleen. Period. Including the civilian equivalent of water-boarding, breaking and entering, mauling and general mayhem on the evildoers."

"Evildoers?" said Tank.

"Evildoers. Snoop is a big fan of George W. He said it on our last case. Those bad guys were Chicago mobsters. Since Snoop's in a coma in Cedars Hospital, in his honor I can safely say that the scumbags who shot him and kidnaped Doraleen are, in fact, evildoers."

"As I remember," Tank added, "George W. said he would bring the evildoers to justice or he would bring justice to them."

I lifted my coffee cup. "I'll drink to that. Once we finish here, buy yourself and Al new phones that the FBI doesn't have taps on. I keep a second phone under my Mexican name, Carlos Calderone. That way we three can communicate without the FBI listening. We'll figure out a way to send a message to Moffett with the new phone numbers so the FBI can't interfere."

Al's cell rang. He stared at it like it was a bomb about to explode. He thrust it toward me. "I never figured Monster would call, since they know we have that tracker on their van."

The caller ID on the screen was a number I didn't recognize. Another burner phone. I answered. "Hello."

"You don't sound like Al Rice." I recognized Moffett's voice from the phone tap I'd heard with Gene Lopez.

"This is Chuck McCrary. I am working with Mr. Rice to get his mother back." I knew Lopez was recording every word with the phone tap. "We can have your $200,000 by five o'clock tomorrow."

"It's $225,000 now. There's more interest due."

I raised an eyebrow in Tank's direction. He nodded.

"Okay," I said, "$225,000 by five o'clock tomorrow. I'll bring it."

"No, I want Rice to bring it."

"Not gonna happen, Moffett. There's a reason Al handed his phone to me: I represent him. If you want the money, I'll bring it." I didn't give him a chance to object. "What kind of bills do you want?"

"Used fifties in forty-five bundles of one hundred bills each."

"Is a soccer bag okay? Easier to carry." I wanted the soccer bag. A briefcase wouldn't fit my purpose.

"Yeah, sure. Whatever. There's a bench on the boardwalk at North Beach near 154th Street that's shaded by four sabal palms. Be there tomorrow at noon with the money. Sit on the bench and you'll receive further instructions. Bring the phone you're using now with you." He disconnected.

I added the burner phone's number to Al's contact list as *Monster*.

I used my Carlos Calderone phone to send a text to the number:

Cannot get the money by noon. Will have it by five. FBI is tapping Al Rice's phone. Communicate with me on this number from now on. McCrary.

I opened the applications window on Al's phone and scrolled to the last page. I found it: the tracker app. I showed the screen to Al. "Moffett must've installed this tracker app on your phone when he kidnaped you and mangled your hand. He used it earlier today and realized that your phone was a couple miles behind him on 115th Street. That's how he knew we were there.

I suspected something hinky about your phone yesterday when I heard the voicemail message he left. He said Tank couldn't hide you out west in the boondocks forever. How else could he know you were in west Port City? A tracker app was the one thing that made sense."

"You'd better uninstall it, Chuck," Tank suggested.

"Nope. Now that we know Moffett can track Al's phone, maybe we can use that against him."

"How?"

"I haven't figured that out." I removed the battery from Al's phone. "But it's something we know that he doesn't know we know. Maybe we'll think of a way to use it."

Chapter 63

THE NEXT MORNING, THERE WAS NO CHANGE in Snoop's condition. Janet insisted I keep his Toyota.

Tank needed a few hours to raise that much cash in used fifties. New fifties were easy, but Moffett didn't want those. We collected used ones from three different bank branches.

I made additional preparations.

The afternoon thunder clouds had gathered over the Everglades by the time I parked in the 154th Street lot at North Beach. The sun wouldn't set for another three hours, but the clouds gathered to our west already shadowed the beach. The beach was practically deserted. My bad luck, the topless women had left for the day. I stuck the battery back in Al's phone and switched it on. Now the FBI would know where the phone was.

My Calderone phone announced, "New message received from Monster." It was a text:

Drive south on A1A at 30 mph.

I headed south at 25 mph. Ninety-nine percent of the traffic drove at or above the 35 mph speed limit. Within three blocks I spotted the Jeep a block behind me. I sped up to 30 and called Tank. "Close up enough to read the license of the red Jeep a block behind me. Then drop back and have Kelly Contreras identify it. Maybe it'll give us a hint where Moffett stashed Doraleen."

Another text came in:

Turn right on North Bay Causeway. Increase speed to
45.

I made the turn. A light rain began to fall.
Another text:

Park in Fishermen's Pier Park.

That was a small island park in Seeti Bay on the north side
of the causeway. The pier had been standing for generations. The
parking lot was sand and gravel. Any real pavement was a
distant memory worn away by decades of trucks and cars
parking under the sea grapes and casuarina trees to try their luck
on the old pier.

The rain stopped by the time I bumped down the driveway
to the rutted lot and splashed through the puddles that hadn't
soaked into the ground yet. The park was always jammed on a
Saturday, but it was late afternoon and many fishermen and
families had left to beat the afternoon showers. I slipped into a
spot in the center of the park and eyeballed my mirror while the
red Jeep passed on the causeway.

"New message received from Monster."

Drop bag in trash can at far west end. The package will
be released after we count it.

I texted back:

No. I want proof of life.

I hit *send*, squeezed into a parking spot, and waited.

My phone rang. It was from another number I didn't
recognize. Had to be another burner phone. "Hello, this is Chuck
McCrary."

"Chuck, this is Doraleen Rice. I'm okay. There's a knife at
my throat. That's all I'm allowed to say." The call disconnected.

I saved the number that the call came from in my contacts
under the name *Proof.*

"New message received from Monster."

Drop bag in trash can at far west end. Continue driving
west on causeway.

I replied to the text:

That was not Doraleen Rice. I need proof of life.

My phone rang. It was from the Monster contact number.
"What the hell are you trying to pull, McCrary?"

"That wasn't Doraleen Rice. I'll ask her a question only she
will know the answer to."

"Screw you. You're gonna get the bitch killed if you don't
stop screwing around with me."

"I have the money; you want the money. I'll give you the
money, but first you gotta prove Doraleen is alive. Take it or
leave it."

"What's the question?"

"Nope. Doesn't work that way. I'll ask her myself and hear
the answer from her own lips."

Moffett groaned and grunted. "She'll call you back."

In a few minutes the Proof number called me again. "This
is Chuck McCrary. Is this Doraleen Rice?"

"Yes, Chuck. Teddy said you wanted to ask me a question."
She spoke slowly, and she had named one kidnapper. Smart
lady.

"Are you on speaker phone?"

Doraleen said, "Is this thing on speaker phone? I'm not sure
what that means."

"Yes, it is on speaker phone." A meticulous accent like
Doraleen had described. It was Scarface.

"I will ask a two-part question, Doraleen, if that's who you
are. What did you call me the first time we met?"

"I called you Chuck."

"No, that's not what I mean. You called me by a famous
poem."

She paused and I listened to the background noise. "Oh, yes,
I called you my Sir Galahad."

I was sure the pause was intentional.

"Okay, second part, Doraleen. Finish this sentence: All-arm'd I ride, whate'er betide…"

She paused again. "Until I find the party girl."

"Okay, Doraleen. I'm satisfied it's you."

Scarface disconnected.

Doraleen had given me three clues in our conversation.

Two minutes later my phone said, "New message received from Monster."

Drop bag in trash can at far west end. Continue driving west on causeway.

Most action in Fishermen's Pier Park centers around the pier. A small beach to the east lies far enough from the pier that the fishing lines don't interfere with the few swimmers. Some people wade from the beach into the warm bay waters near the pier to fish from the bay. The rest use the pier. The rest of the park shore is protected from storm erosion by boulders and rip-rap that keep people away from the water. Few people hang around those areas. They park and walk to the pier or the beach. As a result, the trash bin at the west end is seldom used except by occasional picnickers.

I got out of Snoop's Toyota and glanced around. I lifted the canvas soccer bag from the back seat. The picnic tables under the shelters had been used by families enjoying a spring day with a bayside picnic, like they had done on this same site since 1925. This late in the day, most concrete tables were empty. Even under a shelter, a picnic in the rain isn't much fun. With the rain stopped, at least for a while, some SUVs and vans had their back hatches and doors open, and people set up their picnics and fishing sites again.

At least one vehicle in the lot came for a more serious purpose. Which one?

I ambled toward the west end, dodged the puddles, and studied the parked vehicles that remained. Moffett's gang was partial to SUVs and minivans, but that included most of the vehicles in the park. One blue Honda SUV had two men in it, wearing light jackets as they sat with their windows up, air conditioner blasting. I wore a jacket myself to hide my shoulder holster. I slipped out my phone and stopped as if I was punching in a number. I held the phone to my ear and walked behind the Honda. I snapped a picture of its license as I passed. It was the same color and model Gene Lopez had described as a TCL vehicle. Lopez had given me the license number, but I didn't recall it.

I reached the trash bin, sweating in the humidity left by the rain. One paper Burger King bag lay in the bottom, soaking wet, along with plastic bags, crushed paper cups, and paper scraps stuck to the bottom with the glue of spilled drinks and other sticky substances I didn't want to think about. Other than that, the bin was empty. I dropped the money bag over the edge. I hoped I hadn't bruised the Burger King.

I examined the image of the Honda's license. It was the missing fourth car that belonged to TCL Enterprises. I texted Kelly with the *Proof* contact phone number and a message:

Ping this phone. Doraleen Rice is there.

I returned to Snoop's car. I watched the blue Honda in my mirror while I splashed my way from the rutted lot back to the causeway. The man on the passenger side got out and walked toward the trash bin.

I drove west on the causeway.

Chapter 64

EXCEPT FOR FISHERMAN'S PIER PARK on the north and the bridge to Pink Coral Island on the south, North Bay Causeway is a narrow strip dredged from Seeti Bay in 1925. Technically, the causeway is wide enough for four lanes of traffic to stream between Port City and Port City Beach. Maybe it was wide enough in 1925, but, with 21st Century traffic and vehicles, there was no way to pull over and slip in behind the blue Honda except on a perilously narrow shoulder that should be marked *No stopping unless you want to be rear-ended*. The two thugs in the blue Honda might not know I'd spotted them. If I'd been that lucky, I didn't want to blow it.

I called Flamer. "What you got on Bernard Prevossi?"

"No criminal record, which is no surprise since he's got those liquor licenses. The state is picky about who they issue those to. He's forty-five years old. Born in Crestview, Florida. Graduated Florida State with a degree in business. Worked for a Certified Public Accounting firm in Tallahassee for two years. No record of him passing the CPA exam. Married once. No children. Divorced twenty years ago. Bought a small pub in Tallahassee. Kept it for eight years, sold it to move to Port City. Never mentioned in a single court case or civil lawsuit, which is a surprise, considering all his business interests."

"Who handled his divorce?"

"Guy named Oswaldo Duran."

"Okay, check if Leonard Satin or Oswaldo Duran are the Lone Ranger types or has either one ever been in a law firm.

Find out what law firms they've been with the last twenty years. No, make that twenty-five years."

"Give me ten minutes," Flamer said, then disconnected.

While Flamer and I had been talking, Kelly sent me a text:

Phone not GPS type. While it was on, it pinged from tower in 8100 block of NW Charles Boulevard.

That was the neighborhood where the three strip clubs were. I replayed Doraleen's brief phone call in my mind. The first clue from her call was Scarface's name. The second was the music playing in the background, *The Stripper* by the David Rose Orchestra. The third clue was her answer to the quote from *Sir Galahad*. She changed the line from "holy grail" to "party girl." Doraleen was held at a strip club, and I remembered where I'd heard *The Stripper* before.

How was Moffett connected to the Orange Peel?

I popped the battery from Al's phone. I didn't want Moffett to know I was on the way, nor Gene Lopez. I headed toward the showdown.

Chapter 65

FLAMER CALLED. "Oswaldo Duran and Leonard Satin were both of counsel to a big law firm with, like, seven or eight names in the title."

"You said 'were.' What about now?"

"Satin is still of counsel, Duran moved to Port City ten years ago."

I slowed down and moved to the right lane. "What does 'of counsel' mean?"

"That's an attorney who offices with a law firm, or the firm uses him for a special few clients, or he consults on a particular case. Neither one is a partner and they file their legal stuff in their individual names, no firm name involved. It could be a simple office-sharing arrangement."

"So the big firm's partners wouldn't necessarily be involved?"

"In this case, with over a hundred lawyers in the firm, they wouldn't know what either of these guys did."

"Examine Oswaldo Duran's time in Port City. Find what he's been up to."

"I did. Duran never married. He's of counsel with a big firm here in Port City. He was one of the lawyers who got Florida's same-sex marriage ban overturned. He's gay."

"*Hmm.* Being one that overturned the same-sex marriage ban doesn't mean he's gay," I said.

"Doesn't mean he isn't either."

"What difference does it make?"

"His home address is the same as Bernard Prevossi's and has been for eight years. Think about it, Chuck. Prevossi was married a year, didn't have children, divorced, never remarried. Duran is single, never married. They've lived together for the last eight years. Do the math; they're gay."

"Okay, but so what?"

"So Prevossi owns gay bars and strip clubs and is involved in ugly sex trade stuff. It's bums like him who give gays like me a bad name."

"They can't all be like you and Kennedy, Flamer, like all straight people aren't like Tank and me. Thanks for a good job." I disconnected and sped back up.

Tank's voice came from Snoop's radio speaker. "The guys in the blue Honda found the first tracker. They dumped it in the parking lot before they got on the causeway."

I had slipped the first GPS tracker in a side pocket of the money bag and zipped it closed. I sewed the second, smaller one, under the bag's false bottom. "Let's hope they don't think about there being a second one. Where is the bag now?"

"Would you believe it's in the Orange Peel?"

"Yeah, I'd believe that. I'm on my way there. You and Al meet me there." I told him about my proof of life conversation with Doraleen. "I'm gonna call Gene Lopez. We gotta get the FBI over there before they move her again. They arrived too late the other two times."

"Let's hope third time's the charm," Tank said.

"Maybe we'll have a nice reunion scene with Al and Doraleen after we rescue her."

I texted Moffett:

Where can I pick up Doraleen Rice?

My phone rang. I accepted the call and Moffett's voice came from the radio. "You crazy bastard, I have half a mind to kill the old lady right now. I warned you not to screw around with me. Where's the rest of my money?"

"Moffett, I gave you half the money as a good faith gesture. Now it's your turn to have a little faith. Turn Doraleen Rice loose and I'll give you the rest of the money. Where can I pick her up?"

"You can pick her up in hell," he shouted over the phone.

"Don't be silly. You don't want the woman; you want the money. I have the money; I do want the woman. You're the one who's screwing around. Let's do this thing, and we both get our lives back. Where do I pick her up?"

"I'll get back to you." He disconnected.

NGOMBO SAT IN THE OFFICE at the Orange Peel and listened to Moffett's tirade on the phone. This was bad, very bad. Bones had warned him that Moffett was… *off* in some way. This was not the strong, smart criminal Ngombo went to work for six months ago. He had respected and admired that man as the leader that he, Ngombo, aspired to be.

Moffett was now a loose cannon, bouncing around the deck in a suddenly stormy sea and threatening to sink the entire ship. But what could he do about it?

First Moffett had insisted Bones drive the four of them to the Orange Peel when they left the Tri-Patron building. The logical choice was the Tuscan site, but Moffett shouted and cursed at Bones when he suggested it. The Tuscan site was easy to get the woman into without being seen; no one was around at night. The Orange Peel was crowded with strangers at night. Even the back rooms might have a dancer or bouncer wander around at any time.

It was insanity to hold the woman there. Yet Moffett had insisted.

Ngombo and Bones had waited with the woman in the van for several minutes until the rear lot emptied of people. Moffett had gone around front and opened the rear fire door for them to drag the woman inside. Ngombo had brought Doraleen Rice to the office like Moffett ordered. Later Moffett gave him the key to a storeroom in the rear of the club to lock her in for the night. It was a small room, little more than a closet. At least it had a toilet and sink, if not a shower or tub. Maybe it was a dressing room used by the club's previous owners. A speaker near the ceiling broadcast the music played in the showroom. Now it contained files, boxes, cleaning supplies, and extra chairs.

After McCrary demanded proof of life, Moffett had sent Ngombo with a new burner phone to the storeroom. Following the first call, he had let himself out, locked the woman in, and reported to Moffett in the office. When McCrary was not satisfied, Moffett screamed and cursed like a crazy man before he sent Ngombo back to the woman again.

This place was evil. Ngombo had known at some level about the human trafficking business Moffett ran with his other men, but this was the first time he had confronted the actual result. He couldn't ignore that these women were prostitutes. This was not a fit place for a warrior. He wondered why the gods had conspired to bring him here.

Chapter 66

I CALLED LOPEZ. When we connected, I got back on the road toward the Orange Peel. The longer we delayed, the more likely he would miss her again. I briefed Lopez while I sped across town. "Moffett has Doraleen Rice at the Orange Peel Gentlemen's Club. If you hurry, you can raid the club before they move her. I'm on my way there to make sure they don't escape."

"I've heard that before. The other two times they flew the coop before we got there and you lost them."

"If at first you don't succeed..." I said. "The money bag is there. Her proof of life conversation came from there, but time's wasting. They might move her any minute. I'm meeting Tank and Al Rice over there. We're on our way."

I didn't tell him Moffett had said he'd get back to me over an hour ago. I felt the sweat run down my ribs, and it wasn't from humidity this time. Had I pushed it too far by giving him just half the money? I shoved the thought aside; Tank and Al had agreed to the strategy. No battle plan survives contact with the enemy. I hoped Moffett hadn't gone off the rails. If he had; all bets were off. I punched the accelerator harder.

Lopez brought me back to reality. "We executed a search warrant on Tri-Patron Imports yesterday."

"Oh?"

"We found a dormitory with twenty beds. We think they're involved with human trafficking in addition to this kidnapping. We found evidence they were holding Asian women there."

"What evidence?" I had a disturbing mental image of Miyo being held against her will. Miyo's doppelganger, the stripper Tammy I had met at the Crazy Lady, might have been captive in that very room.

"It's technical stuff that involves DNA markers and other scientific mumbo-jumbo. My CSU guys turned the place inside out, and our lab geeks tell me someone at that warehouse has run Asian females through there—a lot more than twenty. I have to believe my own experts."

"*Hmm*. There were Asian strippers and waitresses at the Crazy Lady who barely spoke English. One girl practically offered to do me right there on the table. There were other Asian women at the Orange Peel who I didn't talk to. Moffett may smuggle in illegal Asian women and force them into prostitution and dancing in strip clubs that belong to a man named Bernard Prevossi."

"Bernard Prevossi?"

"Yeah. Does that ring any bells with you?"

"No. What's the connection to Moffett?"

"I don't know. I do know that Tri-Patron Imports is a corporation whose registered agent is Leonard Satin, a Tallahassee attorney who is trustee of a Florida Land Trust that owns the building where they held Doraleen. Satin connects the same way to the other strip clubs. Prevossi holds the liquor license on three strip clubs on Charles Boulevard and others around the state. Maybe in other states too, but I'm concerned with the ones in Port City. Maybe he gives Moffett a commission for bringing in the girls."

"Wouldn't be the first time."

"Unfortunately, no," I agreed. "But maybe we make it the last, at least for Prevossi, Satin, and Moffett."

MOFFETT ENTERED THE ORANGE PEEL OFFICE.

Ngombo set his coffee down beside the couch. Bones and Moffett had gone to the showroom to watch the girls dance. Ngombo stayed behind to avoid the impure women. Moffett grinned at Ngombo and sat in the big leather chair behind the desk. "You're missing a great show, Teddy. Finest pieces of ass in the whole country. Enjoy yourself."

"With respect, Monster, I am a warrior. I wish to remain here."

Moffett shrugged. "Your loss, Teddy."

Pete the bookkeeper opened the door. Ngombo had seen Pete twice before, once at the Tri-Patron site and once at the Tuscan site. On those occasions, Pete and Moffett retreated to a private office to conduct business.

Moffett rose from the chair behind the desk and walked around to shake hands with the bookkeeper. "Pete, you want a drink?"

"This isn't a social call, Monster." He sat in the big leather chair behind the desk and motioned Moffett into a visitor's chair. That surprised him; Pete acted like the boss, and Moffett acted like the employee. Perhaps he misunderstood the relationship between the two Americans.

"What the hell were you thinking to bring that woman here?" demanded Pete. "We have secure locations for things like that."

Moffett spread his hands and hunched his shoulders. "I thought—"

"No," Pete interrupted, "you didn't think. Or you were thinking with your dick, which is the same thing. You brought her here because you wanted to ogle Jasmine again, didn't you?"

"Her name is Jennifer now," Moffett replied weakly.

"I don't give a fart in a whirlwind what her name is this week. She's a product that I sell, and don't you *ever* forget it." He shook a finger at Moffett. "I loan her to you as a favor—an employee bonus, if you will—but she belongs to me. They all belong to me. Don't press your luck with me, big boy."

Moffett cut his gaze toward the African.

Pete followed his glance. "Teddy, isn't it?" he asked.

"Yes, Teddy Ngombo."

"Why don't you wait outside, Teddy?"

Ngombo left.

Chapter 67

AFTER I REACHED THE ORANGE PEEL, the rain pelted down again. I circled the building. The silver Caravan was parked near the fire door in the back. The rain was a blessing in disguise; no one hung around the parking lot. I stopped in the driveway, ran through the rain, and stuck another tracker under the rear bumper.

I called Tank. "I'm parked at the Orange Peel where I can observe the front entrance. You and Al park in the rear where you can watch both fire doors. The Caravan is parked back there. How long before you get here?"

"We're twenty minutes out," said Al. "Tank's driving; he handed me the phone. His Mercedes doesn't have a Bluetooth."

"Isn't that supposed to be a superb product of German engineering?" I asked.

"Maybe that was a different model."

"Must be. Okay, call back when you get close. The FBI may get here before you do."

I punched on Snoop's music system and listened to Willie Nelson. *Blue Eyes Crying in the Rain* fit in while rain fell in the Florida night.

The silver Caravan emerged from behind the building and splashed its way across the front lot. The headlights hit raindrops on my windshield and blinded me with scattered light.

I paused Willie, booted my tablet, and fired up Snoop's car. "Call Tank," I told the Bluetooth.

"What's up, Chuck? My GPS says we're still seven minutes out."

"The Caravan has left the Orange Peel. I stuck another tracker on it and I'm following."

"Do you buy those things by the case?"

"I should; I go through so many."

"Was Momma Dora in the van?"

"It's raining here and their headlights blinded me when they left. I couldn't make out the inside of the car. She might still be in the Orange Peel. Where is the money bag now?"

"Al, check the tablet for the money bag. Where is it now?" I heard Tank say.

There was a mumbled reply.

"Still in the Orange Peel, Chuck," said Tank.

"Okay, it's up to you, but I suggest you two stay at the club and wait for the FBI if you get there before they do. Doraleen may be with the money. I'll follow the Caravan in case she's in that. Let me know what the FBI finds."

I disconnected and played Willie again. I needed something to sooth my anxious mind. Come to think of it, that was a good title for a country song, *Come Sooth My Anxious Mind*, or maybe *Sooth My Anxious Heart*. Too bad I'm not musically inclined.

I stayed a half-mile behind the Caravan. By the time it reached I-495, the rain had stopped, or maybe we drove out from under the cloud. The Caravan followed the loop west at two mph below the speed limit with me in warm pursuit. Their speed meant they would take no chances of getting stopped; Doraleen must be with them. *Damn, that means that the FBI will miss her again.*

They hit the big curve and followed the loop south to the NW 115th Street exit. Surely, they wouldn't return to Tri-Patron Imports? They drove east on NW 115th Street to NW 103rd Avenue and went south. Once they passed 108th Street, I knew they were headed somewhere else. But where?

Chapter 68

TANK SHOOK HANDS WITH GENE LOPEZ. "Thanks for getting my money back, Special Agent Lopez." Chuck had advised him to always use FBI titles.

Lopez grinned. "Please, call me Gene, Tank. It's a real pleasure to meet you after watching you on TV all those years. I've been a Pelicans fan practically forever. You guys were robbed in that Super Bowl game. If it hadn't been for that bad call, you would have a Super Bowl ring instead of an AFC Championship ring."

Tank touched his ring self-consciously. "It is what it is, but thanks for your comments."

Lopez continued. "I don't want to raise false hopes, Tank. The money may be yours, but it's also evidence in a kidnapping and in a human trafficking case. Might be a long time before the cases are settled and the money is released from evidence."

Tank shrugged. "Again, it is what it is. Fortunately, it's not like I need the money right away. Take all the time you need to make your case. Now if you'll excuse me, Al and I have errands to run."

"Do those errands involve Chuck McCrary and the whereabouts of Doraleen Rice?" Lopez asked.

Something made Tank hesitate. "Like I said, we have errands to run."

Lopez grasped Tank's arm; he couldn't reach Tank's shoulder. "What kind of errands?"

Tank stared down at Lopez's hand until he removed it. "Gene, am I under arrest, or is Al?"

"No, no, of course not."

"Then we'll leave. Have a nice day."

TANK CALLED ME. "The FBI raided the Orange Peel. Momma Dora wasn't there. They did recover my money, but it'll be a year or more before I get it back. What's happening with you?"

"The Caravan drove back out to the same neighborhood where the Tri-Patron Imports is. They're driving two miles under the limit, so I'm pretty sure Doraleen is with them. Lopez and the FBI are liable to be tied up at the Orange Peel for hours. Head this way. I'll text or call you after I know where they stop."

"You want me to bring Al in with me? He doesn't know shit about shooting."

"Al didn't stay at the Orange Peel?"

"He said he wanted to rescue his mother. Something about being less sheep and more tiger."

"It's up to him. There will be at least three shooters holding Doraleen. Any addition to the arsenal has gotta be better than nothing. You have those vests from yesterday?"

"Yeah."

"Put them on before you come after me."

"They're bulletproof?"

"Let's hope so; I'll be wearing one exactly like them."

The industrial neighborhood where Tri-Patron Imports was located began development at NW 90th Street in the 1980s and worked its way north as new sites where sold. The further south we drove, the older the buildings were. The map displayed on my tablet showed the van had turned east on NW 95th Street and drove into a parking lot on the south side. I stayed a half-mile behind. This late at night there was no traffic in the area, and I would stand out like a bonfire on a beach.

I parked in a lot with two other cars in it off NW 103rd Avenue south of NW 96th Street. That positioned me around the corner from where the Caravan stopped. I strapped on my own armored vest, locked the van, and mentally crossed my fingers for luck. I moved along the warehouse wall where I was less noticeable.

The 10200 block of NW 95th Street looked like dozens of blocks around it. The parking lots were empty or nearly so. The widely-spaced streetlights lit the street well enough, but they didn't reach the lots or buildings. The industrial tenants had few or no outside lights; it was pointless in a neighborhood largely abandoned after business hours. I slipped along the walls across the street until I stood opposite the unit where the silver Caravan sat.

The Caravan was parked in front of another long structure with four units, similar to the arrangement at Tri-Patron Imports except the building had two stories. Two other vehicles sat in the lot, both SUVs. I hoped they had parked overnight and that their drivers had caught a ride with someone else to the Tri-Patron location or elsewhere. At least the windows on this side were dark. I couldn't see the back, but I didn't risk wasting the time to reconnoiter the alley.

There were small signs above the main entrance door and the cargo door I couldn't make out in the dark. A pylon near the street gave me the street address. I texted it to Tank with instructions to park where I parked and approach on foot. I switched my phone to silent.

As I snuck across the street, a light came on in a second-floor window, then one in the next window. I jogged faster, hoping no one in the lighted room inside could see me in the dark outside. I raced across the pavement, jumped the flower bed, and trotted to the all-glass entrance. I could read the two signs now: *Tuscan Carriage Lights—Office* and *Tuscan Carriage Lights—Deliveries.*

Tuscan Carriage Lights, was that *TCL Enterprises Inc.*? *Hmm.*

I stood under the roof over the office door where I was invisible from above. Nine p.m. As far as I knew, Flamer never slept, so I texted him:

Tuscan Carriage Lights, 10266 NW 95 St. Need corporate info and building ownership. ASAP of course.

Within seconds, my phone signaled a reply:

Of course. What else is new?

Chapter 69

AL WAS JARRED FROM HIS THOUGHTS when Tank's phone screen lit the Mercedes interior and announced a new message from Chuck McCrary. "Al, would you get that?"

He fished the phone from the cup holder between the front bucket seats and read the message. "Chuck says to park on NW 103rd Avenue south of NW 96th Street. Says we'll spot his van. Momma is at Tuscan Carriage Lights, 10266 NW 95 Street. Says we should wear vests. She's in imminent danger and he can't wait on us or on the cops. He's going in. We're supposed to call the cops, preferable Kelly Contreras. He says to let her make the collar. What's that mean: the collar?"

"Don't you watch cop shows on TV?" asked Tank. "It means the arrest."

"I haven't watched much TV in the last few years." He'd been too busy with drugs and alcohol and self-pity. *Maybe I'm addicted to all three?*

"Enter that address in the GPS," Tank said. He accelerated up the entrance ramp to I-495. "Then call Kelly Contreras. Her number is in my contact list."

Al grabbed the GPS and punched in the destination, clipped the unit onto the dashboard stand. "Who is Kelly Contreras?"

"She's a Port City police detective. She's Bigs Bigelow's partner."

"*The* Bigs Bigelow as in the Bigs Brigade? Your old playing partner?"

"The same."

"He's a cop?" Al asked.

"Geez, you *have* been out of the loop, haven't you? Welcome to the real world. Bigs has been a cop for several years. Once he retired from the NFL, he went to the police academy. He started as a patrolman and now he's a detective. He and Kelly are the ones who found your car abandoned beside I-95 earlier this week. Chuck and I met them there the afternoon of the day you came back to Momma Dora's. That's when Kelly gave me her card. I think Bigs wants to fix me up with her. Oh, I forgot to tell you, your car is in the police impound, whenever you want it back."

Al's mind raced in multiple directions. Where had the last decade gone? Tank had finished his football career and gone on to the next chapter of his life. Bigs Bigelow, whom he knew by reputation, became a police detective. *What have I become? A drunken junkie who ran through most of a million dollars of another man's hard-earned money.* He felt lower than a snake's belly.

"Hey, wake up, Al," said Tank. "Call her and put it on speaker."

Al snapped back to present time and called the police detective, switching the phone to *speaker.*

"Kelly, this is Tank Tyler. Chuck texted me the address where Doraleen Rice's kidnappers are holding her. It's in the same industrial district as Tri-Patron Imports. He said you might want to make the collar. Steal the FBI's thunder, I guess."

"What's the address?"

"I'll forward his text to you once we hang up. He's there now and I'm on my way as backup. With Doraleen in imminent danger, he won't wait for backup."

"I'll need five minutes to organize the logistics, but, yeah, we'll have a SWAT team there within twenty or thirty minutes. Can you wait for us?"

"Chuck says she's in imminent danger. You can read it yourself. Let me hang up and send it to you." He cut his eyes to Al. "Hang up and forward Chuck's text to her."

Al did as he was told. He said, "How many guns did you bring?"

"Two Glock 19s and a Browning .380 in an ankle holster, why? You don't intend to run in there, guns blazing, do you? This ain't the movies, ol' buddy. A guy could get killed."

"This whole mess is my fault, Tank. I'm carrying a load of guilt that feels like a hundred-pound sack of rocks. Maybe if I help rescue Momma, it'll feel like I removed some rocks from the sack. Lighten the load, so to speak." He grabbed the GPS on the dashboard and moved the screen where they both could watch it. "So, yeah, I'm going with you, if you'll give me a gun. Hell, isn't that why I have the bulletproof vest?"

"We hope it's bulletproof. Okay, I'll loan you a Glock. You ever fire a pistol?"

"No, but how hard can it be? You point and pull the trigger."

"Shooting is like golf, Al. The pros on television make golf look easy, but when you're on the driving range, you find out it's tougher than it looks. Two things to remember: First is, you don't *pull* the trigger; you *squeeze* it."

"Don't pull the trigger. Squeeze it. What's the second thing?"

"Aim at the center of the guy's body. Never aim for anyone's head or arm or leg; you'll miss every time. Aim for the center of his body."

Al swallowed hard. "Aim for the center of his body."

"Now that I think about it, there's a third thing: Beware of the slide. That's the top part of the Glock. It slides back a couple inches every time you fire. If your hand is in the way—like if you use the wrong two-handed grip—it'll cut your hand and you'll drop the gun, sure as hell. If you do use a two-handed grip, place your left palm *under* your right hand to support it. The other way, it'll bite you every time."

Tank reached over and squeezed Al's forearm, never taking his attention off the highway. "There's plenty of guilt to go around, Al. If I hadn't stood by when Bettina Becker was drunk... If I had made y'all leave her alone, you wouldn't have been kicked off the team. You might have..." He lapsed into silence before he spoke again. "You feel guilty for what you *did*. I feel guilty for what I *didn't* do. Plenty of guilt to go around, bro."

Chapter 70

BIG NUMBERS WERE PAINTED ON THE GLASS DOOR in silver with black trim: *10266.* A decal on the window wall beside the entrance warned that the property was secured by a burglar alarm system. I peered through the glass at the alarm panel mounted on the wall. It glowed green. Did green mean *disarmed?* Or did green mean *armed and secure?*

I slipped an electrical current sensor from my pocket and passed it around the edges of the glass entrance door. The alarm contacts were usually at the top of the door, but I tested both sides and the top. If the transmitters were active, the indicator light would glow amber when it passed across them. The indicator stayed dark. Green meant the system was disarmed. Moffett's men deactivated it before they entered and forgot to re-arm it, but they might remember to re-arm it at any second.

I tried the door, but it's never that easy. I removed lock picks from my jacket and attacked the door. It took longer than it should. I was sweating buckets again by the time the lock surrendered. I eased the door open and stepped inside.

My vision acclimated to the dark. Dim light shone through the glass wall from the streetlights. On the right were the stairs and two more doors, one painted light blue and one painted beige. No light came from underneath the closed doors. I surveyed the rooms to make sure I didn't have an unexpected visitor behind me after I went upstairs. They were both small dormitories for ten people each like the one Lopez described at the Tri-Patron unit. I couldn't see a whole lot with the light from my cellphone screen, but the rooms smelled faintly of women.

Since Tuscan Carriage Lights kept illegals in the dormitories from time to time, I knew the alarm wasn't hooked to a police monitoring service. If it went off, it would notify only Moffett or one of his henchmen.

As I reached the stairs, the alarm panel caught my attention. It had turned red; they must've re-armed it from the top floor. I left the entrance unlocked for Tank and Al. I knew all hell would break loose when they opened it. Any second, Moffett might find out the Orange Peel had been raided. No telling what the nut would do to Doraleen once he learned the FBI had recovered the ransom money. I couldn't wait for backup.

I texted Tank a warning about the entrance alarm and told them to charge upstairs as fast as they could gallop. I needed those reinforcements.

NGOMBO SAT AT A CATERING TABLE near the rear of the big room and watched Moffett pacing back and forth. Moffett clapped his huge hands together every few seconds like he was swatting at gnats. The cannon was rolling around the deck in the storm, bashing its way through the ribs of the ship. Ngombo felt panic rise in his throat, but none of it showed on his warrior face. His stomach felt like a hot coal burned inside.

Moffett was in another world, paying no attention to him or Bones. Ngombo had already locked the woman in the second room.

Bones raised his hands. "Boss, it ain't the end of the world. We ain't never killed nobody. They can't get us for murder, even if they do catch us, and nobody knows this place exists."

Moffett stopped pacing. "Pete knows this place is here."

"Pete is free and clear. Far as anybody knows, he's merely the bookkeeper. They can't pin nothing on him."

Moffett snorted. "They will if they dig deep enough—*when* they dig deep enough. Kidnapping is a capital offense, Bones. Do you want to spend the rest of your life in a federal prison as another convict's bitch?"

"Not hardly, boss."

"I didn't think so."

"We have the old lady, boss, and McCrary has over a hundred grand for you. You swap the woman for the money and we both split for Grand Cayman. We got a fortune stashed there. We use McCrary's money to charter a private plane to fly us to Cayman. We give the rest of the dough to Teddy as a bonus for a job well done. We'll be home free. We can retire. Teddy's young; he'll hook up with another gang without no trouble."

Moffett glared at Bones. "I suppose that next you'll want me to write a reference letter for Teddy for his new employers. 'Dear *capo de capo*, allow me to recommend Teddy what's-his-name for assorted strong-arm and leg-breaking duties. He has valuable kidnapping experience and is skilled at mutilating cats.' Is that what you had in mind?"

Bones slumped into a chair beside Ngombo. "Boss, you're the boss. What do you want to do?"

Moffett began pacing again.

"I'm gonna fix us coffee, boss." Bones left the room.

Ngombo fingered his knife where the scabbard was strapped to his left forearm. Moffett, the man he once admired as a thinker, a leader, as fearless, was scared shitless and didn't have a clue what to do next. Moffett had been audacious when he faced no meaningful opposition. He had used his great size like any other bully. Now, he had encountered a strong enemy like this McCrary, and he was impotent. All he did was pace and clap his hands together. He was a caged bear pacing the confines of his zoo pen. This situation wasn't a gnat he could smash. Ngombo considered his own bleak future with this madman in control of his destiny. He didn't like the future he perceived. He fingered the knife again. A true warrior's weapon. A warrior creates his own destiny.

I ASCENDED THE STEPS, EYES FULLY DILATED. The light strip under the door at the top of the stairs provided sufficient illumination for the climb. The stairs were concrete, so an errant squeaky step wouldn't give me away. As I climbed, the sweat trickled down my ribs on both sides. I reached the top and drew my Glock. I took a calming breath and let my heart rate slow.

Beyond that door, I would confront three armed men, maybe more. Every one, subject to the death penalty or life without parole. They had nothing to lose. As for me... Doraleen needed me, and nobody lives forever.

I twisted the knob and stepped through the door.

Chapter 71

QUICKLY, I DREW THE OTHER GLOCK and pointed one at each man. Where the hell was the third man? Three doors on the front wall were painted yellow, purple, and black. Two on the back were fuchsia and Prussian blue. A green door was to the right down the same wall as the door I had entered through.

"Hands where I can see them." I kicked the stair door all the way open behind me.

Moffett stopped in mid-stride.

"Don't even think about it, Moffett. You're such a big target that I couldn't miss. You, Teddy, hands where I can see them. Where is Bones?"

I had a logistical problem. Aiming two guns kept both my hands occupied, but I needed to disarm Moffett and Scarface. While I was a cop, I'd learned that I was most vulnerable when I frisked someone. When I touched *them*, they're touching *me*. I was close enough to grab, one hand was occupied, and my attention was diverted. That's why a cop needs another cop for backup. I wished.

It's hard enough to frisk one man when you're alone. I wouldn't attempt to search two, and the missing third man was the *unk-unk*, the unknown unknown.

I felt like a one-armed man hanging wallpaper. On a ceiling.

The best way to incapacitate a man is to make him sit cross-legged and lean back on his hands. He can't move quickly that way. But I needed to control their weapons first. "Moffett, use your left hand, fingertips only, and remove your pistol."

He glared at me but didn't move. He shifted his weight onto the balls of his feet. He flexed the fingers of both hands. He took a deep breath.

Before he could leap, I shot his kneecap. The sound was earsplitting in the enclosed space. He crumpled to the floor, screaming. The acrid gunpowder stench filled the air. Or was it the smell of fear?

Scarface made a small step.

I centered the other pistol on his stomach. "Teddy, the next move you make will be your last. You're a lot bigger target than a kneecap."

To my right, the green door opened a few inches. Fortunately, the hinges were on the side toward me. Whoever stood behind the door saw only the unoccupied back of the room with the empty table and chairs. I hoped it was Bones, and he was alone back there. Better for me if he stayed in that room for a while. It's hard enough to keep two men covered; I didn't want to try for three, or, God forbid, more. I ignored the third man's presence for now.

Neither Scarface nor Moffett noticed the door move, but they knew Bones was lurking back there anyway.

I pivoted to Moffett. "Don't make me tell you again."

He grunted and hauled a revolver from his belt holster, grimacing with pain.

"Slide it over here."

He gasped and pushed it a few feet. Not far enough. If I moved to kick the gun away, I would need to turn my back to that green door, so I let it go. With Moffett somewhat incapacitated, I couldn't ask him to sit cross-legged.

"I'm bleeding bad here, McCrary," Moffett groaned. "Call 9-1-1."

"You call them, Moffett. You have a phone."

He glared at me. He figured I would holster one gun and look at my phone to dial, then Scarface could make a move, or he could holler for Bones to charge in from the back room. I didn't take the bait.

The purple door on the front wall was padlocked. That must be where they had stashed Doraleen. This deadlock between me and at least two armed men was as volatile as a flask of nitroglycerine. It could blow up at any second. It was safer to get Doraleen out of the building and away from all these guns. She could wait for the cops in the parking lot. The padlock required a key to open.

"Who has the key to that lock?"

No one spoke.

I aimed at Scarface's knee. "Who has the padlock key?"

"I do," he said.

"Use your left hand, fingertips only, and remove your pistol."

He did.

"Slide it over here."

He slid it a couple feet.

I sidestepped to the gun and kicked it to the back of the room, behind a folding table and chairs near the rear wall.

"Sit cross-legged facing that wall over there."

He did.

"Move slowly, and show me the padlock key."

"I cannot reach the key when I am sitting down. It is in the pocket of my pants."

"Lie flat on your back and get it from your pocket."

He laid on his back, stuck his left hand in his pocket, and pulled out a key.

"Stay on your back. Toss the key over here."

The key tumbled and clinked and stopped near my feet.

I needed one hand free to unlock the padlock and that task would require me to glance away from the two gangsters for an instant. Not a good plan. I changed my mind.

"Get up, Teddy. Unlock the door yourself."

I backed further out of reach while Teddy jacked himself to his feet.

He picked up the key and moved to the purple door. He unlocked the padlock, removed it from the hasp, and opened the door. "Mrs. Rice, you may come out."

"Wait, Doraleen—" I was too late.

She stepped through the door. Scarface grabbed her around the waist and held a knife to her throat. "Drop the guns, McCrary. I have nothing to lose."

Chapter 72

IF EVER THERE WERE A *VERY-OH-SHIT!* MOMENT, THIS WAS IT. I had no one to blame but myself. If I'd thought the process through, I would have made Scarface leave the opened padlock hanging in the hasp. I should have forced him to step away from the door and resume his cross-legged position. I could have warned Doraleen not to come out until I made the situation more secure. *Shoulda, woulda, coulda.*

Didn't.

It was too late. Ngombo held a razor-sharp knife tight against Doraleen's throat. Must be the same one he mutilated Race Car with. I felt stupid again. I hadn't searched him for the knife. I set both guns down and stepped back.

"Step back further, all the way to the wall behind you."

I did.

"Good work, Teddy," said Moffett. "Kick my pistol over to me."

Scarface ignored him and moved over to where my Glocks lay forlornly. Suddenly, he shoved Doraleen straight toward me and scooped up a Glock in his left hand. He pointed my own pistol at my head while he stored his knife somewhere up his left sleeve. His gaze remained riveted on me while he stuck the other Glock in his belt. He switched my pistol to his right hand and gestured with it. "Mrs. Rice, please go sit at the table."

Doraleen cut her eyes in my direction.

I nodded. "Sit in the chair on the right."

She moved across the room and sat where I needed her to sit.

"Teddy," said Moffett. "Hand me my pistol and help me to my feet."

Scarface ignored him again. "Where is the other half of the money, McCrary?"

I'd never witnessed a palace revolution, but one had happened under my nose.

"In my office," I replied.

"Where is your office?"

"Teddy," Moffett said in a tight voice. "I said hand me my pistol."

Scarface spun to Moffett and shot his other kneecap. "Be quiet, Moffett." The gunpowder smell filled the air again. He twisted back to me. "As I said before I was so rudely interrupted, where is your office?"

Scarface called his former boss Moffett instead of Monster. The king is dead. Long live the king.

"My office is at 3300 North Bayfront Boulevard."

"I know where that is," Scarface said. "None of this was my idea, McCrary. I am a warrior; I do not attack innocent women. Throughout this unfortunate affair, I have treated Mrs. Rice with courtesy and respect. She will confirm that."

I smiled at him. "I thank you for that."

"I never killed anybody, at least not in the United States. I do not wish to start now."

"I don't blame you. There's no statute of limitations for murder." There isn't one for kidnapping either, but I didn't tell him that.

"I will no longer work for Moffett, but I must have something to show for my involvement in this unfortunate and misguided, uh, escapade."

"I understand." Good old agreeable McCrary, especially with the man who was pointing my own gun at my head.

Scarface considered that a moment. "You offered to trade Mrs. Rice for the other half of the money."

"It's $112,500 in used fifty-dollar bills."

"I am willing to make that trade. How do you suggest we go about it?"

Bones opened the green door behind me. "What's going on out here? I heard gunshots."

Bones must have heard my conversation with Scarface. I expected him to burst through that door with his gun drawn the instant I shouted at Doraleen to wait. He must have heard Scarface tell me to drop my guns, yet he remained hidden. Why did Bones wait so long to show? Maybe he'd waited to see who won. Or maybe he was a coward.

Scarface jerked my other Glock from his belt and stepped back where he could cover us both. "I am in charge, Bones. Stand beside Moffett. With your left hand, fingertips only, remove your pistol."

Scarface learned fast.

"Kick it over to the wall back there, then sit down cross-legged with your back to me."

A real fast learner. Now two guns laid on the floor behind the table.

"How do you suggest we make the exchange?" he asked.

"That's a problem, Teddy. It's not practicable." I made a small step toward the green door Bones had hidden behind.

"Practicable? I do not know this word."

"Practicable. It means 'capable of being accomplished' or simply 'doable.' Getting the money to you isn't doable, Teddy." I ooched another step. "I can't get you the money in a way that will satisfy you. For example, suppose I gave you my word, would you trust me to leave and return with the money?"

"No, I would not. You would return with reinforcements." His shoulders drooped a little.

"That's exactly what I would do." One more step. "Suppose I gave you the keys to my office and the combination to my safe. Would you leave us here to get the money by yourself?"

"No, I would not. I would not know you gave me the right combination. Also, you would call the FBI after I left you alone."

"And you couldn't kill me for the same reason: The combination might be wrong." I didn't want Scarface to forget that he needed me alive.

"It is not... practicable?" he said.

"That's the correct use of the word, for all the good it will do you. And these guys..." I pointed at Bones and Moffett while

I moved another step. "…would you trust them to get the money while you held both Doraleen and me hostage?"

"No. They would not come back for me. They would… abandon me, no? Abandon is the word?"

"Abandon you, yes."

"It is not practicable." He slumped a little more.

"You burned that bridge when you shot Moffett. Do I smell coffee?" I curved toward the door and ooched another step. "Bones, did you make coffee in there? Is that a kitchen for the girls you keep downstairs?"

Scarface raised the Glock. "Stay where you are, McCrary." His body language became tense, like a deer surprised in the forest.

I stopped, but I had moved six feet closer to the table while we talked. I winked my right eye at Doraleen, the one Scarface couldn't see from his angle. "Doraleen, you should go into the kitchen. We could use a little coffee." I pivoted to Scarface. "Would you like coffee, Teddy?"

Doraleen rose from the table. Her chair grated across the linoleum floor.

Scarface waved a Glock in her direction. "Stay where you are, Mrs. Rice." The faint sweat stench oozed from him. Small perspiration beads covered his forehead. His scars glistened in the fluorescent lights.

I made another step. "You're all alone, Teddy. Your best bet is to walk out of here before the FBI arrives." I pointed at the door and moved another few inches. "You have a chance to escape. Don't waste time. The FBI raided the Orange Peel. They're on their way here. Run while you can."

I motioned to Bones. "Toss him the keys to the Caravan."

Bones held out the key fob.

Scarface's pupils dilated. His breath came quicker. He was panicking. "Bones said no one knows this place except Pete the bookkeeper."

Pete the bookkeeper? Maybe the nice catholic single father was not what he appeared.

Scarface was panicking. It was time to turn up the heat. "Of course, the FBI knows about this place. We all know. How do you think I knew to come here? Every cop in the whole world knows." I looked sideways at Doraleen and twitched my chin toward the kitchen.

She nodded.

I pointed at Scarface. "You'd better run while you can, Teddy." I made a final step and stood by the green door.

"Stop." He fired a shot through the door. "The next one I shoot between your eyes. I will not leave without that money. If you will not help me, we will all die." He waved both Glocks around the room. "I am a warrior. I am not afraid to die."

We locked gazes. No one spoke.

The tension grew.

Then all hell broke loose.

Chapter 73

THE BURGLAR ALARM SOUNDED LIKE THE HOUNDS OF HADES were loose in the room.

I jerked the green door open, grabbed Doraleen's arm, and shoved her inside. "Hide behind something and lay on the floor," I shouted after her.

I slammed the door behind her. A slug slammed my vest in the back, cracked a rib, and knocked me off my feet. The gunshot noise was lost in the raucous klaxon of the alarm system. I scrambled behind the table, knocking aside the folding chairs. I scrambled for a gun with my right hand and overturned the table with my left. The tabletop had less chance of stopping a bullet than a car stalled on railroad tracks had of stopping a speeding locomotive, but at least, it made me harder to target.

A bullet smashed a hole in the table top next to my ear. Wood splinters and Formica chips peppered my head and neck. Another shot crashed against my vest beside my heart and more splinters flew. I felt another rib crack. The siren made it hard to concentrate, but I had expected the caterwauling and Scarface had not.

Tank and Al burst through the open door as I leapt from behind the table. I rolled toward the far wall, wincing from the broken ribs, and rapid-fired at Scarface. Five of the six shells missed him. The sixth hit his right shoulder and spun him around while I slid to a stop against the far wall. He fell, his body jerking when Tank's and Al's bullets found their marks.

Bones dived for Moffett's gun and swung it toward Tank and Al, squeezing off shots. All four of us fired as fast as we could. Gunfire echoed off the walls like rolling thunder. Concrete chips flew from the wall behind Bones as Tank and Al fired at him chaotically. Bones jerked when someone's bullet slashed through him. Somebody's bullet hit the alarm box and the siren and klaxon stopped. My shots blasted holes in the wall and doors at the front until my gun clicked empty. Bones's slugs punched holes in the wall behind Tank and Al.

Bones fell across Scarface's body.

Moffett held his one good hand in the air. The other arm had caught a stray bullet. "Don't shoot. Don't shoot," he shouted.

The room fell silent except for the ringing in my ears. The burnt gunpowder stink stung my nose. I felt myself sneeze, but I couldn't hear it with my damaged hearing. I hoped it would come back in a few minutes—or hours.

A phone rang, muffled. It was hard to pinpoint it when it sounded like I was listening through a pillow over each ears. I narrowed it down to Bones. I found a phone in his jacket. *Tuscan Carriage Lights* was the caller. I accepted the call. "There is an intrusion. There is an intrusion. There is—" I disconnected.

I could breathe again. I picked up the other gun from the floor. It's good to have a spare.

"Where's Momma?" shouted Al.

I pointed at the green door. "She's hiding in the kitchen."

Al pointed a Glock at Moffett. "I told you I'd kill you if you went after my mother."

Moffett raise his good hand and tried to lift his wounded hand too. "She's safe, Al. She's safe. I didn't hurt her. I wouldn't ever hurt a woman."

Al pointed the pistol. "Squeeze, don't pull." He shot Moffett once, then again, and again. Then the Glock clicked empty.

I barely heard the shots, even though my hearing was recovering.

Blood ran down Al's neck. He didn't realize he was wounded. Maybe it wasn't as bad as it looked.

Al stumbled two steps toward the green door. He collapsed in a heap, and Tank rushed to his side. Maybe Al's wound *was* as bad as it looked.

This building remained a danger zone until every room on both floors was cleared. Where were the gang members who drove the other two cars parked out front? Were they hidden behind one of the doors in the back wall? Maybe they went to dinner in a third car and might return any second. This wasn't over.

I hurried to Bones's body and stuck his gun in my pocket. I yanked my Glocks from Scarface's hands. I once saw a dead man come to life in Iraq and shoot at me. I popped out the expended magazines, replaced them with full ones from my pocket, and returned one to my shoulder holster.

I had a man down. "Tank?" I asked.

He pressed his hands to the side of Al's neck. "I don't know how bad it is."

"I'll call 9-1-1." In the distance, sirens screamed closer, but the PCPD might not have brought an ambulance. I called 9-1-1 and requested ambulances for four persons. It was possible Scarface, Moffett, and Bones were alive, but not likely.

I couldn't do anything for Al that Tank wasn't doing already. I drew a Glock and cleared the rooms behind the fuchsia and Prussian blue doors. They were restrooms and unoccupied. I removed the Glock from Al's side and handed it to Tank. "Al doesn't have a concealed weapons permit. You did all the shooting, right?"

"Right."

"PCPD," a shout came through the stairway door.

"We're clear up here," I shouted back. "All clear. Three friendlies, make that four, and three hostiles down." I holstered my Glock again and raised my hands in the air. My cracked ribs grated against each other. With the adrenal wearing off, the ribs hurt like hell.

Chapter 74

KELLY CONTRERAS CAME THROUGH THE DOOR FIRST, her police-issue Glock drawn. Her glance encompassed the whole tableau in seconds. She saw me and lowered her weapon.

"Those three over there are the bad guys," I said. "I called for four ambulances. That's Al Rice lying there. Tank you've met. Doraleen Rice is behind the green door."

Bigs came through the door behind Kelly. Both cops holstered their guns. Three more uniforms squeezed into the room.

I opened the green door. "Doraleen, it's safe to come out. Al's been shot."

"Oh my God." She rushed to her son's side. "Al, honey." She knelt and grabbed his hand. Tears ran down her cheeks.

First Snoop and now Al. At least Doraleen was safe.

TANK AND I ARRIVED AT CEDARS OF LEBANON HOSPITAL at the same time. At one in the morning, it was easy to find a parking spot. I parked my minivan beside his Mercedes and hoped the German car didn't feel insulted. We walked inside together. I walked very gingerly to keep my ribs from grating together. I hadn't even removed my vest; I couldn't move my arms through the pain.

My heart did a little flutter when I walked through the emergency room doors. I'd ridden to this same hospital in the ambulance with Snoop the previous Wednesday afternoon. Now it was early Sunday. Last time I asked, Snoop was still unconscious. Al could be in ICU or surgery. Whatever they did, it would take hours. I left Tank with Doraleen and went to check on Snoop.

I stopped at the nurses' station near Snoop's hospital room. At least the doctors had moved him out of intensive care. That was good, right?

"I'm Chuck McCrary. I'm Raymond Snopolski's friend. I know it's late, but I brought a friend into the ER and I wanted to ask about Snoop while the doctors help my other friend. Has there been any change?"

The nurse gawked at me wearing the armored vest.

"I have some broken ribs," I explained. "I couldn't remove it without grating on my ribs."

"Are you a police officer?"

"Private investigator."

"You should go to the ER," she said.

"I will, but first I want to know about Snoop."

She read her computer screen. "Are you Carlos McCrary?"

"Yes, ma'am."

"Good. You're on his list of people it's okay to discuss his condition with. His wife is asleep in a chair in his room. Snoop regained consciousness last night at eight o'clock." She smiled at me. "We expect him to make a full recovery."

I'd been holding my breath for the last four days. My fatigue lifted, even the ringing in my ears stopped. "Wow, what a relief. If you were on this side of the counter, I'd hug you, except my ribs are cracked."

She appraised my disheveled appearance with amusement. "That won't be necessary, Mr. McCrary." She grinned. "Is there anything *else* I can do for you?"

I thanked her and returned to the ER. I walked gingerly to the admissions desk. Now that the adrenaline was leaving my bloodstream, I was sore as hell. They X-rayed me, taped my ribs, and gave me a purple scrub top to replace my messy shirt. A half-hour later I returned to the ER waiting area to reassure Tank and Doraleen that I was okay.

Doraleen stood when I came over. "I'm sorry, Chuck. You've spent a lot of time in this hospital because of me. And now you really should be a patient too."

"Not at all, Doraleen. This is Monster Moffett's fault, not yours." I didn't add *and not Al's* because that wasn't true. It damned sure was Al's fault, but Doraleen didn't need me to remind her of that. Snoop and I both knew the risks of our chosen profession. "I have good news. Snoop regained consciousness last night and is expected to make a full recovery."

"God answered my prayers. *Those* prayers," Doraleen amended. She grabbed Tank's hand. "Let's keep praying."

A woman in green surgical scrubs came through the door. "Mrs. Rice?" She shook hands. "I'm Doctor Donoghue. I have good news. Alfred will be fine. The wound was not as bad as we first thought. We'll keep him twenty-four hours for observation. Oh, wait, it's the middle of the night, isn't it? We'll keep him thirty-six hours, then release him."

"Now God has answered all my prayers." Doraleen hugged the doctor, then Tank, then me. I cried out. We'd both forgotten about my cracked ribs.

Chapter 75

WE HAD A TABLE AT BARNEY'S, a local bar and restaurant near the North Shore Precinct frequented by cops and former cops like Snoop and me. Tank was picking up the tab for the party to celebrate Doraleen's rescue.

Doraleen had sent her regrets. She said she was an innocent bystander and she would be in the way at the party. "Besides," she told me, "at my age, I'm in bed at 10:30 every night. I don't want to be a party pooper. Have a glass of sherry in my honor."

I lifted the glass of sherry like I'd promised. The ribs hardly bothered me. "To Doraleen's rescue."

I took a reluctant sip of sherry as we toasted. My duty was done. "Anybody want the rest of this sherry?" There were no takers. I set it aside and ordered a Port City Amber. I wished Snoop and Janet could have been here, but he was recuperating at home and Janet wouldn't leave his side. Bigs begged off because his son had a school concert. My artist girlfriend, Miyo, was at a gallery show in New York City. Tank's secretary tried alternate dates for everyone, but someone always had a conflict. That's life.

Gene Lopez lifted his mug. "You sure it's okay for a fed to come to a cop bar?"

Kelly Contreras said, "I got you a guest pass, Gene. I told Barney you were a civilian." She leaned against Tank's massive shoulder. "Civilians are always welcome." From the look she gave Tank, I could assume she was over any alleged crush she had on me. It would be a long time before Tank called that forward for the Port City Flames. My old friend Lieutenant Jorge

Castellano had told me Kelly had the hots for me ever since I'd been on the job. I'd doubted it, although she was quite a flirt.

Al put his arm around Janice Jackson a/k/a Jasmine a/k/a Jennifer a/k/a God-knows-who-else. The cast was off his hand and the wound on his neck was covered by a small bandage.

"Janice," I said, "you saw Gene Lopez when the FBI raided the Orange Peel, but I doubt you were formally introduced. May I present Eugenio Lopez, Special Agent in Charge of the Port City FBI office."

She stretched her hand across the round table. Gene stood to shake it. They exchanged hellos. "Gene, I want to thank you for getting me and the other girls out of that club. I didn't mind the dancing, but turning tricks with the customers... that was a nightmare. Then Monster Moffett got the hots for me, and that was even worse."

"It's called 'human trafficking' and it's the politically correct term for slavery," Gene said. "Leonard Satin and Bernard Prevossi both pled guilty to that and a host of other crimes ranging from kidnapping to loan sharking to money laundering. Just doing my job."

Typical Gene, he didn't toss any credit my way or Tank's way. Oh, well, I might have one or two faults myself.

"I never knew his name was Bernard," Janice said. "To me, he was Pete the bookkeeper."

"He was the brains behind the whole operation," I explained, "He owned strip clubs staffed with illegal Asian women who thought they were coming to America to work as nannies. Then he forced them into prostitution. He also owned gay bars in several states where he forced the servers to turn tricks with the customers."

She faced Al. "And I especially owe you. Monster Moffett would do something real bad to you if he knew about our former relationship. That's why I pretended not to know you. I felt terrible about it, but I didn't want to get you in trouble with Monster. You know what a... a... Monster he is."

"Was," I corrected.

"It was impossible for me to get in any more trouble than I already was with Monster." He sipped his club soda. Al was on the wagon, but we all watched him like a hawk.

"But I didn't know that, Al," Janice said. "It felt awful to pretend I didn't know you."

Al hugged her. "You can make it up to me later."

Tank lifted his glass. "And I want to lift a glass to Chuck McCrary. A good friend who showed me that it's not okay to stand by when something bad happens to someone else. To our own Sir Galahad." He grinned at me.

I hoped I wasn't blushing.

The end

Enjoy this book?
You can make a difference

REVIEWS ARE THE MOST POWERFUL TOOLS an independent author like me has to get attention for my books. Much as I'd like to, I don't have the financial muscle of a New York publisher. I can't take out full-page ads in the newspaper or put posters on the subway or bus. (At least not yet, anyway!)

Instead, I have something more powerful and effective than that—something those publishers would kill to get their hands on: I have a committed and loyal bunch of readers.

Honest reviews of my books help bring them to the attention of other readers.

If you enjoyed this story, I would be very grateful if you would spend just two minutes to go to www.amazon.com and www.goodreads.com and write a review (it can be as short as you like) on the book's page.

Your entertainment is the reason I write. I would love to hear from you now that you've finished reading my story. Email me at Dallas@DallasGorham.com. Tell me how you liked my story and what you'd like to see Chuck McCrary do next. Or tell me anything else on your mind.

All the best,

Dallas

CARLOS McCRARY
WILL RETURN

AS A WRITER, I LOVE TO BUILD RELATIONSHIPS WITH MY READERS. I occasionally send newsletters with details on new releases, special offers, and other bits of news relating to my mystery/thriller novels.

If you sign up on my VIP Readers Group email list, I'll send you advanced notice of my new releases (no spam!). Almost always discounted! Also, I'll send you opportunities to WIN cool prizes in special giveaways. Such as free books written by me or by other mystery/thriller authors I recommend and more!

You can get the advanced notices, and access to the special giveaways FOR FREE by signing up at:

www.DallasGorham.com

Also by Dallas Gorham

I'm No Hero

A special forces suspense thriller short story introducing Carlos McCrary when he was a sergeant in the U.S. Special Forces in Afghanistan. Available (in electronic editions only) at all major internet retailers.

ON A CLEAR NIGHT IN JUNE 2006, Special Forces Operational Detachment Alpha 777, the Triple Seven, gets their mission: Free an Afghan mountain village from a ruthless Taliban blockade that is starving the people to death. The village's crime? They educated girls in the village school.

A courageous young boy from the village sneaks through the hot summer night to escape the Taliban blockade. He runs ten miles barefooted to get help, arriving at an Afghan National Army garrison with bloody feet. He seeks the help of Afghan Major Ibrahim Malik. But Malik knows that his ANA small force is no match for the well-armed Taliban terrorists. Malik and the boy come to the Green Berets of the Triple Seven for help.

The Taliban have a larger force, heavily armed with Kalashnikov AK-47s and rocket-propelled grenades. The Americans must rely on their equipment, their training, and themselves.

This is a story of Sergeant Carlos "Chuck" McCrary, a Mexican-American Green Beret, and his team of soldiers who risk their lives to save two thousand Afghan townspeople they have never even met. Chuck and his fellow Special Forces soldiers live the motto: "We own the night." They set off in the darkness to defeat the Taliban and break the blockade. But when the soldiers of the Triple Seven don their night vision goggles and show up in the dark hours to liberate the village, they are surprised and outnumbered by an ambush of heavily-armed Taliban terrorists.

The soldiers of Team Triple Seven must fight for their lives, or the villagers won't be the only ones the Taliban wipe out.

Six Murders Too Many

Book 1 of the Carlos McCrary, Private Investigator, Mystery Thriller series, available in electronic and print editions on Amazon.com. Free to Kindle Unlimited members.

The plan was perfect;
all it took was two simple murders...

Then an over-zealous assassin exterminated an extra victim and things got out of hand.

On his first big case as a newly-minted private investigator, Carlos "Chuck" McCrary must untangle a web of fraud, arson, adultery and murder before he becomes its next victim.

A Billionaire's Estate Is Up For Grabs

Ike Simonetti and his model-slim wife, Lorraine, tell Chuck that Ike's stepmother is trying to steal $400 million from Ike's father's estate. But is Ike Simonetti the only surviving heir of billionaire real estate developer Sam Simonetti? Or is there another contender for the fortune—a baby girl born to the dead billionaire's hot young trophy wife six months after Sam's death? The investigation takes Chuck from the sun-splashed beaches of South Florida to the burned-out Cleveland home of two dead daughters.

The Stakes Go Way Up

When mob hitmen ambush Chuck, the case becomes a matter of life and death. To save his own life and that of the supposed infant heiress, Chuck must discover if one of the billionaire's surviving family members is the real puppet master behind the murders.

Double Fake, Double Murder

Book 2 of the Carlos McCrary, Private Investigator, Mystery Thriller series, available in electronic and print editions on Amazon.com. Free to Kindle Unlimited members.

MOB BOSS GARRISON FRANCO IS GUNNED DOWN IN THE STREET, and the police think they know who did it—Jorge Castellano, one of their own homicide detectives whose wife had been threatened by Franco. Castellano claims he's been framed and pleads with private investigator Chuck McCrary to find the real killer.

Chuck discovers a mysterious teenager who ran away from an abusive foster home who may have witnessed the murder. But the boy doesn't trust anyone and won't tell Chuck what he saw. Chuck must gain the boy's trust before he can solve the crime.

Chuck's prime suspect is Ted Rayburn, a disgraced, former police detective and convicted blackmailer, now out of jail and plying his trade again. With shameful secrets and millions of dollars at stake, three of Rayburn's super rich victims try to hire Chuck to kill Rayburn. He refuses, but days later Rayburn is found shot to death with Chuck's gun. Chuck is arrested for murder.

Now Chuck must not only find out who killed Franco and framed his friend Castellano for the murder, but must solve the new murder or face a lifetime in prison himself.

Chuck must deal with millionaires and billionaires on the one hand and hoodlums and drug dealers on the other.

DALLAS GORHAM SENDS READERS ON A WHITE-KNUCKLE RIDE from the crime-filled streets of a South Florida ghetto to the waterfront mansions and high-rise condos of mega-millionaires in pursuit of the mysterious and elusive killer.

Quarterback Trap

Book 3 of the Carlos McCrary, Private Investigator, Mystery Thriller series, available in electronic and print editions on Amazon.com. Free to Kindle Unlimited members.

PORT CITY IS EXCITED TO BE HOSTING THE NEW YORK JETS and the Dallas Cowboys in the first Super Bowl in its fabulous, new billion-dollar stadium. Chuck McCrary's old friend from high-school football, Bob Martinez, is starting quarterback for the Jets.

One week before the game, Martinez's supermodel fiancée, Graciela, disappears in the middle of the night from the Super Bowl headquarters hotel. Martinez hires Chuck to find her, but he won't let Chuck involve the police.

That same day the odds on the Super Bowl game change dramatically when someone bets a hundred million dollars that the Cowboys will beat the point spread. Is it Vicente Vidali, the New Jersey casino owner and mob boss? Did he kidnap Graciela?

Chuck discovers that Graciela has a secret that places her life in danger, regardless of the outcome of the game. Was she really kidnapped, or did she run away from her own secret life? Bob Martinez also has a dangerous secret that threatens to destroy his multi-million-dollar career in the NFL.

Chuck's search for the missing supermodel takes him from the dangerous streets and drug dealers of a South Florida ghetto to the waterfront high-rises and private island mansions of billionaires, movie stars, and crime moguls.

QUARTERBACK TRAP SLICES LIKE A SCALPEL through the hidden world of organized crime, mega-million-dollar scams, and the hidden secrets of an outwardly glamorous world where careers–and lives–can be lost in a heartbeat.

Dangerous Friends

Book 4 of the Carlos McCrary, Private Investigator, Mystery Thriller series, available in electronic and print editions on Amazon.com. Free to Kindle Unlimited members.

A FAST-PACED ACTION THRILLER ABOUT ECOTERRORISM, political corruption, and felony murder.

Chuck McCrary is a wisecracking former Green Beret turned private investigator with a special genius for helping people in trouble—especially if they can pay him for his efforts.

Michelle Babcock, the granddaughter of South Florida's legendary restaurateur and Chuck's friend, Hank Hickham, has disappeared. She wakes Chuck with a 4:30 a.m. phone call, desperate for help. James Ponder, her drug addicted boyfriend, has involved her in a double murder that could put her in prison for life unless Chuck can find her a way out.

Michelle only expected free tutoring in college chemistry when she slept with James Ponder, a graduate student obsessed with global warming protests, who has a talent for ecoterrorism. Instead, she is sucked into an unhealthy circle of friendships surrounding an amoral professor whose secret agenda has yielded him millions of dollars with more loot to come. Michelle is swept up in a nightmare of political corruption, terrorism, and mega-million-dollar crimes.

Chuck uncovers a conspiracy involving arson, murder, and the Chicago mob. A mysterious millionaire has masterminded a string of mega-million-dollar stock market scams that reach back for five years. The mastermind intends to cut his losses by murdering anyone who can lead the cops back to him. That includes Michelle, Chuck, and the conscienceless professor, who becomes Chuck's unwilling ally.

ONE REASON PEOPLE KEEP TURNING PAGES in *Dangerous Friends* is to watch the gripping character of Chuck McCrary. The skill with which he handles clients, police detectives, mob assassins, and FBI agents—all while controlling the outcomes of the case—is as remarkable as the clues he uncovers. Chuck seeks justice without regard for the legalities involved and tries to leave the world just a little better than he found it.

McCrary's Justice

Book 6 of the Carlos McCrary, Private Investigator, Mystery Thriller series, available in electronic and print editions on Amazon.com. Free to Kindle Unlimited members.

NEBRASKA FARMER WILBUR JENKINS receives three cryptic text messages from his missing daughter, Liz, claiming that she is a sex slave in sun-splashed Port City, Florida. Jenkins grabs the next plane and begs the Port City cops to find his daughter. But Liz left home of her own free will, and the texts came from the cellphone of Antonio Crucero, a corrupt diplomat from a Caribbean tropical paradise. Crucero's diplomatic immunity protects him from U.S. law, and he refuses to cooperate.

Police detective Jorge Castellano sends the distraught father to Carlos "Chuck" McCrary.

McCrary is a wisecracking private investigator with a special genius for helping people in trouble. McCrary left the Port City Police so he could do the right thing without worrying about trivialities like *due process* and *probable cause*.

McCrary uncovers a cesspool of sex trafficking and drug smuggling that stretches from South Florida to Switzerland to the Caribbean. And Crucero has his pudgy fingers all over the operation.

Crucero's diplomatic status protects him from the reach of U.S. law, but it won't protect him from Carlos McCrary. McCrary has his own brand of justice and sets out to destroy Crucero any way he can—diplomatic immunity be damned.

FROM SOUTH FLORIDA'S GOLDEN BEACHES to a Caribbean paradise, from trendy Coconut Grove to the perilous Florida Everglades, *McCrary's Justice* slashes like a machete through a treacherous jungle of sexual predators, drug cartels, and new and fearsome enemies.

COMBINING AN INTRICATE PUZZLE OF A PLOT AND AN EXCITING PURSUIT OF JUSTICE, Dallas Gorham puts Carlos McCrary through his paces and sends readers on a white-knuckle ride that circles back to McCrary's own home, where he must confront the worst nightmare he could imagine.

Yesterday's Trouble

Book 7 of the Carlos McCrary, Private Investigator, Mystery Thriller series, available in electronic and print editions on Amazon.com. Free to Kindle Unlimited members.

YESTERDAY IS DEAD AND GONE. OR IS IT? For Cleo Hennessey, her past threatens to destroy her future.

A young, naïve country singer, Cleo just wants to make music for her thousands of adoring, newfound fans. NBA superstar Marvelous LeMarvis Jones, Cleo's fiancé, bankrolls her first concert tour. Then an unbalanced cyber-stalker takes issue with the couple's interracial relationship.

Cleo won't take the threats seriously, but LeMarvis hires Private Investigator Carlos McCrary to provide security for Cleo's *Summer Fun Concert Tour*. At the tour's first stop, a backup singer with a dangerous past is murdered onstage. Was the bullet meant for Cleo?

Despite Carlos's urging, Cleo refuses to cancel the tour, even as more bodies pile up on the tour's journey across Florida. In Jacksonville, the stakes are raised when the killer tires of Carlos interfering with his quest to do God's work.

What is Cleo hiding? Has the yesterday she thought she'd escaped finally found her?

With the killer outsmarting Carlos and the cops at every turn, has Carlos finally met his match? Will he wind up taking a knife to a gunfight?

Acknowledgments

MY THANKS TO MY EDITOR MARSHA BUTLER. She makes me a better writer. Her website is

ButlerInk.com.

My thanks also to my cover designer Michael Butler of Michael by Design. I enjoy working with him. His website is

MichaelByDesign.com.

About the author

DALLAS GORHAM IS A SIXTH-GENERATION TEXAN and a proud Texas Longhorn, having earned a BBA at the University of Texas. He graduated in the top three-quarters of his class, maybe.

Dallas (the writer) and his wife moved to Florida years ago to escape Dallas (the city) winters (*Brrr.* Way too cold) and summers (*Whew.* Way too hot). They live in Florida in a waterfront home where they watch the sunset over the lake most days and where he has followed his lifelong love of reading mysteries and thrillers into writing them in his home office. He is a member of Mystery Writers of America and the Florida Writers.

Dallas is frequent (but bad) golfer, playing about once a week because that is all the abuse he can stand. One of his goals in life is to find more golf balls than he loses. He also is an accomplished liar (is this true?).

Dallas is married to his one-and-only wife who treats him far better than he deserves. They have two grown sons whom they are inordinately proud of. They also have seven of the smartest, most handsome, and most beautiful grandchildren in the known universe. Dallas and his wife spend *waaaay* too much money on their love of travel. They have visited all 50 states and over 90 foreign countries, the most recent of which were Indonesia and Malaysia, where their cruise ship stopped at Bali and Kuala Lumpur.

Dallas writes a blog at DallasGorham.com/blog. It's sometimes funny, but not nearly as funny as he thinks. His website, DallasGorham.com, has more information about his books, including the characters, which are recommended for anyone who enjoys action and suspense with a touch of humor and plenty of twists and turns. If you have too much time on your hands, you can follow him on Twitter at Twitter.com/DallasGorham or Facebook by going to Facebook.com and searching for "Dallas Gorham Books."

His Amazon Author Page is
Amazon.com/Dallas-Gorham/e/B00J4LISCS

A preview of

McCrary's Justice

Chapter 1

LIZ LAY STILL AS A CORPSE IN THE DIM LIGHT, watching the fat man's chest rise and fall. Was he asleep?

Earlier, the springs had screeched in protest, the bed bouncing like a dinghy in a hurricane. The clock on her dresser had flipped over to *1:11*, while he hammered away inside her and grunted like a pig.

The massive arm sprawled across her felt like a fallen tree trunk. The thick hair on his forearm chafed her naked skin like steel wool.

Her chest felt as though a steel band had tightened around it. She fought back the tears, trying to overcome her feeling of helplessness. Her clothes were locked away in a closet. She never needed them except to dress for meals. The remainder of the time, she spent imprisoned in her room, languishing naked on the filthy bed, waiting for the next john. Day after day, night after night, men violated her. She wasn't a prostitute; she was a sex slave. She wiped away an escaped teardrop and swore she wouldn't be helpless much longer. Soon, very soon, she'd be free... or dead.

Tommy had told her to treat the fat man right. This john was an ambassador from a Latin American country, the Republic of San Something-or-other. But who knew? Tommy lied just for fun.

She'd trembled when Tommy told her the ambassador had returned and the creep asked for her. For an entire night. Again.

"Show him another good time, Liz," Tommy said, squeezing her breast hard enough to hurt. One more reason to hate Tommy.

She'd almost protested, then remembered the fat man's phone and kept quiet. Tommy kept his girls away from cellphones, but when the ambassador visited, Tommy let him keep his. He was a big man in more than waistline. She wanted that phone. With a phone, she had a chance. If Tommy caught her, he'd make the other girls watch while he killed her. And she wouldn't die quickly. She shuddered when she remembered Evelyn. Free or dead.

Tommy had kidnapped six women, addicted them to drugs, and rented them out for sex. He called them *Tommy's Angels*. Now there were five. Three weeks ago, they'd watched Evelyn die by Tommy's order. "Angels, this is what we do if you try to escape." He'd taunted them while he and three gang members raped and strangled her. "Don't make the same mistake Evelyn did."

Ironically, Evelyn's gruesome death had rekindled Liz's burning desire for freedom—a desire that drugs and depravity had dulled to the brink of extinction. Since Evelyn's murder, Liz only pretended to swallow the pills Tommy gave her every day. When he turned away, she spat them out and hid them under her mattress. If all else failed, she'd accumulated enough pills to kill herself.

Tommy called her an angel, but she lived in hell with the devil. She'd rather die.

There was nothing good about "good times" with the fat man. He provided drugs for them both, including blue pills for him. He looked young enough not to need chemical help, but maybe he liked to last extra long. He demanded rough sex in repulsive variations for an endless two hours. The previous times the drugs kept her from realizing how disgusting he was, but when she stopped the drugs, the reality of her situation sank in. She almost wished she had swallowed the last pills instead of palming them. They would have made her pain and humiliation more bearable. The fat weirdo left her sore for days.

She shivered through the night, unable to sleep through the snores of the rancid, sweaty john. He kept the air-conditioning on high and the room was as cold as a meat locker. Still the stench of his sweat polluted the air. She stared at the ceiling in the icy room trying not to breathe the foul air. She dreaded the morning when he would awaken, take another blue pill, and rape her again. He always did.

He tipped her well, but no tip could compensate for her degradation. With no place to spend money in captivity, she stashed the tip money in a plastic bag hidden in the toilet tank. If she escaped this brothel—no, *when* she escaped—she would have money to get home. The hope of escape gave her a reason to stay alive.

After an eternity, the john's breath slowed to a regular rhythm. His lips puffed a few ragged breaths. He rolled onto his side, and his bulky arm rasped like sandpaper across her skin. The cheap mattress bounced like a bowl of Jell-O with his movement. Heavy musk from his after-shave mixed with the dirty socks smell of sweat and sex. She gagged and choked back the bile that rose from her empty stomach.

Tonight was her first chance to call for help since she'd decided to escape or die, but dare she move? What if Jabba the Hutt woke? Would he throw his disgusting body on top of hers, groping for her breasts with his slobbering mouth, trying to mount her?

She scooched a few inches away from the ambassador toward the edge of the bed. It moved ominously, but he didn't wake. He snorted once and rolled over.

She used his movement to disguise hers as she inched closer to the edge of the bed. She wiped cold sweat from her forehead, trying not to jiggle the bed. The fat man squirmed onto his back, and she moved enough to dangle one leg off the bed, feeling for the floor with her foot.

The clock on the dresser flicked over to *2:17*.

Do it before you chicken out. She shifted more weight to the foot on the floor and held her breath.

As gently as a lava flow, she slid the other foot off the bed and lowered it to the worn carpet, alert to the slightest change in his sleep. She started to sit up, but stopped mid-motion when the springs vibrated. Her heart felt as though it would burst through her chest.

His snores halted. She froze. The john wasn't breathing. *Sleep apnea.* She'd learned about it in high school. *Don't panic. He'll breathe in a few seconds.*

She felt pressure in her chest. *Damn,* she was holding her breath. Only when he snorted like a pig did Liz exhale. He resumed snoring, louder this time.

She sat upright, shifting more weight to her feet, and lifted her butt off the mattress. The springs remained quiet, and she breathed a silent prayer of thanks.

The john's clothes were draped over a chair in the corner. Sliding his phone from the holster clipped on his belt, she moved silently toward the bathroom, never taking her eyes off the sleeping john. The phone was different from the one she had owned before Tommy imprisoned her. She fumbled with it in the dark, trying to turn it on. Her hands shook so much that she dropped it. Liz froze as it clattered on the tiled floor of the bathroom. *I'm a dead woman.* No one could sleep through that noise. Breathing deeply but quietly, she looked back towards the bed. Jabba snored on.

When the ambassador had checked his messages earlier, he hadn't noticed her peering over his shoulder. Now, she pushed every button on the phone until the light from the screen cast an eerie glow in the dark bathroom. *Free or dead,* she whispered as she pushed the messaging icon.

Chapter 2

MY OFFICE PHONE RANG. "Wilbur Jenkins on line one."

"Thanks, Betty." I tapped the other button. "This is Chuck McCrary. How may I help you?"

"Are you the guy who shot that crooked cop?"

I have to list the phone number of McCrary Investigations. Who would hire a private investigator with an unlisted number? I hoped this wasn't another nut job accusing me of murder. Such is the price of fame. Or is it notoriety? Sometimes the caller is a new client. Those are my favorites.

"I prefer to accentuate the positive and say I rescued a woman whom the crooked cop had kidnapped," I answered modestly.

"So you are that guy?"

"The one and only. How can I help?"

"I'm Will Jenkins. My daughter's been kidnapped. I want you to find her."

"Have you contacted the police?" There's no point wasting someone's money to do a job the cops do for free.

"That's the first call I made. They're working the case mighty hard, but they ain't got shit, excuse my French. Lieutenant Jorge Castellano, he said to call you, and he give me your phone number. That Castellano fellow, he's the police detective that you sprung from that murder charge, ain't he?"

"He didn't tell you?"

"Maybe the lieutenant weren't too proud of that murder charge, even if he did beat the rap."

"Maybe."

"The main thing he said was you might could find my daughter."

"Can you come to my office?"

I STUCK OUT MY HAND. "I'M CARLOS McCRARY."

My visitor switched his faded John Deere hat to his huge left hand and shook with his right. "Will Jenkins. Friends call me Will."

"And I'm Chuck." I handed him a business card. Too bad it didn't have a magnifying glass logo like the search boxes on websites.

"The lieutenant, he already give me one of your cards."

Will's callused palm matched his sunburned face. With his worn blue jeans, faded cotton shirt, and scuffed work boots, he reminded me of my father. His forehead was white below his thin brown hair.

I got him coffee and led him to my conference room. "What did Lieutenant Castellano say?"

"First, you oughta read these texts my Lizzie sent me early Tuesday morning." He handed me his phone.

The first text was sent at 2:22 a.m.

Daddy, held captive in Port City FL by white man named Tommy Flannigan, five foot ten, thirty to forty years, medium build, palm tree tattoo on left forearm, pierced left ear with diamond stud. Sex slave. DO NOT CALL OR REPLY TO THIS TEXT. HE WILL KILL ME IF HE LEARNS I USED THIS PHONE. It belongs to a john. Love, Binky

I read *sex slave* and my stomach clenched like a fist. It stirred a memory of my cousin Emily. No, not a memory, a fear.

The second text was sent at 2:25 a.m.

Four other girls held too, maybe more. Sex slaves. Jill from Chicago, Tawnya from Philadelphia, Delores from Shawnee, and Morgan from Cleveland. Don't know last names or any addresses. DO NOT CALL OR REPLY TO THIS TEXT. Binky

The last one was sent at 2:30 a.m.

Held in house with three stories, 30 feet wide 80 feet deep, on busy street with two lanes traffic and parking on both sides. Sex slaves. Three gangsters. Scruffy, black, skinny, fifty. Vince, white, medium, forty. One big bald guy no name. DO NOT CALL OR REPLY TO THIS TEXT. Love, Binky.

I swallowed hard and composed myself. "What did the police say?"

"I'll get to that in a minute. First thing I got to know is, can you find her?"

"Did she leave of her own free will, or was she kidnapped?"

"She went to Disney World. Her and her friend Jennifer."

"Jennifer?"

"She and Jennifer, they been friends since they was this high." He held his palm three feet off the floor. "Jennifer lives on the farm next to ours, maybe a half-mile down the road. Jennifer's parents give her a new car for graduation and the two of them decided to drive to Disney World. I fought it, but Lizzie, she saved the money herself and she was legal age. There wasn't nothing I could do to stop her." He dropped his head. "We wasn't getting along too good, her and me, since her mom died."

Will didn't say anything else, so I prompted him. "She and Jennifer left for Disney…"

He looked at his hands in his lap. "She was so mad she wouldn't return none of my calls while she was gone. After three weeks, Jennifer come back without her."

"Where was Liz?"

Will sighed. "At Disney, Liz and Jennifer met a group of young'uns on a high school trip from Brazil. Liz, she was real taken with one boy in the group. The Brazilians was going to visit Fort Lauderdale after Disney. Liz decided to go with them. Jennifer, she drove back by herself."

"Drove back to where? Where do you live?"

"Butler County, Nebraska. I'm a farmer. Mostly I grow corn."

"If you live in Nebraska, how did you hear about my gunfight with the cop who kidnapped that woman?"

"When the lieutenant give me your card, I Googled you. Then I Googled him."

"I would've done the same thing." I wrote *Butler County. Corn.* "How long since she left?"

His eyes glistened. "A little over a year."

"Did she send you any letters, emails, anything like that?"

"Nope. Not even a postcard."

"Did she leave Jennifer a note with the boy's name or address, maybe a phone number where you could reach her?"

"Oh sure. She didn't sneak off or nothing. She gave Jennifer the boy's name and phone number. But she made Jennifer promise not to tell me what she done until she—that is, Jennifer—until she got back home to Butler County."

He pulled a handkerchief from his hip pocket and wiped his eyes. "By the time Jennifer come home, the Brazilian boy, he was back in Brazil. I called him long distance. He said the last time he seen my Lizzie was at the Miami airport when they was leaving for home."

"You hadn't heard from her before those texts?"

"Nary a word."

"Was her cellphone on your plan?"

"Yeah. When Jennifer come home, I called the sheriff in David City—that's the county seat. He tried to do a phone trace, but Lizzie's phone wasn't on the network. The phone company said the last time her phone was used was in Port City a week after them Brazilians flew home. The Brazilian boy, he wasn't involved."

His eyes were moist. "I pay for her phone every month... I know it's lost or stolen or somesuch, but I keep hoping someday she'll turn it back on. The preacher, he says a faint hope is better than no hope, and I should live with faith."

"Are these texts the only clues?"

"Yep. Can you find her?" Will cleared his throat.

"With so little to go on, it won't be easy. I'll do my best."

Will sat straighter. "Mr. McCrary, I got one of the biggest farms in Nebraska, and if my Lizzie don't come back, I got no one to leave it to and nothing to live for. Corn prices are real good; I can pay."

"I figured that. I just don't want to raise false hope."

"I understand; no guarantees." He stuck out his hand.

I shook it. "Of course I'll help. What's your daughter's name?"

"Elizabeth Marie Jenkins. Everybody calls her Liz."

I noted that. "Date of birth?"

She was nineteen. So young to be the victim of sex slavery. But any age was too young.

"Do you have a recent picture?"

He pulled two wallet-sized portraits from his shirt pocket and looked at them. "This is her high school graduation picture. I took it last year." He looked at one and handed me the other. "Keep it. I have plenty more." His eyes glistened.

The world froze for a moment. It was his daughter's picture, but, except for the hairstyle, it could have been my cousin Emily. Sun-lightened, shoulder-length hair, pale blue eyes, and a wide innocent smile that knew no fear and saw no evil anywhere in the world. She smiled just like Emily did.

I swallowed hard and blinked. "I suppose you showed these texts to Lieutenant Castellano."

He nodded. "When the first text come in, my phone whistled like they do. That sorta woke me a little. You know how you kinda hear something in your sleep, but it don't, like, *register*?"

I nodded.

"The second text, the phone whistle woke me all the way. I was reading it when the third text come in. When I read it—" His voice broke. He put his hands over his face.

I handed him a tissue.

Will wiped his eyes again. "I tell you, I prayed for strength not to call her back then and there. She felt so close... so close..."

I looked at Liz's photo again to avoid watching her father weep. How did that innocent girl see the world now, a year later?

"I held that phone another half hour, praying my Lizzie would send another text. I finally give up and I called the airline to catch the first plane to Port City. When I rented a car, I asked the clerk where the nearest police station was. That's where I met Lieutenant Castellano. That was Tuesday afternoon late."

He pulled a paper from his shirt pocket and studied it. "The lieutenant, he ran the other girls' names through the missing persons' notices. There was nothing for that Jill girl or nobody named Tawnya, but that Dolores girl, Lizzie misspelled her name. It's not D-E-L; it's D-O-L. She gotta be Dolores Cherry from Shawnee, Oklahoma. That girl Morgan, she's Morgan Putnam from Cleveland. Their parents, they reported them missing a year ago. Lieutenant Castellano, he called the police in Shawnee and Cleveland. Nobody has no leads and the girls' parents, they ain't heard from them. I promised them both I'd contact them if I found anything."

"The text mentions a man named Tommy Flannigan. Did the lieutenant find anything on him?"

"There's no Tommy Flannigan in the police records, the phone book, or nowhere else. This Tommy fellow, he must've gave my Lizzie a phony name. Over a hundred criminals named Tommy in Atlantic County fit his description. The lieutenant, he assigned two detectives to check out criminals named Tommy, but it takes time. Castellano says he's feared this Tommy, maybe he don't have no criminal record."

I glanced at his phone again. "What about Scruffy and Vince?"

"The lieutenant, he couldn't find nobody named Scruffy, white or black, with a criminal record. He did find a folk singer on Google. But he's white and seventy-three years old. Lives in Nashville. The lieutenant says there are two hundred crooks in South Florida named Vince. They're checking."

He slurped his coffee, now cold, and frowned.

"I'll call the receptionist for fresh coffee." I did. "Could the lieutenant do anything with the house description?"

"His computer geek, he ran it every which way through the property appraiser website and the Department of Transportation map database. He had the sergeants brief every precinct for all the patrol units Wednesday, Thursday, and this morning. Nothing yet."

"What did he find out about the phone that sent the text?"

Will referred to his notes again. "It's a Washington, DC number. It took a couple of days, but yesterday he learned it belongs to a fellow named Pablo Antonio Crucero Obregon. He's the ambassador from the Republic of San Cristobal."

"Did anyone interview the ambassador?"

"The lieutenant, he said the ambassador lives in Washington, but he's been in San Cristobal for the last three weeks."

"Somebody else has his phone."

"That's what the lieutenant said."

"The lieutenant, he said the FBI can't do nothing."

"He's right. Technically the girls are missing persons. Liz left home of her own free will. The only evidence your daughter is held against her will is three texts sent from a phone with a diplomatic connection. That's not enough to involve the FBI. Sorry."

"That's what I figured."

"Okay if I call the lieutenant after you and I are through here?"

"You can call him now if you like."

"I'll do it later. I have some boring cop stuff to discuss with him."

"Nothing about my daughter's case will bore me."

"I'll call him later."

Betty knocked twice on the door and brought in fresh coffee. I nodded my thanks and waited for her to leave.

Will cleared his throat. "Is there something you want to discuss with the lieutenant that you don't want me to hear?"

I sipped my coffee while I decided how to answer. "It would take a literal miracle for the cops to find your daughter. That's why the lieutenant sent you to me."

"I don't understand. Why can't the cops find my Lizzie?"

"Jorge Castellano is a LEO—a law enforcement officer—sworn to uphold the law. LEOs follow state laws and the U.S. Constitution—things such as search warrants and Miranda warnings that protect people's rights."

"Okay, but so what? My daughter was kidnapped for crissakes. Her life's in danger, not to mention the other girls."

Will smacked the table with his palm. "We got to get a move on."

"The cops follow due process to obtain evidence, or the prosecutor can't use it in court."

"You mean that legal stuff I seen on the TV cop shows?"

"Right."

"I don't need to convict nobody in court. All I want is to find my daughter." His eyes glistened with unshed tears.

"Jorge knows that he can't find Liz if he follows due process of law. It just isn't going to happen. He sent you to me because I'm *not* a LEO. I couldn't care less about due process. Sometimes I do things which are, ah, outside the law."

"Such as?"

"Suppose I find that three-story house Liz described. I would need to search the house to find her. As a private citizen, I can't get a search warrant, so I might pick the lock or break down the door. If Liz or another of the captives were inside, nobody would raise a ruckus that I broke the law when I freed them. You follow?"

"Good P.R. makes you bullet proof."

"Right, but if the girls are not there—say the kidnappers moved them somewhere else—I wind up in jail if I'm caught in a B&E."

"B&E?"

"Breaking and entering."

Will rubbed his chin. "You take big risks."

"Goes with the territory. Also, as a private citizen, I don't give Miranda warnings when I question a witness. I get them to talk to me however I can—whatever works."

Will caught the implications. "Jesus Christ. If you question somebody, and they don't answer you—"

I nodded. "Sometimes, I... *persuade* them to cooperate."

"How?"

"Are you sure you want to know, Will?"

His eyes became icy. "I want my daughter back, whatever it costs, whatever it takes."

Chapter 3

Lieutenant Jorge Castellano answered on the second ring. "*Hola, Carlos.* Did a man named Will Jenkins call you?"

"He just left. I'm gonna take the case. Thanks for the referral, I think."

"Good. You know our hands are tied, but you…"

"Right. What did you turn up on the names in the texts?"

"We're checking every Vince and Tommy, but nothing's popped. I have two guys on it. Unfortunately, our records don't always include tattoos and identifying marks."

"The tattoo could be new anyway. Any luck with the house description?"

"We screened the property appraiser's data base for houses over six thousand square feet. There aren't many houses that size in the county and none in the area within three miles of the cell tower."

"How about the street she described?"

"Do you know how many streets in Atlantic County have parking on both sides?"

"Thousands of miles of streets."

"We briefed the patrol units in all precincts. We told them at morning muster to watch for three-story houses of any size on a street with two lanes of traffic with parking on both sides. Nobody's seen anything suspicious so far."

"Tell me about the phone that sent the texts."

"We ran into a brick wall."

"How so? It's pretty simple to check out a phone number."

"Usually. We got a warrant using the phone number and obtained the tower's location from the cell carrier. No problem. The problem came when we tried to identify the owner. The phone's registered address is the Embassy of the Republic of San Cristobal in Washington, DC. We called the U.S. State Department to learn that it belongs to the ambassador, Pablo Crucero. We checked him out with the DC cops and the State Department. Pablo is not the guy. He's been in San Cristobal for several weeks for knee surgery."

"Who has his phone? A family member?"

"Yeah. The ambassador owns four cellphones, all with diplomatic immunity, which means we can't get a warrant to do anything with the phone, such as trace back its GPS locations. He has a wife, a thirty-year-old son, and a daughter who attends Georgetown University. The wife and daughter went with Daddy to San Cristobal, so the phone that sent the text may belong to the son."

"Jorge, you saw the texts. This girl was kidnapped. Can't you do an unofficial GPS backtrack on the phone?"

"Are we on speaker?"

"No."

"I tired, but the phone has its GPS locator disabled. Whoever this guy is, he has something to hide."

"What's his name?"

"You're gonna love this, *amigo*. It's Antonio Ricardo Crucero *Calderone*."

"With my luck, this idiot is a distant cousin." My Mexican mother's maiden name is Calderone and my legal name is Carlos Andres McCrary Calderone, after the Mexican custom.

Jorge laughed. "San Cristobal is a long way from Mexico, *amigo*. If he's kin, he's an eighth cousin or some such."

"Where's Antonio now? Does he live in Port City or is he here on vacation?"

"Funny you should ask. When we asked about the son, the embassy stonewalled us. A snooty embassy fart reminded me the ambassador and his family enjoy diplomatic immunity. The embassy would release no personal information, not even the son's whereabouts. And we can't question them without the father's permission."

"I suppose you asked for permission."

"Do cats have hair?"

"And their answer was…?"

"Go piss up a rope. They used fancy diplomatic words to tell me to take a long walk off a short pier. That's when I told Mr. Jenkins to call you."

"Which cell tower did the texts use?" I wrote down the address and the name of the cellphone carrier. "You have pictures of the two girls you identified?" I checked my notes. "Dolores Cherry and Morgan Putnam?"

"I'll email them to you."

"Thanks. Anything else to tell me?"

"The DC cops couldn't come out and say it, but one cop called them 'diplobrats'—that's what DC cops call the children of diplomats who ignore local laws. The mild offenders park illegally or break the speed limit, then tear up their parking citations and speeding tickets. The worst ones commit felonies like drug smuggling or assault. They had a diplobrat commit murder once. All the cops could do was ask the State Department to declare the perp *persona non grata* and make his country recall the guy."

"Is that the situation here? Human trafficking or drug smuggling?"

"God, I hope not. We don't even know if he lives here, but his phone pings on Port City Beach. If Antonio Crucero is a criminal, which we don't know, our hands are tied."

"But mine aren't."

"*Exactamente, amigo.* That's why I told Jenkins to call you. We'll keep working names from our end. If anything pops, I'll keep you in the loop."

"I may not keep you in the loop from my end."

"Of course, I have deniability. Next time you see Jenkins, tell him you saved my freedom and my career. Hopefully, you can save his daughter."

Chapter 4

LIZ SAT ON THE EDGE OF THE BED AND WATCHED as the john closed the door behind him. Maybe he was the last one for the day. She was tired and sore from servicing a dozen men. She didn't bother to hope her day was over. Hope made no difference. Another stranger would come in the door or else Tommy would. One was as bad as the other.

Liz washed in the bathroom before the next john showed. She didn't bother to dress. Tommy would tell her if the john wanted to play dress-up. She returned to the bedroom and lay on the bed to wait for the next whoever—or *whatever*. It didn't matter, did it?

Some men opened the door and walked in like they owned the place. The fat ambassador for example. Others knocked like they needed permission to enter. They pretended this was a date even when she opened the door naked as Venus on the half-shell. Months ago, she told several johns that she was a captive. She asked them to call the police. They laughed, so they knew. Still, it was funny how many johns knocked. Maybe they sought the illusion of a normal romantic relationship. Liz had no illusions left.

Benson Broady had been her first romance. They met at David City High School and dated for two years, he the basketball player and she the head cheerleader. She remembered their first clumsy love-making on the blanket behind the grain elevator. He had been so sweet, so tender, so... romantic. Wasn't that the way love was supposed to be?

Benson left for the University of Nebraska. She planned to follow him the next year. He drove out to see her on weekends when he came home from Lincoln. They used the blanket behind the grain elevator again and again. She thought of it as *their* place. She didn't understand when Benson's visits became less frequent and then before Thanksgiving they just stopped. Maybe it was the weather turning colder as autumn set in. At Christmas, he swore everything was fine between them. He had been busy, but he didn't call. If he came home on a weekend, she didn't know it. Easter weekend, she borrowed her dad's car, drove to David City, and confronted him in his living room. Benson confessed he was seeing another girl, a freshman.

That romance had been an illusion. Was it any different than the illusion the johns wanted? Sometimes she couldn't tell the difference between real passion and fake. She sighed and looked back at the door.

She never knew which john was the last until Tommy came in. He *always* opened the door without knocking. Of course, he did own the place. He would say her day's work was done, and he would screw her one more time himself. Every day.

She heard the doorknob turn. No knock.

It was Tommy. "Hey, Angel. You had a good day today. I got compliments from three clients. They said they'd ask for you next time."

He called them *clients*, as if they were somebody special. They weren't special to Liz. To her they were an endless drudgery of sweat, body fluids, and sore muscles. If johns complained about her sexual performances, Tommy would beat her. She sighed. At least Tommy wasn't going to beat her this time.

Tommy smirked. He never smiled, only smirked. "You know what I want, Angel." He pushed her back on the bed.

After it was over, she dragged herself to the bathroom one more time. At least he was the last one for the day.

She stood under the hot water a long time in a vain attempt to scrub away the dirty feeling Tommy left her with. It didn't work. It never did.

For her thirteenth birthday, Liz's mother gave her a pink flannel nightgown. When her mother died from breast cancer two years later, Liz wore it every night. The nightgown made her feel like her mother was there, even as her father became more distant. She washed it so often, it faded almost to white. She packed it first when she left for Disney. It was her link to the home she loved before her mother died. Before Daddy changed.

Then she met Tommy. He was nice at first. He gave her a new phone to replace her old one. The old phone was so *last year* he said. They laughed when she threw it into the Atlantic. She abandoned her old life, her old character. He partied with her, gave her drugs and alcohol. After a week as her lover, he asked her to have sex with a friend of his. She refused and he hit her. He brought her to this place and made her watch as he burned her clothes in the alley behind. "Your past is dead, Angel. This is your future. I'll give you everything you need." He dragged her inside nude and locked her in this room for two days without food. She drank from the lavatory in the bathroom.

When he did show, she was so grateful that she met all his demands. Better than starving to death, wasn't it? Now she wasn't so sure.

She returned to the bedroom where she worked and slept. Tommy had burned her nightgown. The only underwear any of his Angels owned was kinky stuff some johns told them to wear. The small chest of drawers overflowed with thong underwear, crotchless panties, pushup bras, and sex toys. The closet held a few normal clothes she wore for meals downstairs. The rest was a nurse's uniform, a maid's uniform, and see-through negligees in red, white, and pink for the johns. None of them felt comfortable for sleeping.

Liz sat on the bed and stared at the door. Tommy always locked it from the outside when he left. The bed felt warm where she and her kidnapper had lain. She stood. She couldn't sleep yet—not on a bed still warm from a man who just raped her. She grabbed tissues from the box on her nightstand, dried her tears, and blew her nose. She had slept nude for eleven months, but she'd never gotten used to it. She felt exposed and vulnerable, even when she pulled the covers over her head and made a little tent the way she did when she was a child.

Where was Daddy? Why hadn't he found her? He might be mad at her for leaving, but he was her father. Did he change cellphone plans and get a different number? Maybe he didn't receive the texts she sent. It had been a week with no action. Her spirits fell further.

If he didn't come soon, she would kill herself. Had she hidden enough pills for an overdose? How many would it take? If she tried to escape and failed, she'd be tortured to death. No, it would be escape, rescue, or overdose. Whatever she did, it had to work the first time.

She flopped back on the bed. She'd give Daddy two more weeks to come through for her. Two more weeks and she was through. For good.

Chapter 5

ANTONIO CRUCERO WAS THE TYPE who shared his personal life on social media without hesitation. He had accounts on the first three websites I checked. I found all the information the San Cristobal embassy wouldn't share with Jorge.

Crucero lived on Port City Beach in a rented apartment. He called himself Tony Crucero—very American. I got both license plate numbers from pictures of his Glacier Silver Metallic BMW sedan and his Torch Red Corvette convertible. Diplomatic plates on both—easier to park in loading zones and by fire hydrants. He posted the names and pictures of exclusive bars and nightclubs he frequented. He was proud of the view from his waterfront apartment's balcony. I downloaded selfies of him with different beautiful women, his black hair blowing in the wind when it wasn't in a ponytail. The women were nines and tens. Most looked six feet tall; Crucero was five-foot-six. Diplobrat rated a three, maybe a four. What did they see in him? A jerk like him needed more than money. Or were these women professional escorts?

I filed that question away for future research.

Using the backgrounds and angles in the photos, I figured out where his apartment was and the approximate floor he lived on.

Saturday afternoon late, I staked out his building and waited for the Corvette or BMW to show.

Another gorgeous South Florida sunset lit the sky over the Everglades as Crucero's Corvette squealed down the garage ramp and headed south on Ocean Drive.

He first stopped at the Pelican Roost, a thatched-roofed restaurant on an island in Seeti Bay, and a favorite on his Facebook page. He left his Corvette with the valet. I intended to stick a GPS tracker under his car, but if I failed, I needed my white Dodge Caravan accessible to follow when he left. I found a spot in the self-parking lot fifty yards from the rustic plank steps of the restaurant entrance. I backed in for a fast exit.

The Corvette was parked too close to the valets for me to place the GPS tracker.

I told the restaurant host that I was the first to arrive of a party of four. No, we didn't have a reservation. Yes, I realized it was Saturday night. Yes, we would wait an hour-and-a-half for a table. The host jotted down the fictitious name I gave her. "When your table is ready, Mr. Washington, this pager vibrates and flashes red lights like this." She tested the pager and handed it to me. "You can wait in the bar for your party."

The Pelican Roost sticks all customers in the bar long enough to order a drink before showing them to a table. Sure enough, Crucero slouched over a stool at the Tiki Bar, smack under a ceiling fan. His hair was longer than it looked on his social media page. He looked fatter in person than he looked on the internet, maybe because he was so short. I was surprised he fit into a Corvette. His XXXL Hawaiian shirt made a vain attempt to disguise his bulk. He left three buttons open in the tropical heat. Three gold chains hung halfway down a chest that could double for a bearskin rug. He wore two rings on each hand. He had no visible tattoos. Not surprising, since his arms and chest were so hairy a tattoo wouldn't show through the fur. He sipped a Coco Loco with a paper umbrella and a bougainvillea flower stuck in the top. South Florida chic. The flower swayed in the breeze.

Crucero glanced at his heavyweight gold watch and scanned the crowded bar. He'd probably made an 8:30 reservation and his date was late.

I grabbed a corner table and ordered a club soda with a twist. Whoopee, it was party time for the hard-working private eye. The Pelican Roost made great banana daiquiris. Too bad I was on duty.

As I sampled my yummy club soda, a six-foot blond piece of arm candy walked into the bar wearing tropical sandals and a gold outfit. The neckline plunged to her waist and revealed the best cleavage money could buy. Miss Cleavage parted the crowd proudly with her chest as she strutted over to Crucero and presented her cheek to be kissed. She whispered in his ear and rubbed her assets on his arm. From the lack of tan lines on her chest and back, I surmised that she sunbathed nude, or at least topless. Crucero grinned and squeezed her behind as she perched on the barstool next to him. Miss Cleavage ordered a white wine. Ten minutes later, they had a bayside table with a skyline view. Reservation or not, this guy had clout.

I watched them for an hour from the bar. The ceiling fan stirred the humid night air without conviction. I could work up a sweat lifting my drink.

My pager buzzed and flashed. I leaned toward a party of four at the next table. "Excuse me, my party hasn't arrived. Would you like a table now?"

They would.

I swapped pagers with them. "Tell them you're the George Washington party. Enjoy."

I watched for another hour, then followed Crucero and Miss Cleavage to an exclusive private nightclub with a velvet rope and a bouncer in a tuxedo at the entrance. Their parking lot was not as well-guarded as the Pelican Roost's. I attached the GPS tracker to the Corvette and watched from my minivan. At 2:30 a.m., the couple staggered to his car. Crucero stuck his hand down the front of Miss Cleavage's dress as he helped her into the passenger seat, and she stroked his private parts through his slacks as he closed her door. Driving home, he weaved from lane to lane and narrowly missed causing two collisions.

Chapter 6

MY CONDO WAS A MILE FROM CRUCERO'S. I hired an off-duty cop, Robby Gorski, to watch Crucero's parking garage in case he used the BMW, but I figured he would use the Corvette again. Miss Cleavage looked more Corvette than BMW. I monitored the GPS tracker from home. The Corvette moved shortly after noon on Sunday. I dismissed Robby and headed down to my Caravan.

Miss Cleavage must have arrived at the Pelican Roost in a taxi or Uber, because Crucero didn't take her to retrieve her car. I caught the Corvette and kept it in sight as he and Miss Cleavage crossed the Beachline Causeway, top down in the South Florida sunshine. Crucero didn't speed. Maybe Miss Cleavage was reluctant to mess up her hair with the top down. He wore his hair in a ponytail, so he didn't worry about the wind. I followed them to Coconut Grove. I recorded Miss Cleavage's trendy address and left Crucero and his arm candy to enjoy their afternoon delight. What did a cover girl dish like her see in a short, fat blob like him?

I drove to Crucero's apartment. He'd be occupied for at least an hour as he climbed the Twin Peaks in Miss Cleavage State Park. From there it was an hour's drive to his apartment. I would monitor the Corvette's movements with the tracker app on my smartphone. Technology makes a PI's life easier when you ignore inconvenient privacy laws.

Crucero's apartment was in a rental high-rise, not a condo. The security was limited to a few cameras. I parked my Caravan in the loading zone and removed a flower arrangement I'd bought at Walmart along with items to disguise my appearance. I carried the flowers to the reception desk. I held the bouquet high to obscure my face, but I could see the house phone. "Flowers for Tony Crucero."

"Just a moment." The receptionist grabbed a house phone and punched Crucero's apartment number.

Bingo. Apartment 1212.

He hung up. "Mr. Crucero doesn't answer. You wanna leave them? I'll make sure he gets them when he comes back."

"Sure." I set the flowers on the counter. "How about my tip?"

The guy shrugged. "You can come back later, or you can leave them. Your choice."

I left the bouquet. Let the poor schlub collect the tip when he delivered the flowers.

I drove the minivan back home and switched to the sedan I had rented the previous day. Returning to Crucero's high-rise, I piggy-backed under the garage gate on the bumper of a resident's car and spiraled my way to the top floor and into an unassigned space.

I hiked down the ramps three floors until I found Crucero's BMW. I attached a tracker device to it and hid behind a pillar to watch the keypad door lock. Another resident's car squealed up the ramp and parked. A woman grabbed a Macy's bag and walked to the door. I was too far away to read the numbers, but I watched her hand movements as she punched four digits on the pad. Top left, lower right, lower left, ending with a tap on the right.

Three possible combinations. The second one worked. The World's Greatest Private Eye on the job. I stored the number in my phone for future use. Most of these places wait a year or more before they change codes, if they ever do. I never know when another case—or this one—will bring me to these same apartments again.

Elevators always have security cameras, so I climbed the fire stairs to Crucero's floor. My mouth was dry as I checked the Corvette's GPS tracker again. A little pre-action jitters, routine before a mission, even one as simple as a B&E. Crucero was in

Coconut Grove knocking boots with Miss Cleavage, having more fun than I was. I opened the door to the elevator lobby. As empty as the space behind the moon.

There were five apartments on the floor. A discreet brass plaque with the coat of arms of San Cristobal was mounted on his door.

I picked the lock in two minutes. My heart rate climbed a little higher. The last tumbler clicked and I turned the knob.

As I stepped inside, the alarm system beeped. Damn. I knew this was going too well. The alarm would go off in forty-five seconds. I found the keypad beside the door and punched the disarm button. *Enter code* flashed on the screen. It's incredible how many people use *1-2-3-4* as their alarm code. If that failed I had forty more seconds to try Crucero's birth year, his birthday in both day/month and month/day format, both of which I found on his social media, then the apartment number.

If those failed, I would run like a scalded dog.

"Who the hell are you?" A bulky man in a gray suit and striped tie came from further inside the apartment. He had *bodyguard* written all over him as plain as if it were tattooed on his forehead. Dark skin, black eyes, and beaked nose. Black hair parted in the middle and pulled tight over his ears. Probably had a ponytail at the base of his neck, but I couldn't tell from this angle. His face looked chiseled from limestone, an Indian from southern Mexico or Central America. The Colt M1911A1 muzzle he leveled at me measured .45 inches in diameter. Pointed between my eyes, it looked black as a cavern and big as a cannon.

A Special Forces instructor said, "When the balloon goes up, if you stop to blink twice, you might be dead." Sometimes you have less than a second to make a life-or-death decision.

If I went for my gun, that .45 slug would shred a hole in me big enough to throw a baseball through. If I didn't reach for my gun, he might kill me anyway. I chose Plan C.

I raised my hands to waist height and answered in rapid Spanish. "I'm the maintenance man. Mr. Crucero reported his ice maker was broken."

Striped Tie responded in Spanish. "Where's your tool box?" He lowered the .45. Nobody fears the maintenance man.

"In the hall," I answered in Spanish. "I'll get it." As I moved toward the hall, I grabbed a brass sculpture from the ornamental table beside the door. I hurled it at his head and dived out the door. He fired two shots that slammed into the wall and echoed in the marble-floored elevator lobby. The brass horse and rider must have hit him, because he didn't chase me as I sprinted to the fire stairs. Either that or he paused to enter the alarm code. I raced down five flights of stairs to the rent car.

I caught my breath and felt my heart slow to normal as I drove back to my own parking garage. I switched out the fake license plates for the real ones. On the way to the airport to return the car, I tossed the baseball hat, surgical gloves, and fake eyeglasses into a dumpster behind a grocery store. The security cameras wouldn't help if Crucero reported the break-in, but I'd bet he wouldn't involve the cops.

How many solid citizens post an armed guard in their apartment? What was Striped Tie guarding that was so valuable? Jorge mentioned that some diplomats smuggled drugs. One thing for sure, Crucero was into something dangerous.

Made in the USA
Columbia, SC
30 April 2018